A ROMANCE
OF FLIGHT

A ROMANCE OF FLIGHT

To Ed and Wilma: Read, enjoy, and keep flying

DONALD PATTILLO

MOUNTAIN ARBOR
PRESS
Alpharetta, GA

This is a work of fiction. Names, characters, businesses, places, and events are either the products of the author's imagination or are used in a fictitious manner. All historical persons and events are written in the interpretation and understanding of the author and do not claim to be absolute truth.

Copyright © 2021 by Donald Pattillo

All rights reserved. No part of this book may be reproduced or transmitted in any form or by any means, electronic or mechanical, including photocopying, recording, or any information storage and retrieval system, without permission in writing from the author.

ISBN: 978-1-6653-0034-6 - Paperback
eISBN: 978-1-6653-0035-3 - ePub
eISBN: 978-1-6653-0036-0 - mobi

Library of Congress Control Number: 2021905760

Printed in the United States of America   033121

☉This paper meets the requirements of ANSI/NISO Z39.48-1992 (Permanence of Paper)

Wilbur Wright photo courtesy of Special Collections & Archives, Wright State University

To my Peace Corps family

Wilbur Wright

"For some years I have been afflicted with the belief that flight is possible to man. My disease has increased in severity and I feel that it will soon cost me an increased amount of money if not my life. I have been trying to arrange my affairs in such a way that I can devote my entire time for a few months to experiment in this field."

Wilbur Wright to Octave Chanute, May 13, 1900

* * *

"... the fact that the brothers and their sister were unmarried fascinated the public after 1908. When queried about his marital status, Wilbur simply replied that he did not have time for a wife and an airplane.

"Perhaps. But Wilbur, with his extraordinary sense of his own strengths and limitations, may simply have felt that freedom from family responsibilities was an essential element in his ability to concentrate his attention and energies.

"Rumors of romance would continue to plague Wilbur to the end of his life. None was ever confirmed. It seems unlikely that he would ever have trusted himself so far with anyone outside the family."

Tom Crouch, *The Bishop's Boys*

* * *

Wilbur and Orville walked almost four miles to the town of Kitty Hawk, where they telegraphed their father:

"Success four flights Thursday morning against twenty-one mile wind started from level with engine power alone average speed through the air thirty-one miles longest 57 [*sic*] seconds.

Inform Press home Christmas."

Prologue

Kill Devil Hills, North Carolina
December 14–17, 1903

Wilbur and Orville awoke early, to the sound of whistling wind. Their primitive cabin was extremely cold, and they rushed to light the stove. As the room gradually warmed, they prepared a simple breakfast and ate. They then checked outside. The wind was high, perhaps over twenty miles an hour, as they had hoped. Their machine had survived the night undamaged, and they judged that conditions were right for another flight attempt. The brothers were determined to get it right this time, since they needed to return to Dayton by Christmas.

They had been there since September 26, working steadily to assemble and ready their flyer for testing. Orville had needed to return to Dayton early in December to fashion new steel propeller shafts to replace those that had cracked, and he had returned on December 11. On December 14, conditions had looked favorable, and after flipping a coin, Wilbur had won the right to make the first attempt. They had recruited five local men to help and set up the launch rail in the direction of the wind. Wilbur had taken his place on the lower wing, the engine had sputtered to life, and the flyer had slid down the rail. As it became airborne, Wilbur had pulled up too sharply, and the craft had nosedived into the sand. Damage had been slight, but the attempt was a failure. They had spent the next day repairing the damage. They had been ready to make another attempt on the sixteenth, but there had been no wind.

Now, on the seventeenth, the wind was again favorable. It was also near freezing, an important factor since dense, cold air gave the wings more lift. They raised their signal flag for the five men from the village to come over. Everything was ready soon after ten in the morning, and Wilbur set up a camera to record the event. It was now Orville's turn, and he was calm and confident. He lay down atop the lower wing and gripped the controls. Fuel was primed into the cylinders, and the battery coil box was plugged in to start the engine. The propellers started turning. Wilbur steadied the right wingtip as the flyer began to move along the rail. After a run of forty feet, it lifted off. The wind held the flyer in the air for twelve seconds, after which it settled into the sand, still under Orville's control. It had flown one hundred and twenty feet.

The crew carried the craft back to the launch rail. At 11:20 a.m., Wilbur took his position on the wing and took off smoothly. His flight covered 195 feet. Twenty minutes later, Orville made his second flight, of 200 feet. Finally, at noon, Wilbur flew again, this time remaining aloft for fifty-nine seconds and covering 852 feet. The flyer was slightly damaged on landing but had proved it could sustain flight. Wilbur was convinced it could fly for twenty minutes, if not longer. This time, it took a major effort for the crew to drag the machine back over that distance, since it weighed some seven hundred pounds.

After lunch, the crew was relaxing and talking when a sudden strong gust of wind caught the flyer and flipped it over, causing severe mechanical damage and cracking many wooden ribs. That ended testing of the first flyer, but the brothers were not unduly upset, since it had succeeded.

Chapter One

Mrs. Wagner

Miami International Airport, October 5, 1962

It was a good day to fly. The weather, as usual, was warm and sunny, and the airport was busy. The boarding announcement for the Miami–Chicago flight, with an intermediate stop at Cincinnati, came over the public address system. Passengers waiting in the lounge quickly made their way through the departure gate to the boarding apron. Among the first boarders was a slightly stooped elderly woman who, although carrying a cane, climbed the stairs to the huge Boeing 707 jet airliner without assistance. In welcoming passengers aboard, the first-class stewardess became mildly concerned for the woman. While well-dressed and appearing quite strong, she was noticeably aged. During her greeting, the stewardess was struck by the woman's rather full gray hair, which framed a deeply lined face and was worn straight and long rather than gathered and rolled behind her head as was more customary among women of her age. The woman returned the stewardess's greeting pleasantly, took her aisle seat in the first-class compartment, and waited quietly as the cabin continued to fill.

After closing and locking the cabin door and making the mandatory safety announcements, the stewardess checked the manifest and identified the passenger as Wagner, Mrs. Ellen. She was further concerned because Mrs. Wagner, in addition to using a cane, appeared to be the oldest passenger aboard and was traveling alone. She decided she would give her extra attention if time permitted, then turned to flight preparations.

The airliner was towed away from the gate and turned toward the taxiway. The captain started the engines and steered his aircraft on the taxiway toward takeoff position, but then was notified by the control tower to hold his position in the line due to a traffic buildup. The captain informed the cabin staff of the delay and that they had been ordered to hold on the taxi ramp until they received takeoff clearance. He then made the announcement to the passengers, adding that he did not expect the delay to be very long. Given the delay, the stewardess walked to Mrs. Wagner's seat to ask if she could provide any particular assistance.

"Mrs. Wagner," she said, looking at the manifest again, "these delays are all too common, unfortunately. I'm sure we will be underway in a few minutes. Could I get you something in the meantime? A blanket, perhaps?"

"Oh, no, thank you. I'm fine."

"I see you are flying with us to Cincinnati."

"Yes, I will depart at Cincinnati, but my actual destination is Dayton."

"Is this your first flight?" asked the stewardess.

"Oh, hardly," Mrs. Wagner replied pleasantly. "I have had some involvement with aviation since the early days, and I have been flying on commercial airliners since the 1930s. In fact, my husband was a pilot, and he finished his career as a captain for Pan American."

Impressed with that statement, and pleased that Mrs. Wagner appeared interested in conversing, the stewardess decided to continue. "So, you are an experienced air traveler."

"I even learned to fly an airplane myself in my younger days," said Mrs. Wagner, "although, I didn't become an active pilot. I have been widowed for almost ten years, and I don't travel much anymore. But I wanted to fly on one of the new jet airliners before I became too old. That is why I took this flight rather than a flight directly to Dayton."

"I'm impressed," said the stewardess. "You are something of an aviation veteran. Are you from Dayton originally?"

"No, but I had occasion to visit there as a young woman. I am going back for the inauguration of the National Aviation Hall of Fame."

"I had read about that. So, you are quite familiar with the city, I suppose."

"I was in past years, but this will be my first trip there since 1948." She paused, then added, "That was when I attended the funeral of Orville Wright."

"Oh? Did you know the Wright brothers?"

Mrs. Wagner's demeanor changed at that question, and her eyes glistened. The stewardess felt that she possibly had intruded too far with her questioning as Ellen Wagner replied, wistfully, that she had.

Chapter Two

Ellen

Pittsburgh, Early Summer, 1904

Ellen Hobson knew her parents would be disappointed. She had been courted for the past several months by Walter Carrington, but had firmly, and finally, turned down his proposal of marriage. Ellen had expected his proposal and was aware that her parents had expected her to accept. She also knew that, in the event he proposed, her father was prepared to give his consent.

Nevertheless, she knew her own mind and did not delay in informing her parents. The next morning, over breakfast, she told them of Walter's proposal and of her decision to reject it. They acknowledged and accepted her decision, but both made it clear to her that they were indeed distressed. Ellen spent the rest of the morning helping her grandmother with a sewing project, then spent most of the afternoon reading a book on American history.

The following morning after breakfast, and after Ellen's father had left for work, her mother initiated a conversation. "Ellen, you are twenty-two years old. That was my age when I married your father. We both think you would have done well in this match, and I can't imagine why you would spurn Walter this way."

Ellen could tell that her mother was not prepared to let the matter rest. She decided to defend herself, even though she felt it unnecessary. "Why should I marry just because it is the thing expected of me?" she protested. "There are other worthwhile things I can do at this point in my life."

A Romance of Flight

"We just want what we feel is best for you, dear, and Walter is a fine young man from a good family."

"I know, but as I explained to you, I simply don't love him, and I don't feel ready to marry at this time anyway. I don't mean that I never intend to marry," she added hastily. "I would like to be a wife and mother someday, and you already know that. But you have provided me with a good education, and I know the expense wasn't an easy burden. I want to use my education for some purpose, and I plan to become employed and earn my way in the world."

"That is all commendable, of course, but I still feel you may come to regret not accepting Walter's proposal. And you may feel at loose ends now that Julia is engaged."

Her mother's remarks caused Ellen to reflect a moment. She had just recently graduated from the Pennsylvania College for Women, a small institution for young women in Pittsburgh founded by the Presbyterian Church and located near the section of the city in which she lived. Afterward, she had felt pressured to marry and enter into what others regarded as a conventional life for a well-bred young woman, a pressure that had increased after she had attracted a suitor. Walter Carrington had seemed a perfect match to everyone but her: her parents approved, her brothers liked him, and his family was rather better off than hers—the Carringtons lived east of the Hobsons, in the Shady Side district just off a street where many opulent mansions stood—and she suspected that was another reason her parents favored the match. But her feelings for Walter were essentially nonexistent. Although respecting her mother's concerns, Ellen felt at the same time that she tended to be rigidly conventional, if not controlling, regarding the future of her only daughter. She found herself feeling slightly resentful, even though she and her mother did not have a history of conflict.

Among other things, Ellen wanted to travel. She had had few opportunities to see the country beyond Western Pennsylvania and especially wished to visit New York, Philadelphia, and

Chicago. As a child, she had been fascinated by the reports of the Chicago World's Fair of 1893. With its great publicity, she had also followed closely the St. Louis World's Fair now underway, wishing she could attend. She longed to see the Atlantic Ocean and felt that an appropriate type of employment might give her both the means and the opportunity.

Ellen understood her mother's pointed reference to her classmate and best friend, Julia Douglas, who was to be married in two months. She emphasized to her mother that Julia's marriage would not mean any change in their friendship.

"Well then, what are your plans?" asked her mother. "How are you going to earn your way in life?"

"You know that I like to write, and I want to learn something of the world. I have been thinking of journalism, of becoming a reporter for a newspaper. I am going to try to find a position on my own, but I'll ask Father for help if it becomes necessary."

"That is no job for a young lady. I have always heard that a newsroom is an unsavory place, that reporters practice foul language and worse manners. And I doubt that a newspaper would pay a living wage to someone with no experience."

"That may be so, but it is what I would like to try. I realize there are likely to be barriers to overcome, but there have been women who have succeeded in the field while young, and I can't think of anything else I would rather do. The only other fields open to me would be teaching and some type of social work, and I don't find either of those appealing. If I do find a position as a reporter, I trust I may still live at home until I become better established."

"Of course you may. I wouldn't have it any other way. You know that your father and I will support you if you are determined to do it. But do you have a specific plan? Which newspaper?"

Ellen replied that she was formulating such a plan.

* * *

That afternoon Ellen visited Julia, among other reasons to

inform her that she had turned down Walter Carrington's marriage proposal.

"I must say I'm not surprised," said Julia. "I like Walter, of course, but I could never detect that you held any feelings for him."

"I know I have made the right decision. My parents aren't very happy with me at this moment, but they accept that it is my life."

"You know that I will support whatever you do," said Julia. "For myself, I feel very happy and confident about what I am doing, but I admire you for wanting to pursue a career."

"That means a lot, especially coming from you. I don't expect it to be easy, but I am fortunate in that I am young, and can always change my plans if events turn me toward another direction."

Julia indicated her agreement. They then turned their attention to Julia's plans for her wedding, in which Ellen would have a role.

* * *

Over the next month, and on her own, Ellen intensively pursued a position. She first contacted by letter the eight general interest newspapers of Pittsburgh, then several smaller dailies in nearby cities. She later inquired of certain newspapers in person, but still met only with frustration. While not entirely surprised by the rejections she received, Ellen nonetheless suspected that they were due more to her gender than any other factor. She knew that female reporters still were not generally accepted in Pittsburgh, or in the entire country for that matter, although a few had been successful. After becoming frustrated with her lack of progress with her own efforts, she turned to her father, hoping that his business knowledge and contacts might open doors otherwise closed to her.

"I will call on the few contacts I have in the newspaper community," he had told her, "but I can't promise anything. I will say again that I'm not at all sure this is what you should be doing at this time in your life."

Ellen thanked him, although understanding that he felt as her mother did, and held strong reservations about his young daughter working in a newspaper environment. He mentioned specifically that he regarded reporters as hard-drinking practitioners of the low life.

Joseph Hobson, nevertheless, kept his word, calling on several of his business contacts and conveying his daughter's interests. Soon after her father's intervention, Ellen gained an interview with managing editor Theodore Rutledge of the *Reporter*, one of Pittsburgh's leading newspapers. She was especially pleased with that development since she knew that the *Reporter*, although not the largest daily, was well-respected. It was an afternoon paper, as most were, and Ellen realized that that would mean a change in her usual daily schedule, but one to which she could adapt. Additionally, she had learned that Rutledge had a reputation as a progressive and that he knew of her father's dry goods emporium in the downtown business district. She thought that both factors probably had helped her gain the interview. Although Ellen had written Rutledge earlier about a position, she decided it would be better not to mention that fact when she appeared for the interview. By his granting an interview now, she doubted that he had remembered her original letter, perhaps even never having read it.

On the appointed day, Ellen traveled to the *Reporter* building. Upon entering, she obtained directions to the office of Theodore Rutledge, and proceeded upstairs to the second floor. She looked out over the busy city room, covering most of the floor, as she approached and saw perhaps a dozen men present, men she assumed to be reporters. She became aware that she was the object of intense attention from some, but was determined that she would not be intimidated by any stares. Somewhat nervously, she knocked on the door to the managing editor's office, and heard an invitation to enter. She entered and was greeted by Theodore Rutledge, who stood behind a large and cluttered desk. Ellen took the proffered seat, and they exchanged brief pleasantries. Ellen noted that Rutledge was of medium height, balding, and exhibited a somewhat formal but still friendly demeanor. She guessed him to be about her father's age. Rutledge then began the interview. "I will ask you first why you wish to become a reporter," he said, rather bluntly.

"I strongly feel this is the best way for me to use my education and to pursue my interest in writing. I think I can help this newspaper. I also want to make my way in the world, so to speak," Ellen responded in an even tone, trying to convey a professional demeanor.

Rutledge acknowledged those points, then began questioning her skills and background for the position. "I've become somewhat open to the idea of adding a female reporter to the staff," he said, "but I would have preferred someone with more experience. I know that you have a good education, however, and that should help."

Ellen had anticipated that he might question her lack of experience as well as her motivation and had rehearsed how she might deal with skepticism. She strongly responded that her education would be an asset.

"I should warn you that you might face special difficulties as a young woman in beginning a position here and trying to establish yourself in a male-dominated profession," Rutledge added. "How would you deal with such difficulties, or how would you plan to win acceptance?"

"First, I am determined to overcome any obstacles, whether they relate to my gender or otherwise. Once I demonstrate my capabilities as a journalist, I can make a contribution to the *Reporter* and to the profession, and I think that should help me win the acceptance of those who may hold doubts at the start."

They conversed for several more minutes and as the interview drew to a close, Ellen felt that she had handled herself well and had answered questions appropriately. She hoped she had impressed Rutledge with her determination as well as with her realistic expectations. At the conclusion of her visit, Rutledge stood, and they shook hands again.

"I do appreciate your coming in," he said. "I will speak to some of the staff about you and notify you as soon as I can."

As she departed, Ellen thanked him, adding that she looked forward to hearing from him. She felt confident. Rutledge called her the next day, offering his congratulations and offering her a position, confirming that she indeed had been successful in the interview. Ellen accepted enthusiastically, feeling particularly gratified that she would be the first female reporter hired by the *Reporter*. She had liked Rutledge from the start, as he appeared to possess an even temper and had displayed none of the coarse manners popularly associated with men in his profession. She was optimistic that she would get along with him. Ellen informed her parents and grandmother of her success, and they reiterated their support.

"It certainly speaks well of you that they offered you a position," said her mother. "You have our support in your endeavor."

***

Ellen began work in August, at a salary of twelve dollars a week. On her first day, she reported to Rutledge at his second-floor office, again feeling the curious stares of many in the city room as she entered. She took a seat as she had for the interview, and he began to brief her on her training.

"The main thing we need is a well-written copy. I will expect you to write news stories and cover events with the help of more experienced reporters, and to train under them. As you gain experience, I will consider assigning you to a more specialized field according to our needs. But I must caution you again that your presence will not be welcomed by all, so it will be up to you to win acceptance from the present staff. You will have my support, of course, and I am going to assign Roy Graham to mentor you directly. He is my assistant city editor and is fully briefed as to your capabilities and interests."

"I have always understood that my presence could meet with some resistance," Ellen replied, "but I believe I can deal with it. As I have told you, I think the best way I can win acceptance is by becoming a competent reporter."

A Romance of Flight

Rutledge appeared to agree with her statement and called Roy Graham to his office. As they were introduced, Ellen observed that Graham was neatly dressed and was rather tall, with a slender build and thinning reddish hair. She found him of pleasant enough appearance and demeanor and guessed that he was in his early thirties.

"I will be happy to help you in any way I can, Miss Hobson," he said, "and I also welcome your presence here. I think you can add something to this paper, especially in city news coverage. Please come to my office, and I will help you get settled."

"Thank you very much, and please call me Ellen," she replied.

Graham sat behind his desk in his office, which lacked the privacy of Rutledge's but was still spacious. As they conversed, Ellen could sense immediately that Graham, while rather soft-spoken and formal, was undoubtedly serious about his profession. He also appeared to be congenial, and she sensed, or hoped, that he would regard her as an equal.

"The *Reporter* enjoys a daily circulation of around fifty thousand," he began, "and the typical edition runs from twelve to sixteen pages in length. I can tell you that one reason Mr. Rutledge decided to hire an additional reporter is that our general editor wants to increase the size of an edition, probably to twenty or even twenty-four pages. You should have a chance to contribute more news stories as they happen or as you discover them, and you will have the same access to Associated Press reports as other reporters. On that point, I should emphasize that much will depend on your initiative. If you have an idea for a story, or learn of something that should be covered, bring it to me and I will consider it."

"I appreciate that. I have been reading the *Reporter* for some time now, so I am familiar with the scope of your news coverage as well as with the paper's writing style."

Graham acknowledged her statement. After he completed his briefing, Ellen tentatively concluded that his personality might serve as an effective complement to that of Rutledge, with his courtly and more formal manner. Additionally, she found it encouraging that Graham, like Rutledge, did not appear to affect the hard-bitten, profane manner that she had been warned to expect of reporters and editors.

"Now, if you will come with me," said Graham, "I will show you to your desk. Unfortunately, as the new person on the staff, your location isn't the most desirable, but it was all I could make available at this time."

"I didn't expect anything luxurious," she replied. "I'm sure it will be fine."

Roy Graham then escorted Ellen around the newsroom and introduced her to several reporters who were at their desks that day. They greeted her with varying degrees of warmth, and none demonstrated any enthusiasm for or particular interest in her presence there. Ellen still greeted each in a friendly manner. Graham then introduced her to a man named James Overstreet, the chief copy editor, whose office was next to his. Ellen had already been informed that Mr. Overstreet would be editing her submissions from the start, as all stories were required to be approved by him before being submitted to Mr. Rutledge. She exchanged brief pleasantries with Overstreet, who returned them in what she felt to be a perfunctory manner. Roy Graham continued by taking her on a tour of the *Reporter* building. He first explained to Ellen the operation of the huge presses below street level, which she found fascinating. He then gave an explanation of the newsprint storage room on the fourth floor and brought her to the small cafeteria on the fifth floor where all employees could eat. Graham invited her to join him in a light lunch at that time, which she accepted. She enjoyed the chance to sit and converse casually. She was pleased that she was not the only woman in the building, as she saw three eating together. She assumed they were clerical employees. Afterward, he took her to the payroll office, after which they returned to the city room.

"I hope this has been enough to get you started," said Graham, "but if you have any questions, just ask me. I will be around most of the time."

Ellen thanked him again for his help, and Graham returned to his office. Ellen sat at her desk and started organizing her workspace and spent the rest of the day reviewing recently published articles as well as stories in preparation. At the end of the day, she felt some satisfaction that things appeared to have progressed as she had wished and hoped. As she departed, she suddenly felt tired, probably due to some degree of tension, but she definitely looked forward to the next day.

* * *

"Well, I suppose we can tell our friends and neighbors that our daughter is to become the next Nellie Bly," Ellen's mother said to her a few days after she had started her position.

Ellen thought that her mother was absolutely serious. She replied, "I do admire Nellie Bly, Mother, but I don't expect to emulate her. I simply want to become established as a reporter at this point."

While in college, Ellen had studied the pioneering female reporter, Nellie Bly, born Elizabeth Cochrane, and what she had accomplished in Pittsburgh during the 1880s as a reporter for the *Dispatch*. She shared Nellie Bly's concerns for the conditions of women and for overall working conditions in society, and Ellen especially admired her ability to gain interviews with wealthy and powerful men of the era, including Andrew Carnegie and Henry Clay Frick. She knew that Bly had moved to New York in 1887 to join the *New York World* and, thereafter, had severed her Pittsburgh connections. Ellen had read of Nellie Bly's later fame resulting from her highly publicized trip around the world, lasting seventy-two days and being completed on January 25, 1890. She had beaten the fictional record of Jules Verne's *Around the World in Eighty Days* that had inspired her.

Ellen did not, however, regard herself as a budding social crusader in the manner of Bly, but simply as an aspiring reporter and writer. Further, she felt no imperative to prove that she could do as well as a man in a male-dominated profession, but she did have ambitions beyond reporting on food and fashion, which appeared to be the expected fields for those few females in the male-dominated profession. She thought that she might be more likely to follow the example of Willa Cather, who had worked for a time as a reporter in Pittsburgh and became a well-known writer and was now on the staff of *McClure's Magazine*.

Ellen continued living at home as she and her parents had agreed. She customarily rode the electric streetcar to the downtown area but did not often ride with her father, as her schedule involved starting earlier in the day and also ending earlier than his, as the afternoon edition went to press. Generally, she arrived home in time to help her mother and grandmother with dinner. Her parents no longer mentioned Walter Carrington, and she felt encouraged that they continued to accept her decision to pursue a career. Ellen recognized the adjustment her changed status required both of herself and her parents, from being the youngest in the family to being an independent adult beginning to earn a living.

For the past four years, after her older brothers Edgar and Richard had moved out and established their own households, the home consisted of Ellen, her parents, both in their fifties, plus her maternal grandmother, Ryan, approaching eighty. Edgar, age twenty-six, was associated with their father in his dry goods business, now known as Joseph Hobson and Son, while Richard, twenty-nine, was an accountant with the new United States Steel Corporation. Richard had married more than three years ago and recently had made his parents grandparents and Ellen an aunt. Edgar had also married early last year.

Julia Douglas married in late August, becoming Mrs. John Albright in a colorful ceremony at the Shady Side Presbyterian Church, also the Hobson family church, with Ellen as her main attendant. She and Ellen continued to see each other as before. Ellen's parents maintained their support, although she knew they still wished for her a more conventional existence, and from time to time made comments to that effect. Ellen, while respecting their views, still felt no lessening of her resolve to build a career.

Chapter Three

The Assignment

PITTSBURGH, AUTUMN 1904

After some three months at the *Reporter*, Ellen found herself evaluating her progress almost daily, comparing her experiences to that point with her original expectations. Was she progressing toward what she wanted to become professionally? She knew she had learned rapidly; she understood not only how to write news stories but also how the newspaper business operated and had succeeded at winning at least the tentative acceptance of some of the experienced reporters. She had been consistently deferential to their experience and believed that she had successfully conveyed her eagerness to learn. Despite those positive signs, Ellen still resented the fact that some on the staff had made sarcastic remarks about, among other things, her Bachelor of Arts degree, although she had not mentioned those episodes to either Roy Graham or Mr. Rutledge. She wondered if such remarks were actually defensive, since she had learned few male reporters possessed degrees or had pursued higher education. She disciplined herself to maintain a professional manner at all times, however, ignoring the disparaging and occasional lewd comments made about her as a woman that she sometimes overheard. She had applied herself diligently to her assigned tasks, and after sharing assignments with veteran reporters during her training, had begun pursuing some less significant assignments independently. She had turned out fifteen-hundred-word stories with regularity and had never missed a deadline.

One disappointment for Ellen, however, was that she had not been allowed her own byline. Even articles she had written entirely on her own were published either without a byline or with a pseudonym, but that practice appeared to be ingrained with all newspapers at the time. She had accepted the situation and had not complained to Roy, as she felt that she might succeed in gaining her byline after more time had passed and she had become better established in her position. In her almost daily contact with him, she had found Mr. Overstreet to be aloof, even taciturn, but was nonetheless relieved that he had begun to consistently approve her writing efforts. Ellen also had begun serving voluntarily as a proofreader for the work of others on the staff, after they determined that her skills in spelling and punctuation were superior to theirs. That alone had earned her the grudging respect of certain reporters, as her corrections and revisions had served to protect them from what surely would have been scathing criticism from Mr. Overstreet.

Despite occasionally being tempted to do so, Ellen had not complained about her less-than-elegant furnishings and working conditions, knowing that to say anything would only be likely to reinforce prejudices held by others about the suitability of a young woman in the newspaper world. Also, she had learned that newsrooms in general were sparsely furnished, with simple wooden desks and chairs. But she was frustrated at times with her battered desk and her old Underwood typewriter, as well as with her location in a cramped corner of the city room. Her principal view was of the smoky steel works running along the Monongahela River to the south, but she knew that the environment would improve eventually, as the mills were moving steadily out to the suburbs. To the west, her view was of the district popularly called The Point, where the Monongahela and Allegheny rivers converged to become the Ohio. A major portion of that district was used by the Pennsylvania Railroad, primarily as a large and noisy freight yard.

Ellen enjoyed watching the numerous steamboats and barges

operating on the rivers, and she also enjoyed watching the numerous incline railways running up Mount Washington. She became keenly aware of the busy pace of construction, as downtown Pittsburgh was rapidly becoming more modern. A window near her desk was generally kept open for ventilation, but the smoke and noise from the railroad yard largely counteracted the benefits. The window would be closed with the arrival of colder weather, of course, but that in turn would make the office stuffy and even more uncomfortable. The newsroom was generally noisy, but that condition affected all equally. One noise Ellen did enjoy was the rumble of the huge Goss presses, directly below her, when printing the daily edition. She invariably felt a quiet rush of excitement when the press run started. The final major aspect of Ellen's everyday existence was that the six-day workweek was exhausting, but she accepted it as the standard to which she had to adhere.

Roy Graham was true to his promise and had helped Ellen significantly with her training. She especially appreciated his defending her from the skepticism and occasional opposition of older reporters.

"Ellen, I have been aware that certain reporters have made remarks about you as the lone female on the staff," he had said, "and I have let it be known that they are to treat you with the same respect due their wives or sisters. I think it has had an effect, but if you encounter any new problems, bring them to me. I also know you would like a better desk location and better furnishings, and I will try to improve your situation, but I can't promise anything yet. As you know, the problem is that such improvements are almost always awarded on the basis of seniority."

Ellen replied to Roy that she appreciated his support, but also expressed the hope that he had not phrased his admonitions to the staff as being in direct response to any complaints from her. He stated emphatically that he had not. Reassured, Ellen decided not to press for any workplace improvements so long as there were those who remained resentful of her presence in the first place, but she was also aware that as the lone female she was not enhancing her chances of wider acceptance by consistently declining to join her male colleagues in trips to saloons after work. She acknowledged to her parents that they had been correct in their characterization of most reporters as coarse in manner and behavior; she frequently overheard profanity and other coarse comments, and while she had never been able to ignore them entirely, she disciplined herself not to react. She was gratified that Roy Graham would support—or more accurately, protect—her in such matters. He continued to speak with her on a daily basis, and she felt comfortable in approaching him whenever she needed advice.

One positive development was that she had formed a working relationship with Josh Raymond, an experienced reporter in his thirties, who offered to work with her on a story. She agreed, and they collaborated successfully. "Unlike some guys in the office, I believe we can help each other by working together," Josh had told her. Whenever she had an opportunity to interview anyone outside the office, she readily took it, and Josh helped turn the interview into a story, with his experience in adapting to the *Reporter* style. She made a habit of asking him his advice about reporting in general.

Ellen's private evaluation began with her determination that she had indeed made progress. She felt proud of what she had done, but was still disappointed that she had not been assigned to stories or news events that she could regard as highly significant. She had not been allowed to participate in coverage of the presidential campaign, in which Theodore Roosevelt was elected to a full term in a strong win over the Democrat, Alton Parker. Nor had she become involved with coverage of the gubernatorial election in Pennsylvania. The prevailing view was that since women could not vote, they would have little interest in electoral politics and consequently no place in reporting on campaigns. Reporting on business and financial developments was also closed to her. Stories primarily of concern to female readers, placed in what were informally called the society pages, had represented the majority of Ellen's assignments. In that respect she also worked to expand coverage of women's clubs, church activities, and household advice. She was interested in theater reviews, which all newspapers published regularly, but decided not to ask for such assignments until she had gained more experience.

Ellen also pursued a private goal of learning as much about the *Reporter* as she could. She knew that it had been established more than forty years ago during the Civil War and had grown rapidly in recent years as the newspaper business had boomed. She tried discreetly to learn something also of its ownership and governance. She knew that a general editor and a publisher with offices on the top floor were over Mr. Rutledge, but she had never met either. There was also a board of directors, but she understood little of how it operated or how it affected the city room. Further, those matters were little discussed among the staff, and she decided not to persist with detailed questions.

As a new employee, and especially as a young woman, Ellen knew that her major challenge was in persuading others that she could undertake more important stories and cover major news events. She had become aware that many major national and international stories were developed from Associated Press reports rather than by original investigative efforts, but supposed that was the standard practice for newspapers in Pittsburgh. Those reporters who did not resent Ellen's presence in the city room expressed concerns about her vulnerability if she were assigned to crime or disaster stories and their potentially dangerous conditions. The most positive aspects of her experience to date were that she had learned that she possessed a gift for interviewing, and that she enjoyed writing. But she wanted most to expand the scope of her reporting assignments and felt she could handle stories about business and political events, and perhaps even developments in science.

Despite her demonstrable progress, and her successful adaptation to the conditions of her position, Ellen concluded that she was in danger of becoming bored or frustrated if the scope of her assignments did not expand—and soon. Through wide reading, she had learned what others, including female reporters, were doing in journalism since the time of Nellie Bly. She admired the series of muckraking articles by Ida Tarbell on John D. Rockefeller and the Standard Oil Company that began appearing in 1902 in *McClure's Magazine. McClure's* had been founded in 1893 by Samuel S. McClure, a reporter who had been determined to break down barriers in reporting on those in power. *McClure's*, in the opinion of many, had ushered in the age of muckraking. The issue also struck close to home, since major Standard Oil operations were located in the Pittsburgh area. Ellen learned that the Tarbell articles recently had been published in book form, reaching an even wider audience. She aspired to assignments approaching that level of significance someday, even though she did not necessarily regard herself as a muckraker in the style of Nellie Bly. Nor did she aspire to undertake anything as monumental as had Ida Tarbell.

Ellen decided to speak with Mr. Rutledge, knowing that his support would be essential if she was to have a chance of achieving her goal. She knew she would have to persuade him that she should undertake broader and more challenging assignments. After mentally rehearsing what she would say, and arranging a time to speak with him, she approached Rutledge in his office. He gestured for her to take a seat.

"Mr. Rutledge," she began, somewhat nervously. "I am happy to be here and appreciate all you have done for me. I also think I have progressed in my work, but I have been considering where my future might lie. I feel I should move beyond the types of stories I have been assigned so far. I want to cover news events and pursue stories of greater significance I hope you do not judge me as being premature in my aspirations."

"I have been pleased with your writing so far, Ellen," replied Rutledge, "and you have conducted some effective interviews. Also, we have not had much in the way of interpretative reporting in the past, and I am impressed that you appear to write more in that vein than others. That is an area where this paper needs to become stronger. So, your ambition doesn't surprise me. The question is what more I can offer you at this time."

He thought for a moment.

"I still have concerns that you might be placed in danger if I assign you to cover crimes or natural disasters. If any harm came to you, it would reflect badly on this paper. I don't think involving you in political reporting would be well accepted either."

"I appreciate your concerns, sir," she replied. "Perhaps there are other news developments posing less danger or controversy that I could cover, or there might be social conditions I could investigate. I would also be interested in interviewing leading figures in industry and business and perhaps reporting on developments in their fields. I have even given some thought to reporting on scientific progress. Eventually, I could develop stories as significant as those of Nellie Bly."

"I'm not displeased that you are thinking along those lines, and I know that in time you could do well with such assignments," he replied, "but the problem is that those areas are already covered by others on the staff. I also believe that it takes several years to develop a strong reporter, and I advise you to be patient. You know that I have defended you to those who did not favor a female reporter on the staff, and so has Roy, but I can foresee increased difficulties and resentments if you move into more challenging fields so soon. Let me take some time to consider what you have told me."

Ellen agreed and returned to her desk. She was at least relieved that Mr. Rutledge had not reacted entirely negatively to her ideas.

The next day, Rutledge called her into his office.

"You may be pleased to learn that I have developed one idea for an assignment based on what we discussed. It would involve some travel, if you are open to that."

"Certainly," replied Ellen. "I would welcome the chance to travel. I have hardly left the state of Pennsylvania."

"It wouldn't be across the country," replied Rutledge, with a soft laugh, "only to Ohio. But first, do you know anything about the science of aeronautics, or have you read anything about it?"

Ellen replied that she knew nothing, although she was aware that some men had been aloft in balloons. She was mystified as to why Rutledge would bring up a subject but decided not to say so at the moment.

"I understand almost nothing about the science either," responded Rutledge, "and we have no one on the staff who possesses any interests in that direction. But here is my idea for you: I remembered reading some rather sketchy stories several months ago about two brothers from Dayton, Ohio, who reported that they had succeeded with a powered flying machine. I think some call it aerial navigation. Anyway, these brothers claimed that they had propelled the machine into the air, controlled it, and brought it back to earth safely. They conducted their experiments at some remote location on the North Carolina coast, but I have the impression that they are now continuing their work back in Dayton. I opened a file on the matter at the time, and have added a few notes to it since, but I haven't pursued anything further or thought much about doing so until now."

"I suppose that I have heard some speculation about such flying machines," said Ellen, "but I had no idea one had actually been built and tested. I had always assumed that the idea of man flying about in a machine, or aerial navigation as you said, was impossible."

"So had I," he replied, "and so had many men of science, as I understand it. But I believe that the possibility may be something we should not overlook. It is not that this story would involve major figures in business and industry, as you mentioned yesterday, but if you regard aeronautical development as being at the forefront of science and invention, I suppose this would qualify. It could also turn out to be a development that this paper should be devoting its attention to."

"Unfortunately, I know little of science, much less of aeronautics," said Ellen, "but I could study and learn."

"Then you would be interested in reporting on these brothers and investigating their claims?"

"Yes, sir. And by coincidence, I have visited Dayton twice before with my family, although not for several years. I have a great aunt there, my grandmother's sister, who was the reason for my family's trips. Anyway, I would love the chance to interview the brothers and observe their flying experiments, assuming they are still conducting them. I could then learn for myself if they have done what they claimed."

"Excellent," replied Rutledge. "The fact that you have a relative there makes it easier for you to travel on your own, as that was another concern I had. Since you will be working on a story out of state, that should serve to reduce any resentment about your assignment by others on the staff. I suggest that you contact these brothers directly and determine if they will grant you an interview and allow you to observe their experiments, although I cannot imagine why they would not. It would appear to me that an invention of that significance should have been publicized throughout the country, but as far as I can determine, that has not been the case. I checked and found that the New York papers have printed little, and I don't think the Ohio papers have done that much either. So, if it turns out that there is something to the story, we may have an advantage."

"Do you have their name and address?"

"The name is Wright," he replied. "I don't have a full address, but you may study the information in my file and proceed from there. If you receive a reply from them and get approval for a visit, I shall approve your travel to Dayton. Incidentally, I have met the editor of one of the Dayton newspapers, Luther Beard of the *Journal*, who might be a good source. I will give you his address; you probably should contact him first."

"That sounds like an excellent beginning," said Ellen. "I'm rather excited at the prospect."

"Good. But I would still caution you that the story may turn out to be a hoax, or that this flying machine may not be anything close to what the brothers have claimed. It wouldn't be the first time that a claim for some great invention has turned out to be a hoax, of course. And even if their claims are true, it still troubles me that the story has not been more widely reported and their machine better recognized."

"I understand, but if I can establish that they have not really done what they say they have done, that would be a public service as well."

Rutledge agreed, and turned over the file to Ellen, who returned to her desk and began reviewing its contents. She found some handwritten notes by Rutledge, but there were only three newspaper clippings. The first and most complete was from the Norfolk *Virginian-Pilot*, in which large headlines were followed by a story including a claim of a flight of three miles. The remaining news reports in the file were from the Cincinnati *Enquirer* and New York *American*, but their reports appeared to have extended from that of the *Virginian-Pilot*. All the accounts appeared to Ellen confusing and to some degree contradictory, and none was by an eyewitness. The major point of agreement in the reports was that the brothers Wilbur and Orville Wright of Dayton, Ohio, had reported successful tests of a powered flying machine last December near a town called Kitty Hawk, on the North Carolina Outer Banks.

Ellen saw another newspaper article, reporting on a failed flight attempt by a Professor Langley of the Smithsonian Institution about the same time as that of the Wright brothers. From the illustration in the story, the Langley machine appeared to be large and heavy. According to the report, it had crashed into the Potomac River, but the pilot had been rescued. Evidently, Langley had given up his attempts following the failure. Ellen felt herself intrigued by the problems and challenges posed by flight attempts.

After her initial excitement and mounting interest in the story, however, Ellen found herself becoming somewhat apprehensive. This was what she wanted to happen, but now she felt rather nervous. She would not say so to anyone at the *Reporter*, of course.

She had not imagined an assignment of that nature, nor had she anticipated traveling alone outside the state, although the fact that she had some familiarity with Dayton made that prospect more welcoming. Regardless of any and all possible drawbacks, she saw the assignment as a unique opportunity, and she was determined to make the most of it. Her immediate concern was that she was hopelessly bewildered by the idea of powered flight. What little she had read about those men who had conducted glider experiments and who had made ascensions in balloons constituted her total knowledge.

It continued to puzzle Ellen, as it had Rutledge, that such an achievement had not been more widely recognized and publicized. She thought the Wright brothers' flight claims suspicious in that they took place in such an isolated area, with no reporters or outside witnesses present, rather than in a city or other more accessible location. With further inquiries, Ellen learned that the basis of the original story was not a press release intended for newspapers but a telegram the brothers had sent to their father from Kitty Hawk that was routed through Norfolk. Two freelance reporters had seen the telegram and developed the news story from that source alone, applying considerable imagination in the process.

It became clear to Ellen that proceeding with the story would require her to deal with many wide-ranging questions, with no obvious answers or explanations. She thought, as had Rutledge, that the most likely reason there had been little further publicity about the flight experiments was that there was little substance to them in the first place. Further, and as far as she could understand, even successful powered flight or aerial navigation had little or no practical purpose. That led her, in turn, to question what benefit such a feat would be to the country or to the public. While Ellen still welcomed the opportunity offered by the assignment, it dwelt in her mind that powered flight, even if true, simply carried no real significance beyond the fact that it had been accomplished. Further, she felt that the lack of significance may have been the principal reason why there had been little in the way of subsequent news coverage. Nevertheless, she was determined to find out if there was more to the story.

Late in November, as suggested by Rutledge, Ellen wrote General Editor Luther Beard of the Dayton *Journal*, explaining her purpose. She felt encouraged when she received a prompt reply from Beard. She opened his letter immediately and began reading.

Dear Miss Hobson:

I remember with pleasure meeting Theodore Rutledge, your managing editor, some time ago. Whenever you travel to Dayton, please notify me and I will be glad to meet with you and extend whatever help I can with your assignment. The Wright boys run a bicycle shop, and I have their business address, as follows:

    Wilbur and Orville Wright
    Wright Cycle Company
    1127 West Third Street
    Dayton, Ohio

All three of our Dayton dailies, the Daily News, Evening Herald, *and my* Journal, *carried brief reports on their flight claims after receiving the initial story, but I don't know of any substantial reporting since then. I don't know much about the brothers either, although I understand they are sons of Bishop Milton Wright, who is a man of some prominence here. I have been informed that they are continuing their work at a field outside the city, but I don't know if their experiments are intended to remain secret or otherwise. I have the impression they have not been that open about their work, and I am afraid that I remain personally skeptical about their experiments.*

I do not wish to appear cynical about your assignment or about your prospects for developing a full report; I just regret that I don't have any more information at this time. I will be glad to provide whatever assistance I can when you arrive.

Very truly yours,
Luther Beard, General Editor

Ellen was pleased with Beard's interest and offer of help, of course. She was somewhat perplexed that the business of the brothers appeared to be bicycles, but decided to hold her questions about that matter until later. She wrote Luther Beard again to thank him for his help and promised to notify him when she would be traveling to Dayton.

Ellen promptly wrote the brothers at the address supplied by Beard. Addressing the letter to Messrs. Wilbur and Orville Wright, she identified herself and briefly explained her interest. Early in December she received a reply, which she opened eagerly.

Dear Miss Hobson:

Thank you for your expression of interest in our flying experiments and our machine. We have been quite busy with our flight tests as well as other business, but would be willing to provide you with certain information on our work and permit you to witness our flights in the future. We must point out, however, that we have not been pleased with reportage on our work to this point. Most stories have been distorted or inaccurate, and we find that there are many narrow minds that cannot or will not accept that we have conquered the air. We remain determined to gain recognition, of course, and are willing to cooperate with you regarding our flying experiments, but within strict limits. Generally, we do not grant formal interviews, and it will be necessary to restrict certain details of the design and construction of our invention, since we have not yet secured a patent. Also, we will not permit photographs.

In any event, we have ceased flying for the year, so there would be no early opportunity for you to observe flights. We made a great deal of progress with our tests here and expect to achieve more in the year ahead. We are now designing a new machine that will incorporate improvements over our first two models, and which we expect to have ready in the spring. We recommend, therefore, that you postpone your visit until we are ready to test our new machine. In the meantime, we shall be occupied with gaining the patent and with securing an order from the War Department. We believe our machine possesses military value. If you believe that you can help our endeavors, and you can accept our restrictions, we shall welcome your visit. As always, however, our work must take precedence over any dealings with reporters or with the public. We suggest that you contact us again, possibly in April or May, when the new machine should be ready.

Until then, we remain,
Yours truly,
Wilbur and Orville Wright

Ellen was encouraged that the brothers did not refuse cooperation, but was somewhat concerned in that they appeared less than enthusiastic about spending time with another reporter. She could appreciate their candid statements about their frustration in gaining recognition for their work and how they did not understand the public's reluctance to recognize their accomplishment. On another level, she was favorably impressed with the evident literacy of the brothers, which was more impressive than most correspondence she read in the course of her duties. Ellen reported her findings to Rutledge, who advised her to do as they suggested. He promised again to approve her trip if she could complete the necessary arrangements.

While feeling sympathetic with the Wright brothers about their displeasure over the frequent distorted and disdainful reporting they had seen, Ellen wanted to believe that their true reason for offering to cooperate was a hope that a fresh insight—hers—might result in a more complete, impartial story. She also regarded the assignment as an opportunity to prove that she was a serious reporter. She emphasized those points in her reply.

Dear Messrs. Wright:
Thank you for your prompt response to my query. I understand your concerns about protecting your invention, and I shall abide

by your restrictions. Further, I agree that I should not schedule a visit until your new machine is ready for testing. My chief personal goal is to learn, and only afterward to publish a story on your work. I pledge again that I will strive for accuracy in everything I write.

I will contact you again, probably in April as you suggested, then travel to Dayton after we have agreed on a specific date. I thank you for your response and willingness to cooperate in what I believe could be an important story.

I remain, sincerely yours,
Ellen Hobson, Miss

Afterward, Ellen briefed Rutledge on her progress with the assignment. She also wrote a brief note to Luther Beard explaining that her trip would be delayed. Privately, she felt somewhat crestfallen that she would not be able to make the trip immediately after having developed such enthusiasm for the assignment. But she still looked forward to going in the spring, and she wrote her great aunt of the prospect in the family Christmas card.

Chapter Four

Orville

Dayton, Spring 1905

The months since her correspondence with the Wright brothers passed rapidly for Ellen. She had concentrated fully on stories she had been assigned since and felt that she had made further progress with her journalistic skills. By becoming increasingly absorbed in her daily duties, she had overcome her disappointment that her first independent assignment had been postponed. She especially enjoyed participating in a major series of stories the *Reporter* had undertaken in connection with the fortieth anniversary of the end of the war, involving interviews with Pittsburgh Civil War veterans and lengthy articles concerning their experiences. Ellen conducted many such interviews on her own, transcribed the reminiscences of others, and had worked with several colleagues in developing them into articles. She had included an interview with her grandmother Ryan, who shared her many vivid memories, and her parents also contributed their childhood memories.

Actively maintaining the Dayton assignment in her plans, Ellen attempted to research aeronautics as time permitted but could find very little in the Central Carnegie Library. She read of the gliding experiments of a young German engineer named Otto Lilienthal, and of his fatal crash in 1896. She also found a book entitled *Progress in Flying Machines*, published in 1894 by an American engineer named Octave Chanute. The Chanute book contained accounts of numerous aeronautical experiments, but Ellen could understand little of its technical content. Additionally, she read reports of the airship ascensions in France of a young Brazilian named Alberto Santos-Dumont, including his circuit around the Eiffel Tower in 1902.

She wrote again to the Wright brothers in April, the month in which she celebrated her twenty-third birthday. First referring to her earlier contact, she expressed her hope that their new machine was progressing on schedule, then proposed to travel to Dayton sometime in May if that would be convenient for them. The brothers again replied promptly, informing her at the outset that they were somewhat behind schedule, largely due to the press of legal and Army matters. Because of those factors, they explained, they had not yet begun assembling their new machine, which they now felt would not be ready until sometime in June. Ellen responded, agreeing to postpone her trip until then in order to have the opportunity to witness actual flight tests, and promised that she would contact them again in order to gain their agreement as to a specific travel date.

After that exchange, Ellen devoted much of her attention to stories dealing with President Roosevelt's role as a mediator for the Russo-Japanese War, concluding with the Treaty of Portsmouth. She did not directly participate in reporting the events but assisted with organizing and editing overall coverage while striving to understand all implications of the developments. The *Reporter* did not have an international correspondent, but many reports on the progress of the peace efforts came through the Washington correspondent. Ellen wrote several reports in collaboration with other reporters, usually placing the events into a local perspective.

Early in June she wrote the Wright brothers again, informing them that she would like to arrive on June 21, and asked them to notify her in the event of another delay in testing their flyer. She also mentioned that she would arrange to stay for several days in order to gain enough understanding for an in-depth story.

Ellen then wrote her great aunt Keys to announce her

forthcoming trip to Dayton. Her two previous visits to her great aunt had been with her family, but the most recent was six years ago, and her memories were not that vivid. Since that time, she had maintained contact with her primarily through her grandmother. She asked if she might stay with her during her upcoming visit. As Ellen expected, her aunt Keys replied that she would be happy to have her visit and that she would be most welcome to stay in her home. Ellen's parents expressed some concern about her traveling alone over such a distance, but she asserted her confidence in that it was the twentieth century and that young women could now do such things.

In the meantime, the Wright brothers had replied to Ellen, agreeing to her proposed arrival date and adding that her plans appeared reasonable. They informed her that they had almost completed assembly of their new flyer and would begin tests upon its completion. Ellen sent a brief letter to Luther Beard in which she announced her trip schedule and stated that she looked forward to meeting him. With those arrangements underway, she briefed both Theodore Rutledge and Roy Graham about the status of her contacts with the Wright brothers and with Luther Beard. They met in Rutledge's office.

"Everything appears to be in order for my trip," she began. "The brothers are expecting me, and Mr. Beard has also agreed to see me. I have read whatever I could find on aeronautics at the library, so at least I have learned something. Not that my understanding is very great, but I somewhat comprehend what other experimenters have done."

"That sounds fine," replied Rutledge. "Have you completed your arrangements for the trip?"

"Yes. My great aunt is prepared for my visit, and I have my return train ticket."

"I wish you a successful trip," said Roy, as she stood up to leave. She thanked him, although sensing that Roy lacked enthusiasm about her assignment. But Rutledge appeared pleased with her plans and expressed his approval of her travel schedule. She also mentioned to Josh Raymond that she would be traveling, and Ellen asked him to keep up with developments in the office for her during her absence. He agreed to do so.

Ellen spent the Sunday morning of June 20 with her family, attending church services as usual, then departed for Dayton from the new Union Station of the Pennsylvania Railroad that afternoon. The Pennsylvania Railroad ran as far west as St. Louis, and Ellen felt confident that transportation connections would be reliable. While she had assured her family that she could travel alone without worry, she remained privately concerned since she had very little experience with trains. She was somewhat relieved to find that her seatmate was a woman rather older than her parents, who was traveling to Columbus to visit relatives. They conversed sporadically but pleasantly during the trip. As she watched the Ohio countryside pass by, Ellen could appreciate what she regarded as rapid twentieth century progress. She knew that cities such as Columbus and Springfield, although much smaller than Pittsburgh, boasted tall buildings, and industry was everywhere in evidence. She knew also that Dayton was much smaller than Pittsburgh, with a population of only some eighty-five thousand as compared with more than four hundred thousand for Pittsburgh, but nonetheless was a significant and growing industrial center.

The trip, though only some six hours in duration, had given Ellen time to reflect on her life in the year after her graduation from college. She found satisfaction in having begun a career and enjoyed being out in the world to the extent that she was. She did not mind still living at home, and her relationship with her parents remained good despite their differing aspirations for her. She had been almost totally preoccupied with her work and was not unduly concerned about a lack of gentleman callers, as her mother had phrased it. Her decision to remain single clearly was the correct one, she thought, and that status could always change if her life evolved in another direction. She accepted that she was no beauty—her friend Julia always had attracted more attention from young men than Ellen had—and regarded herself as average in all respects, possessing nothing approaching a Gibson Girl face or figure. While she still felt confident about her life and prospects, Ellen admitted to herself that she experienced periods of loneliness even when surrounded by family or newspaper associates. She also asked herself if she felt somewhat envious of Julia's evident happiness. About the flying machine assignment she had gained no particular premonition, but she still held high hopes that, if successful, it would be advantageous to her career. Without question, this was the closest she had come to an adventure since becoming a reporter, and she felt her expectations about the assignment were not unrealistic. Thus, she passed the hours of the trip in a highly positive frame of mind.

The journey was smooth, and the train arrived on schedule. As the train approached Union Station, Ellen quickly observed much progress in Dayton in the six years since she had last visited. It even boasted a skyscraper, the Conover Building of thirteen stories. Also, the Union Station was new, having been completed since her last visit, and she thought it very impressive. She noted that Dayton, in addition to being smaller than Pittsburgh, was quite different in character in that it was situated in a shallow river valley with its streets laid out principally on a grid, while Pittsburgh was built over numerous hills, with predominantly winding streets. She learned that there was a trolley serving the adjacent southern suburb of Oakwood, where her great aunt Keys lived. She boarded the trolley, taking note of the massive National Cash Register industrial complex along the way, then walked directly to her great aunt's house, only two blocks from the trolley stop.

Ellen found that she remembered the house and its location very well. As she approached, she saw the front door opening before she had a chance to knock. Elizabeth Keys had been watching for her and welcomed her with an enthusiastic embrace. Ellen enjoyed their warm reunion. She was pleased that her great aunt—although having visibly aged since her last visit—was alert and articulate. Aunt Keys exclaimed over and over about how Ellen had grown up. In the course of the pleasant evening, after relating family news, Ellen discussed her plans to report on the Wright brothers and their flying machine and asked her great aunt if she knew anything of the brothers or their experiments.

"I remember meeting Bishop Milton Wright at a church gathering a few years ago," said Elizabeth Keys, "but I don't know anything about the family. With his standing as a bishop, I would suppose them to be highly respectable, but I just don't recall reading anything about the boys' flying machine. I'm afraid I don't keep up with events as well as I should. I suppose if their experiments had been talked much of in the city, I would have heard something, and that leads me to think there isn't much talk. So, I'm afraid I won't be of much help to you."

"I didn't expect anything like that from you," replied Ellen. "I just wanted to tell you about my assignment."

"I do appreciate that, although it all sounds beyond me and my generation. But I am proud for you. Your assignment certainly sounds like quite a challenge for a young lady."

Ellen then turned the conversation to her great aunt's immediate family, since she did not know much about her mother's cousins.

"My two sons live away, unfortunately, one in Cincinnati and one near Indianapolis, but they are very faithful in visiting me from time to time. They are busy with their own lives and families, of course, but I do regret that you have not had the opportunity to know your cousins."

Ellen expressed the same regret. She worried over her great aunt's evident loneliness, but admired her determination to maintain her home and her independence. Aunt Keys stated that she had a part-time housekeeper who assisted with many everyday chores. Ellen found that reassuring. She was also impressed that Aunt Keys had had a telephone installed recently. She had observed that telephones were becoming more commonplace in Dayton, as they were in Pittsburgh.

After breakfast the next morning, Ellen lifted the receiver and asked the operator to connect her to General Editor Luther Beard of the Dayton *Journal*. When he answered, she greeted him by referring immediately to their previous correspondence and to Theodore Rutledge. Beard likewise recalled their contact and invited her to his office that morning, to which she agreed. Ellen traveled to the *Journal* building on Main Street by trolley. As she entered, she noted immediately the sharp contrast between the small, relatively quiet *Journal* offices and her own noisy city room; only a few individuals were present in the newsroom. Luther Beard received her promptly and graciously. He first asked after Theodore Rutledge, and Ellen responded by adding that Rutledge had spoken favorably of him. She sensed immediately that he was a man who liked to speak volubly and decided that her best course of action was to let him do so.

"As I told you," Beard began, "we carried a brief report in our paper on the Wright boys' flying experiments in North Carolina back at the time, which was in December of 1903. We haven't reported anything since. One of my reporters went to their field outside the city last year to observe but did not write a story. I would be glad to let you talk to him, of course, but he is out on an assignment today. I'll tell you that he became somewhat frustrated in trying to cover the experiments anyway. He explained to me that the first day he went there, the brothers did not fly because of weather, then another time they had problems with their engine. But I think the main reason he became disenchanted was that they withheld technical details of their craft, and I have heard that is the reason other reporters have lost interest in reporting on them and their machine. I expect their information restrictions will be the major obstacle you will face, unless the boys have changed their policy since then."

"I appreciate that information," said Ellen. "That is precisely what I need to know in order to succeed with my assignment. They have told me that they still impose restrictions on all reporters, but I made it clear that I am willing to work around those. They also informed me that they have constructed a new machine,

A Romance of Flight

and it is possible they may be testing it already. But I would appreciate any further information you have about them and their work."

"Well," he continued, "about all I know about the Wright boys is that their primary occupation is a bicycle business. They sell and produce their own designs as well as those of others and evidently are fairly successful. But I don't know what scientific training they have that would qualify them as aeronautical experimenters. It does appear that they have gotten themselves into the air in some fashion, but personally I remain as skeptical as I was when we first corresponded. I'm doubtful that they have developed anything of practical value, and at this point I have no interest in reporting further on them. One brother—I don't remember which—came to my office to question our lack of coverage of their flight experiments, but that was more than a year ago. That's about all I can tell you about my paper's involvement."

"That is still helpful to me," said Ellen. "Do you know how they got started with flying machines originally?"

"Not really, although I think they have been active for several years. I have been told that they want recognition, but at the same time they seem to have a penchant for secrecy about the details of their work, as I've been saying. Frankly, I find that somewhat strange, even contradictory, and I suppose that is another reason why I am skeptical. What I do know is that their machine is not patented, and it appears that they are concerned about having their ideas stolen. I expect they may give you that reason for wanting to control your reporting, and I'm afraid that is something you will have to manage yourself."

"They told me much the same thing in their letter. I suppose I can appreciate their viewpoint, but it appears to me, as it does to you, that they will need to become more open if they wish to have their work recognized by the public. Do you have any reason to suspect that they may be frauds? I have gained the impression that there have been some fraudulent claims about flying machines and aerial navigation."

"I don't really suspect them to be frauds, but as I said, I still question that their machine really operates in anything approaching reliability. I also don't know what the practical uses of such a machine would be, and I don't think they have explained that either. I suppose that is something else you will have to learn for yourself, and I wish you well."

"Finally, do you have any personal information on them?" asked Ellen. "Anything about their education, for instance?"

"What I understand is that neither brother is married and that they both still live at the family home. And I don't know anything about their education. I have the impression they are rather reclusive. In fact, before you arrived, I asked my reporter who observed their experiments about that, and he confirmed that he encountered resistance in getting the background information he wanted. He also told me that they were disinclined to permit personal interviews, and I think I should add the caution that you could face another problem in being female. I know there are a few female reporters in large city dailies, but there are none in Dayton. Since the brothers appear to be somewhat guarded with reporters in general, you could experience a problem in that they might be even less comfortable in dealing with a female reporter. I hope you will not regard this as offensive, but I could see that potential problem being compounded by your obvious youth. I did not expect you to be so young, and that may be the reaction of the Wright brothers also."

Ellen decided not to react immediately to that statement, but said instead, "They likewise told me in their correspondence that they generally do not grant interviews. I hope I can draw them out in conversation, and I know it will be up to me to learn as much as I can by observing. I can't do anything about my youth, but I have had some success with interviews even when the subjects have been less than eager. So, I can appreciate everything you have told me, but I think I have dealt successfully with such issues in my position with the *Reporter*, and I am confident I can overcome any doubts about my gender and youth. At least they knew my gender when they agreed to my visit."

She added that Theodore Rutledge had expressed confidence that she could complete the assignment, and that she might even do a better job of reporting on the flight experiments than others had done to that point. Beard nodded, appearing to be reassured by her response, then spoke again. "I thought of something else that may help you in the way of background. Bishop Milton Wright, their father, is quite well known in the Dayton area, as I mentioned earlier. He has been involved in several controversies regarding the governance of his United Brethren denomination, and we have reported some news to that effect. I understand the bishop to be a rather strong-willed, uncompromising individual, but I don't know what influence he may have on his sons in that regard. I believe he is now retired, and I haven't kept up with the status of the church controversies. That may be something you will find out in the course of your visit. The only other thing I could mention in the way of personal information is that I expect you might find the Wrights to be a very close-knit family. I don't have any proof, but that is the impression I have gained.

"I would also caution you," Beard concluded, "that even though the brothers have agreed to your visit, they probably would view with disfavor anything you might do or say that could cause interruptions or distractions from their work. So, this could prove to be a difficult assignment for you in many respects."

Ellen replied that the brothers had already made her aware of their work priorities in addition to their restrictions, and she agreed that it might be difficult for her to develop a meaningful story.

"Another thing that bothers me," he added, "and I could be wrong, is that it just seems that the brothers are taking valuable time away from their business by pursuing this flying machine. They are fairly successful in bicycles, and I think they should stick to what they know best."

Closing the interview, Ellen thanked Beard again for his assistance. He in turn asked her to extend his regards to Rutledge. As she departed, she found herself feeling vaguely discouraged by the overall tone of the information he had provided. Still, given her relative ignorance of aeronautics, she remained determined to learn what she could about the field as well as about the two brothers who claimed to have succeeded with powered flight.

Ellen returned by the trolley to her great aunt's house. While feeling somewhat apprehensive, she used her great aunt's telephone and called the bicycle shop. Her call was answered by Orville Wright, who she assumed to be the younger of the brothers since his name had appeared second in correspondence. Ellen announced her arrival to him and reconfirmed her wish to visit. Orville Wright replied that he remembered their correspondence and, although sounding unenthusiastic, agreed to meet with her that afternoon.

After lunch with Aunt Keys, Ellen walked to the Oakwood trolley stop where she boarded the trolley to the city center, then waited at the busy central platform to change to the trolley for West Dayton. Soon, she approached the West Third Street business district and the Wright Cycle Company. As she arrived, she could sense that the street was the hub of the West Dayton commercial area, and that while not appearing as fashionable as the central business district, it was still respectable. It also was quite busy, with the street and sidewalks teeming with people and traffic. She observed in passing that the neighborhood appeared to be racially integrated, a factor with which she was not accustomed but did not concern her.

She located the Wright Cycle Company, a small storefront establishment, as she traveled by and stepped off at the next stop. As she walked up to the shop, she noted that it was far smaller than her father's dry goods emporium, but decided that its location probably was advantageous, being on such a busy street and also not far from the central business district.

A doorbell announced her presence as Ellen entered, and she saw immediately that no customers were present. She was somewhat surprised in that the interior space was smaller than she had imagined, though she thought it very orderly and efficient in its layout. There was a display space in front for bicycles, tires and parts were hanging along both walls, and a small semi-enclosed office was located toward the back. There were several bicycles of a variety of designs on display. A man she presumed to be Orville Wright walked through an opening in the rear, removed the apron he was wearing, and wiped his hands with a cloth. She assumed the area he had exited was a workroom for assembly and repairs.

"Mr. Wright? I am Ellen Hobson of the Pittsburgh *Reporter*. I thank you for agreeing to meet with me." She offered her hand.

"How do you do, Miss Hobson?" he replied. "I am Orville Wright."

Ellen found him to be an unremarkable looking man, probably in his mid-thirties, with dark, thinning hair and a prominent mustache. She noticed immediately that he was neatly, carefully dressed. She felt his greeting was rather stiff and perfunctory, although that did not especially bother her. While she could not be certain, she speculated that he may have been somewhat startled by her youth, as Beard had warned. Perhaps he was indeed expecting someone older.

"My brother Wilbur usually deals with reporters and other inquirers," he stated immediately. "Unfortunately, he is not available today as he is helping our father on some important church-related business. Our father is a retired bishop of the Church of the United Brethren."

"I learned that recently," replied Ellen, remembering that Luther Beard had thought the bishop was now retired. "Well, I look forward to talking with your brother tomorrow. In the meantime, I hope we can make some progress on a story this afternoon, and that you will have time to answer some of my many questions. I respect your policy on interviews, so I would prefer to think of this as a conversation. It would also be helpful if I could learn something about your work in aeronautics before I witness actual tests of the flyer."

The shop was quiet, and Orville agreed to her suggestion. He excused himself to go back to the repair room for a moment, then returned and escorted Ellen to his office, where he took the swivel chair at the desk and offered her a wooden armchair.

"First, let me explain that this will be a learning experience for me," she said. "I do not pretend to possess any expertise in the field of aeronautics. My editor was interested because he was aware of some brief news reports about your flying experiments and felt that there was possibly an important story here. He gave me the assignment because I am interested in pursuing stories of significance, especially with regard to scientific and industrial progress. I'm still a fledgling reporter, with less than a year's experience, but he felt that I had progressed to the point that I could handle an important assignment."

Orville nodded his understanding.

"I hope you will permit me to profile your work in depth," she continued. "Since you have stated that you have not been pleased with reporting so far, I really believe that what I can write will benefit you as well as the public."

Orville again indicated his agreement but still appeared to be unenthusiastic. Ellen had already decided that she would approach the subject of powered flight as a believer rather than as a skeptic, feeling that that would be the best way to maintain the cooperation of the brothers.

"What I know so far," she continued, "is that you successfully tested your first flyer in North Carolina in December of 1903, which would be about eighteen months ago. Then you told me in your letter about the progress you had made in testing a second machine here last year. Perhaps you could describe the current state of your experiments."

"I'll do so," said Orville, "and we are quite optimistic about our new flyer. We think it will fly much better than our first two models. I should mention that we are continuing our bicycle business while working on our flyer and conducting flight experiments. We make our living in bicycles, and everything we have done on our flying machine we financed ourselves."

A Romance of Flight

He mentioned again that he expected his brother Wilbur to be available tomorrow. Ellen was concerned that Orville was becoming somewhat impatient to hurry her along so he could return to his work, although he continued to speak in an even tone.

"Could you possibly give me some background on your publicity efforts to date?" asked Ellen. "It appears that little recognition has been given to you, and I'm sure you want public acceptance of your work."

"Correct," Orville replied. "After we succeeded at Kitty Hawk with our flyer, we were determined that we would gain recognition. But we found that few newspapers or reporters were interested in reporting on our accomplishment. I think those in Dayton simply didn't believe our account. I suppose one problem may have been that no reporters had personally witnessed our flights there, although there were five witnesses from the local community. Wilbur and I were displeased that the major story reported at the time was stolen from the telegram we had sent our father from the Kitty Hawk weather station, and was grossly distorted." Orville paused, as if to catch his breath. He appeared to think, then continued.

"When we returned to Dayton, we were interviewed at our home by a female reporter, a Bertha Comstock of the Chicago *Tribune*, but no published story resulted. The Dayton papers also carried brief reports, but we understand that was only after they learned that the Cincinnati *Enquirer* had done so. So, after that, we decided to write our own news release on our success and submitted it to the Associated Press just after the first of the year. We found that the Dayton office showed no interest, just as the newspapers had not. It was some time before the AP actually developed a story that it placed into release, but it still was very brief and filled with inaccuracies. Some versions even had us flying out over the ocean."

Ellen nodded her understanding, while assuming that Orville's pointed reference to a female reporter was for her benefit. She could sense that the subject of reporters and newspapers was something of an issue with him, and said to him that she had been aware of the distorted initial reports of their achievement and the deficiencies in reporting. But she could not help feeling somewhat taken aback at Orville's open skepticism, if not hostility, toward reporters. He had not raised his voice, but she could discern some underlying anger. She did not think any anger was directed at her, but she knew she would have to tread lightly in conversing with him.

"My brother and I adopted a policy last year of talking to those reporters who wished to report on our work," Orville continued, "but only on our terms, and that included no photographs by others. We invited several reporters to witness our flights here, but we saw no indication that they gave us any meaningful recognition. We know that some were unhappy with our restrictions, but as we informed you, we must maintain them until we have gained our patent."

"I understand," Ellen quickly replied, "and as you know, I will respect your restrictions." She was glad the shop had remained quiet during their talk, with no customers entering. She decided to steer Orville's attention back to the question she had raised initially. "Can you now update me as to the status of your experiments?"

He complied. "I think it would be better if I started by giving you some background on our tests last year. But before that, I must tell you that we had to leave our first flyer at Kitty Hawk, since we had no means of transporting it back at the time. We were able to go back early last year to crate it and ship it to Dayton, but it is still in storage. We then built a new machine and began testing it on May 26 last year, at our flying field here. We tested it over six months and made about a hundred flights."

Seemingly as an afterthought, he added, "I am assuming you would like specific dates."

"I would indeed." She continued making notes as Orville spoke.

"Our trials with our first flyer at Kitty Hawk had been simply to prove that the machine would fly," he said. "Our second machine was heavier and stronger than our first, and we installed a somewhat more powerful motor. We had some problems with the motor at first, but the machine flew well. The other problem we had was with taking off, since we always had to face the wind to provide us with enough lift. We built a wooden launch rail, two hundred and forty feet long, and we had to position it into the wind every time. That could take so long that sometimes the wind would shift again by the time we finished. We solved that problem last September by devising a catapult launching method that made it easier for us to gain takeoff speed from a shorter rail, and that freed us from dependence on the Kitty Hawk winds.

"From that point we made progress with controlling the flyer, but it wasn't always smooth. Wilbur suffered a serious crackup last August, but fortunately he was unhurt. One problem was that we used pine in the structure, and the spars snapped easily. It took some time for us to make repairs, but last September 20, he made a complete circle in the flyer. That proved what we had set out to prove, that we could not only fly under power but could maneuver through the air. That is what no one could do before. Wilbur went on to make a flight in November lasting over five minutes, to celebrate the victory of President Roosevelt in the election."

Ellen smiled at the statement; her father had been an enthusiastic supporter of Roosevelt as well. "I have heard maneuvering through the air explained as aerial navigation," she said, "and I now understand more fully what the term implies. That also answers the question I had about why you began testing at the North Carolina shore. It was the need for good winds."

"Exactly. Good, steady winds and soft sand. We had to face the wind to get aloft, and we needed soft sand for safe landings."

"You mentioned that you have a flying field here," Ellen said. "I assume it must be smooth and level for your purposes."

"Yes. We are using some property a few miles east of the city owned by the Torrence Huffman family, that we secured rent-free. There is a large field, a pasture really, known as Huffman Prairie, which is surrounded on three sides by tall trees, so that we have a measure of concealment from casual onlookers. We had to level the field ourselves, to make it smooth enough for landing the flyer. All the Huffman family required of us was that we remove their horses and cattle to the surrounding pasture where they could continue to graze."

"It sounds as if the field serves your needs well, but do you also plan to return to North Carolina for future flight testing?"

"I am not fully satisfied that Huffman Prairie affords us the degree of security we want, but we have no plans at this time to move our experiments elsewhere. We may well return to Kitty Hawk sometime in the future, but for now, we can do all we need to do at Huffman Prairie."

"I look forward to witnessing some flights. It would add much to my understanding." Ellen felt it necessary to mention that matter specifically, in case the brothers' concerns with secrecy should have led them to change their minds about allowing her to observe.

"We will permit that, as we have for others," replied Orville. "We have just completed building our new flyer, and it is stored in a shed at the field. We hope to test it possibly the day after tomorrow, unless the weather turns against us. Your visit is very timely in that regard."

"That sounds encouraging," said Ellen. "I understand that you made considerable progress last year, but what do you plan to achieve with your new machine?"

Orville appeared to react with more enthusiasm than he had exhibited before and responded immediately. Ellen felt some relief at his evident change. "The new flyer incorporates all we have learned from our first two models. We have used spruce rather than pine for the spars, and that makes the structure much stronger. It has a more powerful engine and will be more capable in its flight performance. We plan to make long-distance flights and bring it to the point that others can be taught to fly. With that step, it should win the approval of the Army."

"How would the Army use the flyer?" Ellen asked. Immediately she feared that her question might have sounded impertinent or skeptical.

"For observation," replied Orville, giving no indication that he resented the question. "It could provide a capability for battlefield observation that has not existed before. One point we have considered is that if both armies have a flying machine, each could see what the other is doing, what maneuvers they were undertaking, and that should prove a deterrent to war. The flyer also could be developed to transport important items of cargo over long distances, and I believe it will be valuable in carrying urgent messages."

That was indeed a revelation to Ellen, since the question of practical applications of a flyer had been at the top of her list, and she replied that she understood. Orville continued to answer her subsequent questions. She could clearly sense his commitment to his work, although he maintained a degree of formality in his responses. She planned to ask him later about his personal feelings about being in the air. She thought that he was enthusiastic about flying, despite his essentially reserved deportment. After several minutes, he offered Ellen a suggestion.

"Perhaps it would be helpful to you if I showed you some papers on aeronautics that we have on file. There are some articles Wilbur has written, as well as some published accounts by others."

"I would appreciate that. I had hoped to have access to such documents. I'm sure they would be very helpful, even if I can't understand everything."

Ellen gained the impression that Orville wished for a break in their conversation, and she was not displeased to transfer her attention to written records about their machine. Orville indicated that he needed to attend to work in the back room, and she mentioned that she would like to review the documents at that time. He would then be free to attend to business. She began to pore over the information Orville had provided her, and she soon determined that Wilbur was the writer and public speaker of the two. Orville mentioned that Wilbur had published several scientific papers on the subject of aeronautics, and also that both were in frequent contact with the distinguished engineer Octave Chanute of Chicago, president of the Society of Western Engineers.

While she planned to study the printed materials closely, Ellen felt that listening to Orville would be the most productive use of her time, as long as he remained willing to talk. "I discovered the Chanute book on flying machines in the public library while researching this assignment," she said. With that statement, she sensed for the first time that Orville was impressed. He began to volunteer further information about their relationship with Chanute, and she was relieved that he appearing willing to continue.

"We began corresponding with Chanute about five years ago, after learning of his work, and we have remained in touch since. Wilbur was invited by Chanute to address the Society about our developments, and he did so on September 18, 1901, more than two years before we actually succeeded with our powered machine. The Society's journal also published Wilbur's article. We regard Chanute as a valuable supporter."

Orville related the story of Wilbur's Chicago visit with evident pride. He then called Ellen's attention to an eyewitness report of their flights published at the beginning of the current year in a small Ohio journal called *Gleanings in Bee Culture*. Orville explained that the editor—a man named Amos Root, from Medina in northern Ohio—had become acquainted with them and had witnessed several flights last year, including the first complete circle flight in September. He was a technology enthusiast and published his eyewitness account in his journal, although such topics were not its normal content. Ellen said she would read it with interest, then asked Orville if he also spoke publicly on aeronautics and about their experiments. He responded emphatically that that was Wilbur's area, while he concentrated on engineering, business matters, and flying.

Ellen gradually concluded that in his curt manner Orville was attempting to conceal a degree of shyness, but she still found herself somewhat put off by him. She believed that her questions were both respectful and knowledgeable, and Ellen knew that her deportment was thoroughly professional. But she sensed that Orville still did not afford her a high degree of credibility, probably due as much to her youth and inexperience as to her gender. He returned to the episode with the Associated Press. He explained that Frank Tunison, city editor of the Dayton *Journal* and the local representative of the Associated Press, had declined to release a wire service story about their flights at Kitty Hawk on the grounds that he simply did not understand the idea.

Ellen decided that her most productive course was to encourage Orville to describe their initial flight tests at Kitty Hawk, as much to get him off the subject of the press as for the purposes of advancing her story. He readily agreed.

"Our first three flights that day were short, under two hundred feet, but they were under control. Our fourth flight was the longest. It lasted fifty-nine seconds and covered about eight hundred and fifty feet, and afterward we heard that Tunison made a statement that a flight of fifty-nine *minutes* might be newsworthy, but not one of fifty-nine seconds, or some words to that effect." Orville's statement was tinged with contempt.

"So, you may see why we have not been happy with coverage of our accomplishments," he continued, "especially by the local press. I should explain something about the flight distance: It was in the face of a brisk and steady wind. In still air, we could have flown about half a mile in that time."

Ellen again indicated her understanding. She decided not to mention her contact with Luther Beard of the *Journal*, and also decided that she probably could do little to change Orville's views that day.

"I will say again that my conceptual grasp of aeronautics and of how you have achieved powered and controlled flight is meager, but I am making the effort to learn and I will treat your accomplishments with respect. I am prepared to remain here for several days in order to gain a deeper understanding. I agree with you that the published reports I have seen so far have been of a rather perfunctory nature, but I plan to report not only accurately but thoroughly. I hope you will credit me with that."

Orville appeared to accept the validity of her statement, and he answered quietly that he would. Although she did not express the thought to him, it also occurred to Ellen that her lack of technical knowledge might actually work to her advantage. Whereas the brothers might feel threatened by an expert reporter, given that they did not yet possess a patent, they might not hold the same concern about her.

Ellen knew there was much more she needed to learn about their first flight tests but decided to shift the direction of the conversation. She could return to questions about flight tests later. "Could you possibly provide some background information on yourself and your family? That might be helpful to my overall understanding of your work."

Orville seemed hesitant, but still responded. "We try to maintain some privacy for our family, and Wilbur probably could answer such questions better than I, but I will give you some idea of how we became interested in the subject of flight and how we progressed from there."

"That is exactly what I am interested in," she replied.

"Wilbur and I have been equal partners in everything we have done since high school. He had some health problems during his youth and stayed home with little inclination to go out into the world as our two older brothers had done. Wilbur is four years older than I am, but by the time I left high school, I had caught up to him in maturity. I had planned a career in business, initially as a printer, so I established a small printing and publishing business and brought Wilbur in as my partner. We named it simply Wright and Wright, and operated it for four years beginning in 1889, after I left school. Wilbur protested from the beginning that he was not meant for the world of commerce, but he became a businessman anyway. I suppose another thing you could say is that both of us are mechanically minded. We designed and built some of our own printing machinery after we started operations.

"Along with our printing venture, we started two neighborhood newspapers. Both folded after relatively brief lives, unfortunately, but we had greater success with religious publishing. This was where our father could help, since he was a prolific writer on religious subjects. He edited the United Brethren newspaper, and we published it for him."

Orville paused for a minute, then added another point.

"Also, around that time, we published a small newspaper edited by Paul Laurence Dunbar, my friend and high school classmate, a man of color. His newspaper served the colored community. He is a well-known poet, incidentally."

Ellen replied that she was interested in poetry and would look up Dunbar's work when she returned to Pittsburgh. She continued taking notes silently and felt somewhat encouraged that Orville's initial reticence appeared to diminish; he became more articulate in describing their origins in aviation. She had learned already from her brief experience that almost all persons with whom she came into contact were willing to talk about themselves and their accomplishments. With her encouragement, Orville continued his account of their business ventures.

"The publishing business made us a living, but eventually we became somewhat bored with it. We began our move into bicycles in 1892, when they were becoming extremely popular. We opened our first bicycle shop at the end of the year on a street near here as the Wright Cycle Exchange, although largely for repairs and parts. The next year we expanded as the Wright Cycle Company and marketed the European safety bicycle, the type you see now in the shop, with wheels of equal size. We found some success selling the new bicycles and closed our printing business thereafter."

He stated again that he and Wilbur had always been equal partners in whatever they did. "We eventually began making and selling our own bicycles, and our business expanded even faster. We moved to this location in 1897, and we were making a good living by the next year."

Ellen continued to write copious notes, to take full advantage of Orville's increasing openness about their backgrounds. After expressing appreciation for the information on their business developments, she attempted to steer Orville into the origins of their involvement with aeronautics. She still struggled to find a tactful way of asking how bicycles could relate to flight.

"I suppose we always had some interest in flight," he said. "Our father gave us a toy glider when we were boys, and we both found it fascinating. We first became seriously interested in the possibility of powered flight after studying the glider experiments of Otto Lilienthal in Germany; I think the year was 1894. And like Lilienthal, we began experimenting with kites and gliders. We spent a great deal of time in the Dayton Public Library and learned all we could about aeronautics from his writings and the work of others.

"We remained busy with our bicycle business, of course, but we continued to read and experiment with gliders as time permitted. By 1899, or about six years ago, we felt we had acquired enough knowledge to start serious experimentation, and so we designed and constructed our own model glider. We first flew it as a kite, so we could control it from the ground. We had learned enough about the laws of aerodynamics that we could match what others had done to that point, and we incorporated the work of Lilienthal and Chanute in our design. We knew that Lilienthal had been killed, of course, and that others had been killed in gliding experiments. We knew that those men who had flown gliders had just shifted their body weight to force a change in direction, which could lead to a loss of control. So, we understood that we had to move beyond their level of skill to fly safely, and the most important thing we learned was to twist or warp the wingtips of the glider. We built our glider with enough flexibility in the wing structure for us to do that. The warping redirected the flow of air over the wings, enabling us to control the direction of flight, and the mechanism was successful in tests. Another thing I should point out here is that we felt that a winged aerial vehicle had more potential than the airships lifted by gas that others had developed. Anyway, the year 1899 was pivotal for us."

Ellen decided that she should move into asking him about his personal feelings about flying and hoped that such questions would draw him out in conversation.

"I have a question I really hope you can help me with. I cannot imagine how it would feel to rise above the earth, to see buildings and people appear so small. It must be exhilarating. Can you describe how you feel when flying?"

"A good question," said Orville. "Yes, I love the sensation of flying. Wilbur thinks that I love flying even more than he does. The wind rushes past your face, and turning or maneuvering the flyer is always satisfying. I'm proud that we have done something no one else has done, and I believe that once we have perfected our machine and developed safe flying procedures, others will want to fly. That would send us on our way. That's why we are so eager to get on with our new machine."

Ellen was glad that her question elicited the response she wanted from Orville.

Orville provided further details on the current status of their experiments, but appeared to become impatient again. "I hope you will excuse me, Miss Hobson, but there are several matters requiring my attention, and unfortunately, I am alone in the shop today. I suggest that you go to our upstairs office where we have certain materials stored. There is a desk and chair, and you may continue to review these papers, if you wish, and please give some time to Wilbur's published articles on aeronautics. You will also find some illustrations of various aspects of aeronautical design."

"Certainly, Mr. Wright," she replied. "If I may stay a little longer to study these materials, that would be enormously helpful."

Orville consented, and she climbed the stairs to the room while he returned to the repair room.

Ellen concluded that she needed to interview Wilbur Wright in great detail. From what she had gained to that point, especially about his writing and speaking on the subject, Wilbur probably was the more learned of the two and could assist her understanding of aeronautics to a greater extent than Orville. She was particularly struck by a phrase Amos Root had used in his article, calling the complete circle flight "the grandest sight of my life." After another hour of study, and taking notes on what she had reviewed, she walked down the stairs and returned the materials to Orville. She thanked him again and left after confirming their agreement to meet the following morning.

* * *

That evening Ellen, reflecting on what she had learned that day, realized more than before that her assignment could indeed be quite difficult. While she knew she was unqualified to write an article with a comprehensive technical explanation of the design and operation of the flying machine—and would have been restricted from doing so by the brothers in any event—she was also aware that her deficiency would in turn reinforce the views of others about female reporters. She had become convinced, however, that there was something to the idea of manned and powered flight and that she could write a coherent story, using the background information she was gathering, of how the two Wright brothers had developed a successful flying machine. Her impressions gained thus far were sufficient for her to afford the brothers some credibility and to overcome her initial skepticism. She did not believe for a moment that anyone with a demeanor as serious as Orville's could be a fraud or a lunatic. The notion of a hoax receded from her mind.

Chapter Five

Wilbur

Dayton, Spring 1905

When Ellen entered the shop the next morning, she saw Orville at the rear, moving a bicycle from the repair room to the display area. She greeted him as he placed the bicycle against a wall. Orville acknowledged her greeting in an even tone, then said he would telephone Wilbur at their home, nearby at Number Seven Hawthorn Street. He did so, then returned to the sales area. Ellen exchanged pleasantries with him, although somewhat awkwardly. She had already decided that Orville was not a man for small talk. Moments later, Wilbur Wright appeared at the front door, removing his plain worker's cap as he entered. He approached Ellen directly.

"Wilbur Wright," he said simply. They shook hands, and Ellen attempted special warmth in her greeting, but Wilbur appeared to be rather aloof in much the same manner as Orville. She silently made some personal observations. The brothers appeared to be similar in physical stature, although Wilbur was somewhat taller. He was also perhaps more pleasant-looking than Orville, though balding and with a rather long face. While she did not regard either brother as handsome, she was struck immediately by Wilbur's piercing blue-gray eyes. Unlike Orville, he wore no mustache, and also unlike his brother, he was indifferently dressed, with a collarless white shirt and no coat.

Wilbur began fidgeting, conveying to Ellen an impression of

impatience not unlike that she observed in Orville. She decided he had urgent tasks on his mind, yet he conveyed an interest in cooperating.

"I will try to be available the remainder of the week to help you from time to time," he said. "Our father is retired but is still engaged in weighty church matters and frequently needs my help, as was the case yesterday, and unfortunately, we are not yet able to devote our full time to aeronautics since we have the shop to run. But our new flyer is at last ready, and we are going to take as much time as necessary. We will be quite busy over the next several days. Orville has told me that you are determined to report fully and accurately on our work, and that is certainly something we can use. I will be glad to listen to your questions and answer them as best I can."

Ellen was impressed by the precision and organization evident in Wilbur's manner of speaking. It was as if he had rehearsed what he said. She nodded her understanding as he spoke. When he paused, she replied, "I appreciate what you said. I am determined to be accurate, and I only want to learn as much as possible while I am here, but without interfering with your work. I will remain in the background at the field."

Ellen could not detect that Wilbur was disconcerted by her youth, and she assumed that he had been alerted to that fact by Orville. She also hoped that he might still possess a degree of warmth lacking in Orville, although that quality was not evident in his initial greeting, and she felt mildly disappointed that he had given no indication that he appreciated her visit or her interest in their work. Ellen waited as the brothers excused themselves to confer briefly on business matters in the repair room. Wilbur then returned and offered her a chair in the office—the same chair she had used the day before—while he sat at the desk.

"Mr. Wright," she began, "I will first emphasize to you, as I did to your brother, that I regard what I am doing as a conversation rather than a formal interview. I am more interested in what you have to tell me than in asking so many questions. I believe I can learn more by studying and observing than by questioning."

A Romance of Flight

Wilbur nodded in agreement. Ellen then asked him to provide whatever information he wished and made notes as he began.

"I hope I won't duplicate what Orville already told you. We are willing to disclose anything within reason about our experiments and plans, but let me know if you already have the information I may give you."

"I certainly learned a great deal yesterday," she said. "Your brother gave me the full background of how you first became interested in flight and how you constructed your first glider six years ago. I hope you can continue from that point."

Wilbur stated, as Orville had, that they were equal partners in the endeavor. He then began providing more technical details of their approach to the construction of a flying machine. He brought out drawings and photographs, including some that Ellen had already seen.

"You are welcome to study these, but I must remind you that we will not permit such details to be published at this time."

"I will honor that, but I'm afraid I would not be able to understand enough of the material to write an authoritative technical description anyway. It will still be helpful for me to study and learn as much as I can before I observe your flights."

Wilbur appeared to accept her statement.

After several minutes, Orville joined them, bringing in an extra chair, and began to participate in the conversation. As they talked, Ellen became impressed by the obvious affinity of the brothers; each appeared to be the alter ego of the other. She also observed that, whatever the serious manner they had presented to her, they possessed a sense of humor with respect to each other and appeared much more relaxed around her when together than either had when speaking with her alone. They jointly described further details of their first model of 1899, to which they had applied many of their own ideas.

Taking over the conversation, Wilbur said, "I know that Orville told you when we began the study of aeronautics and how we built gliders on our own, but I also began to seek help from authorities in the field. I first contacted the Smithsonian Institution about six years ago, because we had learned that Professor Samuel P. Langley was active in aeronautical research there. We received little assistance or encouragement from the Smithsonian initially, and we soon learned the reason was that they were deluged with inquiries from would-be aviators and had little time to help every person contacting them. They did send us several publications on aeronautics, which helped, but the major benefit from my query was that they referred us to Octave Chanute. We wrote him, and then we started corresponding regularly. We came to regard him as the most knowledgeable experimenter in aeronautics in the country, even exceeding the work of Langley. Chanute had built his first glider about three years before we did and shared his experience. We have kept in touch over the past five years. Mr. Chanute is a man of some years, almost as old as our father, but we are good friends."

Ellen replied that she had learned of Chanute's standing in the field and that she knew the brothers had formed a relationship with him. She stressed to Wilbur that she was ready to learn how they had achieved their current state of development in aeronautics, then mentioned that she would also regard it as helpful to know more about their family background as well, beyond what Orville had provided the day before. Wilbur acknowledged but did not respond to her remarks directly. He returned to his discussion of aeronautics, confirming Orville's statement that their studies of the glider experiments of Lilienthal had provided their initial inspiration.

"Perhaps I should give you some further background on the earlier attempts at flight," he said. "I hope you don't have the impression that work toward powered flight began only recently, because experiments go back over most of the past century. We had developed a strong interest in the subject several years ago, of course, but it was not until I first read of Lilienthal's work in *McClure's Magazine* that I had my epiphany. That is when I learned that men had been trying to solve the problem of flight for a hundred years, so I'll tell you something of those before us. The first was Sir George Cayley in England. He experimented over decades and developed and tested a manned glider over fifty years ago, in 1853. Later there was a Frenchman named Clement Ader, who claimed he had gotten his powered machine off the ground in 1890 but did not develop a way to control it. His work had been financed by the French government, we learned, but there was no further development. Then Sir Hiram Maxim, a name you may have heard in connection with the machine gun, also developed a heavy powered machine. He built something similar to a railroad track for launching and supposedly got his machine in the air—I think in 1893—but he was so frustrated with its problems that he stopped experimenting. As I learned more, I went so far as to say that I had become afflicted with the disease of believing that powered flight is possible for man. I knew that I had found something I could devote my life to. In those days, I probably was more confident than Orville that we would succeed with flight. Sometimes he felt overwhelmed with the problems, but we persisted until we solved them."

Ellen was particularly impressed by that statement and nodded.

"Lilienthal's work probably was more advanced than any of those I mentioned, and we were greatly distressed at his death in a crash. He was killed on August 9, 1896, and we read about it soon after. We regard him as a hero, and I believe that Lilienthal, had he lived, might well have been the first to succeed with powered flight. So, in a sense, we are his heirs. We were determined to carry forward and advance his work, and we did. But I still say that while we benefited from the efforts of many who came before us, the flyer we designed was our own work."

Ellen had begun to form a question about how their design improved on Lilienthal's when Wilbur resumed speaking.

"I believe the most important thing we accomplished was to develop a reliable control system for the glider, something Lilienthal had not done. I think you may know that he simply shifted his body weight to turn and maneuver the glider. That technique was inherently unstable, and he paid for it with his life; he encountered a strong gust of wind and lost control and crashed. There was an Englishman named Percy Pilcher who experimented with gliders and was killed in a crash three years later when he lost control of his glider, for the same reason. I suppose my point is that flight is not without danger, but we learned how to avoid the fates of Lilienthal and Pilcher."

That information had already been provided by Orville, if in less detail, but Ellen decided not to mention the point. Instead, she said, "I have learned much from reading *McClure's* as well, including some things that have helped me as a reporter. I also learned that some glider experimenters had been killed."

Wilbur then made a further statement, and Ellen was impressed by the intensity with which he made it.

"The one thing that we did that no one had done before was in developing flight control. We studied all the experimenters before us and found that all had concentrated on ascending into the air, and not on controlling a machine once in the air."

He then turned to an explanation of how they had solved the problem that turned out to be fatal for Lilienthal.

"We knew we would build a flyer similar to Lilienthal's, but we had to take it that further step. We began by observing birds and began to understand how they flew about on three axes of control. That is, they could bank to one side or the other, climb or descend, and steer to the right or left, and they could do two or even all three maneuvers simultaneously. With big birds like buzzards, we saw that they turned by twisting their wings. We were also helped by our understanding of the mechanics of turning a bicycle, in that if you wish to turn left, you must first begin a right turn to stabilize the vehicle. From those observations of birds in flight, I developed the wing-warping or wingtip torsion system, by using control wires to twist the wingtip trailing surfaces up or down during flight."

Wilbur demonstrated by twisting his hands as he spoke.

"This twisting, or torsion," he continued, "had to affect both wingtips simultaneously, but in opposing directions. If we twisted the trailing surface of the right wingtip upward, and the left downward, the air flow over the wingtips would produce less lift on the right surface and more on the left surface. That would raise the left wing and lower the right, and the machine would bank to the right. I developed the torsion system in 1899 and tried it on our kite, before our actual glider tests. We flew the kite on a tether with control wires, so that we could manipulate the wings from the ground.

"I know this may sound confusing or repetitious to you, but I must reemphasize that there are three directions of control, or three axes of flight maneuvering, on any flying machine: vertical, lateral, and longitudinal. This is what we observed birds doing in flight, and we knew we could apply that knowledge to a manned flying machine."

He continued to gesture with his hands to demonstrate the maneuvers.

"Elevator and rudder control surfaces had been developed by others to control the vertical and lateral, or the up and down and the left and right steering. But what we learned was how to maneuver longitudinally by use of a control surface, that is the wings, rather than by shifting body weight. That is called roll, since you roll partially to one side or the other. We could now better control the glider in flight. We had serious problems with stability and control in our first manned glider, but eventually we proved the system. We learned that we had to combine the wingtip torsion with the elevator and rudder, so that as the glider began to turn, it would avoid yawing and going out of control. By the time we built our third glider, we had all control surfaces coordinated, so that we could control the craft in all directions. That is something that Orville developed for us. We were then completely free of the weight-shifting technique of Lilienthal. I know this is a lot for you to absorb in a short time, but if you study some of the published work on aeronautics, you should be better able to comprehend what I have said."

"I know that is true," Ellen replied. "I have already made some progress in that direction, but I realize I have much further to go. Do I understand correctly that the longitudinal controls enabled you to turn the flyer around in a complete circle?"

"Precisely. And more importantly, we could do it safely. That is what flight control is all about."

Orville excused himself to attend to business, as two customers had entered the shop. Wilbur returned to a full description of their gliding experiments at Kitty Hawk, and Ellen was pleased that he continued to speak openly and with enthusiasm about their work.

"You know about our Kitty Hawk test site," he said. "We went there for three consecutive years, 1900, 1901, and 1902. I first went alone in September of 1900, where I assembled our first full-sized glider from the sections we shipped by rail from Dayton. This was still a very small machine, with only about a fifteen-foot wingspan, and barely large enough to carry a man. Lilienthal had made detailed calculations of how much wing area would be needed to lift a glider of a given weight with a given airspeed, and we relied on them in determining the wing size we would need to support a man in the face of the wind. The size of our glider was also limited by what we could build locally, but it was adequate to test our wing-warping system. I should explain that our glider had two wings, one above the other, the same as on our first kite. Chanute gave us that idea, which he had developed from his knowledge of reinforced structures in building bridges. He had also used Lilienthal's lift calculations and determined that double wings give greater lift than a single wing, so we have continued to use them.

"I had to work alone at Kitty Hawk at first because Orville needed to manage our bicycle shop through the busy season. So, we could carry out our tests only in the later months of the year when Orville was able to join me. There was the danger that we could run into foul weather that late in the year, but we did fly in the glider, and under control. We couldn't perform any maneuvers at the time, of course, but we did progress in that direction.

The main problem was that the glider was deficient in lift, and we could not gain the elevation we wanted. I should mention that Mr. Chanute visited us at Kitty Hawk during our 1901 tests and later visited our home. It was after that visit that he invited me to lecture before his engineering colleagues."

Wilbur digressed into the story of his trip to Chicago in September of that year and his speech at the Society of Western Engineers about his experiments and plans. Ellen was relieved by his digression, since she was having trouble keeping up with his technical descriptions. She told Wilbur that Orville had shown her a copy of his article published in the Society's journal. Wilbur acknowledged her statement and mentioned that the article had been adapted from his speech. Ellen made further notes about the Chicago speech, and she thought privately that it was remarkable that Wilbur had become so absorbed with his descriptions of their work that he could hardly restrain himself in the degree of detail. She felt encouraged that he was so much more articulate than Orville, but then she realized suddenly that she had neglected to ask the most elementary of questions—how a flying machine actually lifted itself off the ground and flew.

"Excuse me, Mr. Wright, but I must return to a very simple question. I do not yet understand how any man-made machine can fly and how it can remain in the air. You mentioned lift, and I suppose that is something I need to learn."

"That is a good question, and one I should have addressed earlier. I had become so involved with explaining the control forces that I neglected to illustrate how the machine flies in the first place. Yes, the machine flies because of the force of lift, which overcomes the force of gravity, or its own weight. The simplest explanation, one that has been understood for more than a century, is that the difference in pressure from air flowing over and under a fixed surface provides the lifting force. The wing, which is the fixed surface and provides lift, must be curved on top to cause that pressure difference. When the wing is propelled forward, its curvature forces the air flowing over the top to flow faster than air flowing underneath, creating a pressure differential that pulls the surface upward, and that is what defines lift. This is another case where the principle is very simple, but practical application becomes much more complicated. We had great difficulty developing a wing that would provide adequate lift, and I will try to illustrate the idea as I describe our tests. First, you need power to move the craft forward and create the airflow over the wing. Wind can generate enough lift for a glider, of course, but you need a mechanical power source to sustain flight."

"Thank you," Ellen said. "That is a great help. Perhaps you could now answer another question I have. I understand why you decided on Kitty Hawk for your tests, but how did you discover such a remote location in the first place?"

"Again, a good question. We simply studied various maps, and learned of its isolation, and also learned from weather reports that it had the favorable winds we needed for launching the flyer. We wrote to the head of the Weather Bureau there, and he confirmed the conditions. Once we determined that Kitty Hawk was suitable, we did not consider any other locations.

"Another thing I should clarify," he continued, "is that while the village is Kitty Hawk, the actual location of our tests was the Kill Devil Hills, a beach area about four miles south of the town. It was in fact so isolated that we were forced to live in a tent on our first trip in 1900, since there were no other accommodations. Incidentally, my first letter to the weather station was not delivered but was returned to the town postmaster, a man named William J. Tate. He read it and replied to us directly that he was interested in our plans, and he offered us room and board with his family until we had developed our campsite and completed all preparations. We took him up on his offer, but we subsequently built a cabin and shed for our 1902 tests."

Ellen encouraged Wilbur to describe their progress with the glider experiments. He proceeded to do so with noticeable enthusiasm, and Ellen wrote brief notes as fast as she could.

"We decided to make our second glider, the 1901 model, much

larger than the first, with a twenty-two-foot wingspread. We thought that would give us more lift, but we still experienced a disappointing performance. We just couldn't gain much altitude with it. We tried a greater wing curvature, but then stability was worse than with the first glider. We also installed a movable elevator instead of the fixed elevator we used before, but it still did not offer any improvement over our first model. I reluctantly concluded that the lift tabulations of Lilienthal, on which we had relied from the start, were erroneous. The wing we built simply would not give us the lift that he had predicted.

"I must confess that I had become so frustrated with both lift and control performance of our glider that on the way home from Kitty Hawk I said to Orville that man would not achieve powered flight for a thousand years. It was the most discouraged I have ever been. We discussed the problem with Chanute, but not even he could offer a solution. Orville said that at least we had proved the work of our predecessors could not be relied on. We would have to develop more knowledge ourselves, and that set us on our course.

"We did persist, and we eventually made two critical improvements. First, we devised a movable vertical stabilizer, or rudder, to make the wing warping system on the glider more effective. We accomplished that by linking the vertical stabilizer with the longitudinal controls so that the maneuvers could be coordinated. All the controls were connected with simple wires. Another thing I should have mentioned is that we lay prone in the glider, using hand controls to move the rudder and elevators and a hip cradle to move the wingtip wires. The movable rudder was, as you know, connected to the wingtip wires. When we wanted to turn, we pressed against the hip cradle. If we wanted to make a left turn, we pressed the cradle left, and that pulled the trailing edge of the right wing downward, which increased its lift and raised the wing. The same movement simultaneously raised the trailing edge of the left wing and caused it to dip, and that began the turn. The shift also moved the rudder to the left to help stabilize the turn. For a right turn we did the reverse. That gave us reliable directional control for the first time.

"The second thing we did was to conduct our own tests on wing lift, and from those we recalculated our lift coefficients. Lilienthal's, as I've said, were seriously in error. With our calculations, our next model had a sharper camber, and that improved the lift. I suppose camber is another term I should explain. It is a French word referring to the degree of curvature of the wing cross-section, and it consequently affects air pressure and the lift force. That is what the lift coefficients calculated. With our new calculations, we knew how to build in the correct degree of camber and were not just guessing as we had been earlier. I hope all this adds to your understanding."

Ellen nodded her thanks for his insights as she made rapid notes.

"Anyway, from that point we designed our 1902 model incorporating all our improvements. It was even bigger than our second glider, with a thirty-two-foot wingspread, and had both a movable rudder and an adjustable elevator. We returned to Kitty Hawk in August 1902, assembled our new glider, and began testing. This model accomplished everything we expected in our tests in terms of lift and control, and we were able to glide more than six hundred feet. We also realized that we had progressed beyond Chanute's knowledge. Orville and I concluded that we had actually solved the problem of controlled flight, something no one had done before. I think this is our major accomplishment, because the problem had frustrated many prominent men of science extending back to Leonardo da Vinci. I recognized that we had the advantage of learning from the failures of others, but we still had done what no one had been able to do before."

Ellen sensed that Wilbur was trying to avoid becoming too technical and was trying to describe flight control and features of the flyer in terms that he felt she could comprehend. She was still bewildered by the principle of lift but realized that what he was describing was critically important to her reporting, and so she continued to write. She knew she could review and organize her notes later. "I am afraid I must interrupt again," she said. "I just realized that I am not clear as to where you built your flying machines. It seems to me that it would take a large factory space."

"Actually, we did almost everything here in our shop, using our bicycle tools," he replied. "We have a separate workroom behind the repair room, and we built our gliders and the powered flyer in components there, then shipped the sections by rail. We could assemble the flyer easily at Kitty Hawk by bolting the sections together. So, it wasn't quite the monumental task it may have appeared to you. We built our second and third flyers in the shop also and shipped the components out to Huffman Prairie by rail. I would show you our workroom, but I'm afraid that you would seriously soil your clothes."

"That information really helps me, and I would like to see the workroom. I'll be careful not to brush against anything. It had seemed to me that the craft would have been too large to be built in one place, but it makes sense now that I know you built the components and assembled them on-site."

Wilbur continued with his account. "Since our 1902 glider was a complete success, it served as the basis for our flying machine patent application. We filed the application in March of 1903, before we flew our powered machine, but we received a prompt rejection from the Patent Office. I think they required an actual demonstration before they would consider it further. Another reason the Patent Office was so cautious was that they had received many applications from people who claimed that they had solved the problem of flight, and most were frauds. Actually, we have had more patent success overseas. We applied for and were granted patents from Belgium, France, and Great Britain last year. But the American patent is what is crucial for us.

"Mr. Chanute began to publicize us in his travels to Europe, even though we didn't think our work was ready for publicity. Specifically, he told the French about our experiments, especially the success of our third glider, when he made a trip to Paris in

April of 1903. But we became aware that the French still believed that Alberto Santos-Dumont was far more advanced with his lighter-than-air vehicles, or airships. We also learned that many in France were skeptical of our work because we did not have financial backing."

"I have seen the name Santos-Dumont in some of my readings," replied Ellen, "and your brother told me that you were financing everything by yourselves. I understand why that would carry some advantages." Ellen attempted to sound supportive, in part to induce Wilbur to keep talking.

"With our third glider, we had solved the lift aerodynamics and established that the control system worked," he said. "Then we were ready for the final step, which was, as you know, to power the machine. For that we needed a lightweight engine of sufficient power, although I still think building the engine was secondary in importance to our development of the control system.

"I shall make this point again: it is critical that you understand why we must maintain control over the design details about our machine. The principles of flight actually are very simple and can be understood by laypersons. Our flying machine is not as complicated as some have supposed, and for that reason we fear having our work stolen."

Ellen felt surprised that anyone could represent that the flying machine was relatively uncomplicated, but she responded again that she appreciated their concerns about patent protection. Wilbur continued to illustrate the basics of aerodynamics, including lift and drag, with the addition of power. Ellen struggled to follow his explanations.

Wilbur then returned to describing their Kitty Hawk experiments. "We stowed the glider in the shed and left Kitty Hawk on December 2, and by that time we knew beyond any doubt that we could succeed with powered flight. We had built a machine with adequate lift and workable controls, and we had developed a design for effective propellers as well. I should explain that a propeller for a flyer is not like a boat propeller; it functions more as a rotating wing itself, with differences in air pressure flowing over the blades creating forward thrust. We found that we could not adapt marine propellers for a flyer, so we designed our own and carved them out of wood. But again, the final step was the engine, and neither Orville nor I felt that we could build the engine. We just weren't machinists."

"Did you use an automobile engine?" she asked.

"No. We found that all existing motors were too heavy to be practical in our flyer. We asked several engine manufacturers to build to our specifications, but not one showed any interest. We found the answer close to home, with our machinist Charles E. Taylor. You will meet him tomorrow at the field."

"Mr. Taylor built the engine?"

"To our specifications, and he did a fine job. He finished in just a few weeks, using a simple drill press and lathe. We had an engine both of lightweight and adequate power."

Wilbur then mentioned that he had returned to Chicago a second time, on June 18, 1903, to deliver a speech to the Society of Western Engineers. After that visit, he felt their work was gradually becoming recognized in scientific and engineering circles, though still not with the public.

At Ellen's request, Wilbur moved on to a description of their success with powered flight at Kitty Hawk.

"We built most components for our powered machine here, as you may remember, and had them shipped by rail as far as we could. We could reach the Outer Banks only by motor boat, and from there we had to transport everything to Kill Devil Hills by a horse-drawn wagon. You might mention in your reporting that there was very little difference in design between our powered machine and our last glider other than adding the engine and propellers, but one other change was that we covered both the top and bottom surfaces of both wings with fabric, to give us even better lift. When we returned to Kitty Hawk late in September, the Tate family provided us with meals and a place to stay as before, until we could set up our camp. They also helped with labor and materials. In fact, I used Mrs. Tate's sewing machine to sew fabric for the wings. We used a strong sateen fabric that helped hold the structure together without any heavy bolts or screws. We remain grateful to Bill Tate and his family for all their help, and you are certainly free to mention that in your story.

"Another thing we did was buy some lumber locally to finish the assembly. But by then we were coming to the end of the year, and the weather was getting colder. We made many more flights with our glider while we worked on the powered flyer but ended those tests in November. So, we stowed the glider and devoted our full attention to our powered machine. One setback was that when we first tested the engine, the propeller shaft broke, and I had to make a trip back to Dayton to deal with that. Charlie Taylor manufactured a stronger shaft for us. But after that delay, it had become too windy and even stormy for daily testing, so we had to wait for favorable weather and winds. On Bill Tate's suggestion, we secured the help of a few men from the Kill Devil Life-Saving Station to build a wooden launch rail. We knew that the flyer was so heavy it would require a rail to give us a smooth take-off, and we built it sixty feet long. The help of the local men was important.

"We didn't have everything ready until December 14, and we also had good winds that day. Orville and I flipped a coin to decide who would be first, and I was the winner. I tried a flight about noon, and I succeeded in lifting the flyer off the ground. But then it nosed directly into the sand, so we couldn't call it a successful powered flight. It may have been my fault in that I pulled up on the elevator controls too sharply, and it couldn't maintain that degree of ascent. As it happened, we couldn't repair the flyer in time for another test that day, so we were forced to wait. We had both good weather and good winds again on the seventeenth, so we pushed it out to the rail to try again.

"We brought over some men from the Life-Saving Station who had helped us earlier, and they also became our witnesses. One thing I regret was that Bill Tate did not come that day; he had thought the weather would be too bad for us to attempt any flights. But we were ready, and it was Orville's turn, so he made the first flight about ten-thirty that morning. It covered only about a hundred and twenty feet in the face of a strong wind and rose only a few feet off the ground, but it was under control. Counting that, we made a total of four flights, two by each of us, with the last being the fifty-nine second flight that Orville told you about. We had planned to make still more flights that day, perhaps even flying the four miles to the weather station. We had enough fuel, but after our last test, a gust of wind flipped the flyer over and caused considerable damage. We couldn't get it repaired quickly, so we ended work for the day.

"I think you know the rest, that we had proved what we set out to prove, that the flyer worked, and that we could fly it under power and under control. We sent the telegram from the Kitty Hawk weather station telling our father of our success, and that was the basis for that distorted report in the Norfolk newspaper you saw. We learned later that the editor of that newspaper had already heard something about us from the trip he had made to the Outer Banks reporting on a ship sinking, which possibly explained his interest in publishing the story. But regardless, since we had accomplished what we had set out to do, we decided to leave immediately in order to arrive home for Christmas. As you know, we had to leave the flyer in the shed."

"One question occurs to me here," said Ellen. "I gather that you had not made any efforts to publicize your experiments before you departed Dayton. Did you in fact conduct those first tests in secrecy?"

"Yes," replied Wilbur. "We did not wish to deal with crowds of the curious, or with skeptical reporters. Also, if we had failed, that probably would have cost us all future credibility. We were determined to succeed without the burden of onlookers, and then there was our concern about exposing our design to those who might steal it."

"I understand, and I think that was the proper way to deal with it, given that you lack a patent." Ellen thanked him again for the background information. Although she had received much the same from Orville, Wilbur's more detailed descriptions had provided her with a much better grasp of what they had done. She was beginning to understand more about flight than before.

"There is another point I should make that might be helpful to your story," said Wilbur. "We didn't feel that we were in a race to be the first to succeed with flight, but we had heard reports that Professor Langley tested his flying machine just before we were ready at Kitty Hawk. He made two attempts to launch his machine from a barge on the Potomac River—the first in October and the second just a few days before we flew—but both failed. That is why we were first. From what we have learned since, we think his design was seriously overweight and had other flaws. I know his engine was powerful, but it was also very heavy. Probably his flyer would not have ever succeeded, but fortunately, no one was killed. To us, the irony of it all was that Langley had generous government funding through the Smithsonian to develop his machine."

"I had read something about Professor Langley last year when I began preparing for this assignment," said Ellen, "and knew his machine had failed. But I also understand that your design was rather different from his."

Ellen then told Wilbur that his information was extremely helpful to her, but she felt she had almost reached a saturation point. Wilbur indicated he understood and mentioned that it would be a good time for him to return to the shop floor to look after business with Orville. Coincidentally, she realized she was hungry, as it was past the noon hour. She informed the brothers that she would like to go out briefly for a light lunch but would return to continue her studies for the balance of the day.

"I suggest that when you return, you take the materials to the upstairs room and study them there," said Wilbur. "You can still ask questions, but Orville and I will be needing to attend to business."

Ellen said she would see them again shortly and went out to a small café she had seen nearby. Afterward, she enjoyed a relaxing walk around the neighborhood then returned to the shop. After greeting the brothers, she proceeded upstairs and again turned her attention to additional papers Wilbur had provided. She knew she was gaining a fuller grasp of how their flyer worked, but she still found their computations of lift data utterly incomprehensible. She decided that questions on that point should wait until a more opportune time. After some two hours of further reading and note-taking, as well as editing her previous notes, Ellen descended to the shop floor and announced that she was ready to depart for the day. She was privately pleased that she had drawn from the brothers what amounted to an interview, despite their expressed opposition to the interview format. She continued to be impressed by Wilbur's enthusiasm in describing their work. Despite her initial concern that he would be reticent, he had in fact spoken so volubly that it threatened to almost overwhelm her.

Thanking both brothers again for their help, Ellen informed them that she planned to spend the evening reviewing her notes on what they had given her, since she would use them as the basis for writing her story. As she prepared to depart for the day, she decided to ask one further question.

"What do you expect your next step to be? Are you ready to begin testing your new flyer now?"

"We will be at Huffman Prairie tomorrow morning for that very purpose," replied Orville.

"I look forward to being there," Ellen replied. "Could you give me directions?"

"I suggest you travel to the field on the Dayton-Springfield Interurban electric trolley," said Wilbur. "Probably, you will want to board at the Main Street platform, then get off at the Simms Station platform. We normally take the trolley line there since it runs directly from Third Street. We will need to be at the field early because we have many preparations to make before we can start flying, but you may come anytime you wish. I can't say exactly when we will make our first flight, but it should be in the morning."

Ellen suddenly felt somewhat tired after what had turned out to be an unusually full day of discussion and study. She bid good afternoon to the brothers and departed, saying she looked forward to the next day.

* * *

That evening Ellen, reflecting on her day, felt relieved that despite what she feared might be the case, Wilbur had not appeared to be especially uncomfortable in the presence of a young woman. She flattered herself again that she did indeed possess a gift for interviewing, drawing forth cooperation from those who, like the Wright brothers, might have been initially reluctant. She also had discerned, or at least wanted to think, that Wilbur felt more comfortable in dealing with her than did Orville. She was relieved that he was more open and articulate than Orville, who still appeared less than forthcoming about many details. She knew both were possessed of a rather reserved manner, including their formal style of speaking, but felt that should be no obstacle to her. If she could continue to draw a stream of information from Wilbur, that would more than offset any reticence on the part of Orville, and her assignment might be successful after all.

CHAPTER SIX

THE EXPERIMENTS

HUFFMAN PRAIRIE, SPRING 1905

The next morning, Ellen, having packed a lunch knowing that nothing would be available at the field, walked to the nearby trolley stop, boarded the trolley, and traveled downtown. She changed to the eastbound trolley at the Main Street Interurban platform and took a seat for the short trip to the flying field. Disembarking at Simms Station as she had been instructed, Ellen walked north across open land toward what she knew to be Huffman Prairie. She saw and greeted Orville and Wilbur as she approached. They were at the base of a large derrick, hoisting heavy weights to the top with a pulley. She also saw a third man working with them, who she supposed was Charles E. Taylor.

Wilbur spoke to her first and made the introduction. "Miss Hobson, this is Charlie Taylor, our machinist. I told you about him yesterday, and you know that he has built the engines for all our flyers. He will be helping us again today."

Ellen guessed that Taylor was about Wilbur's age, with his most distinguishing feature being a large, bushy mustache. Taylor greeted her warmly. She returned his greeting, addressing him as Mr. Taylor.

"Call me Charlie," he corrected. Ellen was pleased that he appeared to be both pleasant and talkative, and they began to converse informally as the brothers resumed flight preparations.

"I look forward to hearing more about your work, Charlie,"

she said, "and please call me Ellen. I'm just here to learn, and I would be interested in anything you have to tell me."

As Wilbur and Orville walked to a large shed and opened the door, Charlie began to describe his work to her.

"Well, I've worked for the brothers full-time for four years now. Among other things, I have kept the shop for them when they are out here as well as when they were at Kitty Hawk. I like to think I have been of value in freeing them to go there for their glider tests, since they were able to travel, by assisting them in Dayton."

Charlie then excused himself to help Wilbur and Orville. Ellen sensed that he was very proud of his association with the Wright brothers, and he clearly regarded himself as important to their success. She knew she would want to talk with him more extensively as time permitted.

Ellen took a seat in a wooden chair provided for her as the brothers continued flight preparations. She had already decided to question Wilbur for most details, as she felt that Orville looked forward to her departure despite her assurances that her reporting would respect their restrictions and would also be accurate. In one respect, she did not particularly mind that situation, since she had decided that Wilbur was by far the more agreeable of the two. She had enjoyed her conversations with him at the shop but decided not to press him or Orville further on this day, expecting that they would be under considerable stress in readying the new flyer for its first flight. She planned simply to observe and listen and to make notes in her journal of all that she saw and heard. She began by writing that it was Wednesday, June 23, which would be the first day of testing for the new flyer.

Ellen noticed soon that two other individuals had arrived at the field, but they stood well away from the small crew. She was mindful that the brothers still were quite restrictive in permitting the general public to observe, and so she assumed that the men, to whom she was not introduced, were there with permission. Although she did not express the thought aloud, Ellen began to

A Romance of Flight

feel somewhat caught up in the adventure of observing aeronautical experiments, adding to her earlier sense of exhilaration in undertaking a significant assignment on her own with only limited experience. She felt even more strongly than before that her future would hold such assignments.

Ellen disciplined herself to remain at some distance from the brothers in order to not interfere with or distract them from their task. She watched as Wilbur, Orville, and Charlie Taylor towed the center section of the flyer from the storage shed onto the field. They then carried out the tail section and the forward elevators separately, since they had been detached for storage in the narrow shed. Assembling the components took only a few minutes.

While she was already familiar with the flyer's construction and configuration from the photographs and drawings she had been shown, Ellen was still surprised at its apparent flimsiness. It appeared to her that a stiff wind could demolish the machine. She had been told that the flyer weighed little more than six hundred pounds without a pilot, and she understood that light weight was critical, but it still appeared dubious to her as a man-carrying vehicle. The simple wooden skids on which the flyer landed did little to increase her confidence in its sturdiness or durability.

Nevertheless, she watched with fascination as the three men positioned the flyer on the wooden cradle from which it would be launched. The cradle rested on the wooden launch rail. The final step was attaching the cable to the flyer, which would accelerate it to the point of takeoff. The other end of the cable was already hooked to the weights that were now suspended from the top of the launch derrick. The cable ran around the launch rail to the end of the track where it ran back to the front of the flyer where it was attached. Ellen then was about to observe in operation what had already been described to her: that the weights, totaling sixteen hundred pounds, would be released, pulling back the cable, which in turn would propel the flyer forward rapidly along the rail. As the flyer reached takeoff velocity, the pilot would release the cable, and the machine would lift itself into the air.

Ellen could sense rising tension in the brothers as they readied the flyer for its launch; there was an edge to their voices as they spoke to each other. She felt that tension in herself as well. However, she was already knowledgeable enough to appreciate that both brothers knew exactly what they were doing as they moved quickly and deliberately through their preparations. Wilbur added fuel to the small tank and undertook final checks and adjustments. He and Orville then conferred on the speed and direction of the wind, and she heard them agree that both were favorable.

Orville was to make the first flight, and situated himself prone in the center of the lower wing of the machine, his hands gripping the control sticks. He performed a test of the controls, including shifting his body to activate the wing-warping system. Then, on his signal, Wilbur and Charlie rotated the propellers, and the engine sputtered to life. Ellen was surprised at the clatter the engine, the chain drive, and the spinning propellers combined to make. She instinctively flinched but quickly realized that the engine was running normally, and its sound reminded her of nothing so much as a loud sewing machine. Wilbur positioned himself at the right wingtip to run alongside to steady the flyer as it gained takeoff velocity. On Orville's further signal, Charlie released the weights from the derrick. The weights dropped steadily and rapidly toward the ground, pulling the cable back and propelling the flyer forward with a lurch. The flyer gained speed and lifted off smoothly at the end of the rail. To Ellen, the entire process seemed to take about two seconds. She was awestruck as she watched it climb higher and diminish in her eyes with distance. The flyer quickly rose above tree level but continued in a straightaway direction for only a matter of seconds before Orville began his turn back to the field.

As the flyer descended, Wilbur, watching intently, cried out that Orville was not leveling off completely on his landing approach. His fears were confirmed as the left wingtip of the flyer struck the ground just before the skids touched, spinning the craft

A Romance of Flight

around and bringing it to a forceful halt. Cracks could be heard from somewhere in the flyer's structure, and the engine sputtered to a stop. Ellen gasped, but forced herself to remain in her chair. Wilbur and Charlie rushed toward the silent flyer, and Ellen was relieved to see Orville pull himself up and walk away, evidently uninjured. Wilbur checked the damage quickly, then walked back toward the shed with Orville. Ellen could tell by their conversation that they were concerned but not discouraged. The important point was that Orville was unhurt.

Despite the landing mishap, Ellen had been able to observe for herself not only how the flyer was launched but also how it rose into the air and how it performed under control. After the brothers had assessed the damage, she approached Wilbur for his evaluation.

"I hope the damage isn't serious. Can it be repaired easily?"

"It is not serious," he replied, "but it will take some time to repair. The wingtip was damaged, and four spars in the tail structure were cracked and will have to be replaced. But we've faced these problems before, and we have the materials on hand, so it shouldn't delay us to any great extent. We'll start the repairs immediately, and we'll get back in the air as soon as we can."

Wilbur, Orville, and Charlie Taylor began the repair work, first unbolting parts of the assembly and replacing the broken spars using materials stored in the shed. Ellen took advantage of the time to review her notes and write her observations of the first flight. After more than an hour of intensive work, the repairs were largely complete. By then it was past the noon hour, and the crew took a break for lunch, as did Ellen. She listened quietly as they discussed their plans for further tests.

After lunch and a brief rest, the three dragged the flyer around and positioned it back on the launch dolly. Then, they hoisted the weights to the top of the derrick as before. They agreed that Orville should make the second flight as well. Ellen continued to watch closely as the flyer was prepared for flight, and Orville again took his position at the controls. The engine started and the launch was as smooth as before. The second flight was as brief as the first and followed the same pattern, but Ellen still was nervous. She felt relieved when Orville brought the flyer in for a landing, somewhat roughly but still safely.

There was still some minor damage to the machine in landing that caused another delay. The crew made the repairs, but Wilbur informed Ellen that since they had experienced control and operating problems, they would not attempt further flights that day as a precaution. Wilbur had taken photographs as Orville flew, and Ellen learned that Wilbur was an experienced photographer and developed the photographs himself. She recorded her observations of each flight as well as describing the ground activity before and after. She was disturbed by the continuing difficulties but decided not to intrude with questions. She had been impressed by the high energy level demonstrated by the brothers and particularly in how Wilbur had moved rapidly when Orville touched down in the flyer, ready to act instantly in any emergency.

As the afternoon wore on, Ellen approached Wilbur to confirm his approval for a further visit at their shop the next morning. He agreed without hesitation, stating that they would need time at the shop to recheck their field repairs and to assess the results of their flights before resuming tests. He also reminded her that, as always, they had a bicycle business to attend.

Ellen returned alone to the city on the trolley, leaving the crew free to complete the day's activities. In the long, warm days of June, ample daylight remained for a pleasant stroll, and she walked the two dozen blocks south from the station to her great aunt's house. She regarded the day as significant in her life, having indeed witnessed man making a controlled flight in a machine under its own power.

* * *

When Ellen entered the shop the next morning, she found Wilbur and Orville already at work. She greeted them pleasantly but still formally.

A Romance of Flight

"Please tell me your immediate plans," she asked. "Are you going to fly again today?"

"No," answered Wilbur. "We could, but we wanted to recheck the repairs we made yesterday, since we made them rather hastily. We need to work in the shop today to make additional structural parts to take to the field. But we are determined to make another attempt to fly tomorrow."

She knew already that business demands prevented them from flying every day, and she gained Wilbur's consent to ask further questions extending from what she had observed of their flights. "From your tests yesterday," she asked, "do you regard the flyer as basically sound in design and construction?"

"Yes," Wilbur replied. "I can tell you definitely that this flyer is a much better design than our first two models. Our difficulties yesterday were not due to any flaws in the flyer's design or construction but because we still make mistakes in controlling it in the air and in landing. We will just need to be more careful in the future, and I'm confident we will get better with experience."

Ellen acknowledged Wilbur's answer and really felt that it was correct. She asked further questions when he was available, but that was sporadic as customers entered the shop frequently. At those times, she was careful to remain in the background to avoid any appearance of interfering with their conducting business. She soon decided to spend time in the upstairs office reviewing her notes and reading more of the articles and papers they had given her earlier.

At noon, a young woman entered the shop carrying a covered tray. Wilbur called for Ellen to come downstairs and thereupon introduced her to their sister Katharine. He explained that Katharine normally brought lunch to them when they worked in the shop and that she sometimes kept the shop when they were flying, as she had yesterday. Ellen greeted her warmly as they shook hands.

"I am so pleased to have the opportunity to learn about the work your brothers are doing," she said. "I knew almost nothing when I came here, but I have since learned enough to recognize its importance."

"Our entire family is proud of what they are doing as well," replied Katharine, adding nothing more. Ellen formed the opinion that Katharine possessed a degree of reserve, similar to that of her brothers.

"Katharine is a college graduate, from the Oberlin College, class of '98," Wilbur added with evident pride. "She teaches at Central High School here."

Ellen reacted with pleasure to that information, feeling that it would provide a point of common interest. As the brothers went to the office to take their lunch, Ellen took the opportunity to engage their sister in conversation. Responding to her questions, Katharine stated that she had begun teaching after completing college, and since she was free for the summer, she was able to fulfill the function of housekeeper to her brothers and father. Ellen quickly determined that Katharine's personality probably was closer to Orville's than Wilbur's but also that she likely was equally protective of both. She could observe some resemblance between Katharine and her brothers but regarded her as being of rather severe appearance, particularly with the pince-nez eyeglasses on the bridge of her nose.

In response to Ellen's request, Katharine provided information on the rest of the Wright family.

"We have two older brothers, Lorin and Reuchlin. Both are married with families of their own. Lorin lives here, near us, but Reuchlin lives in Kansas. I am the youngest, as you may know. Our mother died in 1889, and, except for my time away at college, I have lived at home and helped my father and brothers. My brother Lorin also has helped manage the shop when Wilbur and Orville have been absent, including when they have made their trips to North Carolina. Lorin has traveled to North Carolina with them also."

After that brief exchange, Katharine initiated nothing further.

Ellen attempted to end the vacuum and said, "I met Charlie

Taylor at Huffman Prairie yesterday, and I learned that he also helped with the shop when Wilbur and Orville were away."

"Yes," Katharine replied tersely, with some evident distaste. Ellen inferred that Katharine did not much care for Charlie Taylor, a view she could understand since his personality was noticeably different from those of the Wright family.

"I also had the opportunity to attend college, in my home city of Pittsburgh," said Ellen, still seeking to establish some rapport and to break down Katharine's reserve. "I graduated from the Pennsylvania College for Women last year, and I grew up with two older brothers as well."

Katharine acknowledged her comments pleasantly but demonstrated no interest in continuing a conversation concerning family matters. Ellen could not decide if Katharine was simply unsociable, or was uninterested in her specifically, but tentatively concluded that she had little hope of developing a friendship with her. She evidently was waiting for her brothers to finish lunch so that she could return to the house. With Wilbur and Orville continuing their lunch break, Ellen excused herself to return home for lunch with her great aunt Keys, expressing to Katharine the hope of speaking with her again. Katharine acknowledged her comment without enthusiasm.

Ellen returned to the shop some two hours later and resumed her conversation with the brothers. Wilbur invited her again to sit in their office, where he explained several points in papers he had written and sketches he had made of their designs and experiments. He then expressed his regrets about the press of work but explained that for the remainder of the afternoon he would need to work with Orville in the workroom.

"You are welcome to remain in the office," he said, "but I'm afraid that we can't spare much time for you now."

"I don't mind," she replied. "I think I have gained a level of comprehension of flight and aeronautics that I can better understand your papers and drawings. I can easily occupy myself with them for the remainder of the day."

Wilbur returned to the workroom, and Ellen spent more time in the study. As the day wore on, Ellen thought again of how she indeed appreciated the help Wilbur had provided, regarding it as better than she would have expected earlier. With little more to be accomplished that day, she prepared to leave, making sure to tell the brothers as she departed how she looked forward to observing their flights again tomorrow.

Relaxing at her great aunt's house that evening, Ellen regarded the day as significant in that she had become further persuaded, among other matters, of the remarkable closeness of the Wright family. While she regarded her own family as close in many respects, she saw an added dimension to these brothers in that they appeared to have an understanding to support each other without limit.

In sharp contrast, she remembered vividly from her childhood that her own brothers had argued frequently and that both had, on occasion, complained about her to their parents as the favored youngest child. She could not imagine her brothers becoming partners in any endeavor. Ellen concluded that the closeness of the Wright brothers extended to their sister and to their father as well. She speculated, however, that Katharine might be somewhat closer to Orville than to Wilbur, due to similar personalities and perhaps also due to their closeness in age. How much she would dwell on her observations of the Wright family in a newspaper story remained something she would decide later.

Chapter Seven

The Flyer

Summer 1905

On Friday morning, Ellen traveled to Huffman Prairie by trolley as before, again taking a lunch and planning to spend the entire day there. The brothers planned a full day of flight testing, and she wanted to observe every flight. As she arrived at the hangar, she greeted Wilbur, Orville, and Charlie Taylor. Wilbur, in response, mentioned that the weather promised to be clear and otherwise favorable for flying. Ellen planned to continue asking questions, primarily of Wilbur, as they occurred to her and as his duties permitted but decided not to attempt any time-consuming interviews with either brother, respecting the priority of their flight preparations.

Testing began as it had on Wednesday, with the brothers planning to alternate in making flights. Ellen quickly became accustomed to the routine and no longer felt as tense as she had initially when the motor was started and the flyer was launched into the air. The two flights that morning were of short duration, but both Wilbur and Orville expressed confidence that their new model possessed great potential regardless of the nagging operating problems. Landings still appeared rough to her, with minor damage resulting, and the crew was forced to make repairs and adjustments. She spoke with Charlie Taylor from time to time and continued to be pleased by his friendly, open manner. Although not highly skilled as an illustrator, Ellen began making some sketches, feeling that these would help with descriptions in the story she planned to write. She felt relieved and gratified that Wilbur remained willing to take time to answer her questions, especially since Orville continued to largely ignore her. At noon, the crew stopped work for lunch. Ellen joined them and engaged Wilbur in further light conversation.

She enjoyed watching their flights when they resumed after lunch, but Ellen suddenly realized as the afternoon wore on that her visit there was drawing to an end as well. She approached Wilbur when it appeared that he and Orville would be making their last flight that day.

"Mr. Wright, I must return to Pittsburgh tomorrow, but I want you to know that I have accomplished far more than I dared hope on this trip. I hope you can afford me some time now for final questions."

"Yes, of course," he replied evenly.

"Can you now tell me what the next step in your plans will be? It appears that the machine will be successful."

"I think it will be as well," replied Wilbur. "Everything we have learned from our previous machines we have incorporated into this flyer. It is flying capably, but as you have seen, we are still experiencing some control problems. It is not as stable as we would like, and its performance is not yet improved over our previous flyer, but it is a sound design. Another thing I should point out is that the basic structure is quite strong, so it can withstand our rough landings. Our major problem, as I mentioned, is that we have not learned how to control it skillfully, and this includes the landings. I suppose what I'm saying is that it is one thing to design and build a flyer, and another thing to learn how to fly it. We both have to master that, and we still have a great deal of testing to do before we can go forward with production for the Army or for commercial sales. I'm confident we will get there, but I cannot give you a firm schedule as to when all those things will be accomplished."

"I understand," said Ellen. "But apart from perfecting the flyer, it seems that everything revolves around gaining a patent. Otherwise nothing will follow."

"That is the way we see it," replied Wilbur, "so that remains a critical step. You know about our first patent application two years ago, and for your reporting, the date was March 23, 1903. The Patent Office rejected it on the grounds that we had not actually flown a powered machine, and they would not grant a patent on the basis of drawings. After we had flown the powered machine, we decided to resume the patent process with the assistance of an attorney. We found a good attorney, but the process is just very slow, and we still don't have approval. Our attorney advised us to control information about our invention, and that is the major reason we have continued to do so. We had an invitation to demonstrate our machine last year at the St. Louis World's Fair, or the Louisiana Purchase Exhibition as it was called, but he advised against it because we lacked the patent. I know some reporters have been unhappy with our restrictions, and I suppose that is the chief reason why few have expressed interest in observing us this year. Perhaps your reporting will be more significant, especially if it is as accurate as you say you will write it. It may seem odd, but the articles Orville showed you from that bee culture magazine are the most accurate on our work that have yet appeared."

Ellen responded that she had followed the activities that had taken place in the World's Fair in St. Louis and reaffirmed her understanding of his need for restrictions. She made further notes as Wilbur continued.

"Once we are granted a patent, we can proceed with confidence to marketing. It is entirely possible that we can build a profitable business around the flyer. It will be up to us to teach others to fly it, and we also plan to develop it to the point that a passenger can be carried. The other major breakthrough, as you know, would be to gain an Army order. Assuming our tests are as successful this year as we expect them to be, the coming year will be crucial for us. Some have suggested that we form a company and attract investors to finance us, but I'm opposed to that for now. I don't think we should form a company until we have everything ready, so we will continue to finance our experiments ourselves."

"Have you had offers of financial backing?"

"Yes," he replied, "and that could be another point for you to mention in your reporting. Mr. Chanute once informed us that he was acquainted with Andrew Carnegie and offered to ask him to provide financial backing for us, but we declined the offer. We also received a proposal from the Cabot family of Boston to back our developments, but we declined that also."

"I gather then that you will organize a business on your own," replied Ellen, "but only after sales and production are underway. Is that correct?"

"Yes, exactly, although another factor that could delay us is that I may yet have to take more time away from our experiments and from the bicycle business to help my father. As I think you know, he has been involved in some prolonged litigation with certain factions in the church, which he has had to deal with even though he has retired. Three years ago, I audited the books to prove a misappropriation of funds by a church employee, and that was a difficult period to go through. Some of my father's opponents in the church wanted to turn the case around and use it to oust him, but they failed. I have been his primary help in those matters, and I may still need to devote some time there, but I hope the problems will be over soon."

Wilbur then disclosed that they had received an inquiry from the British government last December, when a British Army colonel from the embassy in Washington traveled to Dayton specifically to visit them. The officer had asked about a possible sale of a Wright machine to his government for military observation purposes, and they had replied that they would consider such an order.

Wilbur returned to describing the next steps in their plans.

"We were rebuffed in our first attempt to sell a machine to the United States Army in January, but we decided not to try to sell to a foreign government before receiving an order from our own. We enlisted the assistance of Congressman Nevin here in contacting the Army. But the Army told us it would consider only a machine developed to the point of practical application, and without any government expense."

It occurred to Ellen to ask if the congressman might be related to the Nevin family of Pittsburgh, who were prominent in the newspaper business, but decided that that line of inquiry probably was not appropriate or relevant.

Wilbur continued. "Actually, I was not greatly disappointed at the Army's initial rejection. Since we didn't have patent protection, we feared the Army might confiscate the concept with no provision for full compensation to us. We have heard that such things have happened to others. For that reason, we did not disclose full details of our flyer at the time, and that may have been a hindrance, but we will pursue further negotiations later.

"We hold out greater hope for the British, but we still will not hold any actual flight demonstrations in advance of a firm order. Our concern, as you know, is that the machine could be easy to duplicate. That is the reality that causes us to continue our restrictions."

"I understand completely," replied Ellen. "I know that now, since I have had the chance to observe the machine in operation and have learned the reasons for your views."

Wilbur then said, "We have written a sales proposal to the government to construct a flying machine that will fly fifty miles carrying two men. We prefer to sell to our government first, of course, but we would consider selling to the British and French if our own government refuses to buy our machine."

Ellen again began to feel almost overwhelmed with the volume of information Wilbur had provided, but she continued to take notes. She told Wilbur that she recognized the validity of their accomplishment and that her reporting would certainly reflect that. Silently, she was impressed by the quiet resolve and confidence of the brothers and also respected their determination to do everything themselves before attempting to attract investors or to otherwise profit from their work. She had already decided that factor would be a key part of her reporting.

"Well," said Wilbur, "I need to help close down things here for the day. I will tell you that despite the obstacles and delays we encountered at every stage of our work, we have overcome them. We made steady progress in flight capabilities with our second flyer, and we believe that this new model will be a major practical advance. We also believe that we can succeed in the business of manufacturing and selling flying machines. But we have a ways to go, and much remains to be done."

Wilbur then excused himself to help push the flyer back into the storage shed. Ellen decided to wait and observe them completing their work for the day. As she prepared to leave, she approached Charlie Taylor.

"Charlie, I must tell you how much I have appreciated your help this week. I'm just sorry we didn't have more time to talk."

"Nice of you to say so," he replied. "I just do whatever I can, and I think the boys deserve success."

"So do I. I hope we can meet again."

"You'll have to return."

"I'm already thinking that I would like to. We shall see."

Ellen silently appreciated Charlie's friendly and helpful nature. She felt he could indeed be a friend in this assignment. She then bid good day to the brothers and started to walk toward the trolley platform. As she did so, Wilbur approached and walked to the edge of the field with her. Somewhat to her surprise, he made a personal remark.

"I heard you tell Katharine yesterday that you attended college. As it happened, neither Orville nor I ever received our high school diplomas. I suppose that is something else you should know, although I wouldn't necessarily enjoy seeing that fact in print. I still think we received good educations in the public schools."

"I'm sure you did," replied Ellen, "or otherwise you would not have been able to do what you have done. I shall exercise some discretion in what I write about your individual backgrounds."

"I know you had expressed interest, so perhaps this is a good time for me to provide something more. I can take the time, unless you are anxious to leave."

"Not at all," she replied immediately, pleased at his willingness to talk further. "Please do." She reopened her notebook.

"I was once interested in higher education. My father planned to send me to Yale for a college course, possibly in divinity, but my mother's health precluded that possibility. He did not feel I was destined for the world of commerce, and neither did I. My mother died some sixteen years ago of consumption, and I remained at home and was her primary caregiver in the last months of her life. There was nothing we could do to cure her, but I believe my care prolonged her life, and I took some comfort in that."

She could indeed understand how his mother's early death could be a transforming event in Wilbur's life. She replied, "Katharine had told me of your mother's death, and I know that is a loss you will always feel. I appreciate your sharing that with me. That helps me in gaining a full understanding of how you have progressed to where you are, but I don't think I would include such information in my articles."

"Anyway," continued Wilbur, looking into the distance as he spoke, "that episode made me highly conscious of health. I had suffered a serious injury while playing hockey when I was only eighteen, and I was diagnosed with heart palpitations. It took me some time to recover. At times, I still worry that my heart is weak. I was twenty-two when my mother died, and I had not settled on an occupation or developed any interests. Orville turned to business, as you know, and that is when we embarked on our publishing and printing venture. He brought me in as a partner despite my doubts about the business world. I had felt discouraged in watching how my older brothers struggled to make a living and support their families. Furthermore, I felt I should have been a teacher, and that is why I became interested in education, even though I never pursued that course. So, I remained in partnership with Orville, and our publishing and printing business at least made us a living, and since we both lived at home, our needs were modest in any case. As it developed, Orville and I spent much time alone during the last decade, as our father traveled frequently on church business, and Katharine was away at college. We became highly independent and learned to cook and take care of ourselves otherwise."

Ellen was interested in hearing the story in Wilbur's own words, even though she already had learned most of it from Orville.

Turning to Ellen, he said, "I suppose we have that in common, that we both have been involved with newspapers." Ellen smiled, pleased at the comparison, but did not say anything in response.

He continued, "I really felt little direction in my life until Orville and I entered the bicycle business. Fortunately, the bicycle market began to grow rapidly, and we progressed steadily in the field."

"I certainly can understand why you felt reluctant to enter the business world," said Ellen. "My father is in business, and I have watched him struggle at times also. I worked as a shopgirl for him during the summers of my college years, and I learned some of the difficulties firsthand. So, I admire those who can make a success of it as you and Orville have done. I suppose my awareness of the difficulties of the business world had something to do with my desire to become a journalist. I could at least receive a regular wage."

"In truth, the bicycle business is not exactly a passion for me," Wilbur said. "It makes us a living and that is all, but I still appreciate that it has provided us with the means to undertake our experiments. I estimate we spent about five thousand dollars by the end of 1903 to bring the flyer to the point of success."

His remark about the bicycle business completely surprised Ellen. But she recovered and continued that line of conversation. "I think I can understand what you say about the bicycle business, but I know you could not have succeeded with anything without such a close partnership. You and Orville seem to agree on everything."

"Oh, we have arguments about technical points. We haven't always agreed on how to proceed, and Orville thinks I am too much of a perfectionist. He is very much the inventor, however. He once said he was glad no one had solved the problems of flight before us, so that we could have the opportunity. In fact, I would say that much of the process of invention for us was accomplished in our private discussions, just in rethinking what we were doing. As you have probably learned, we both have our suspicions of the press, but perhaps Orville has them to a greater degree than I do. I hope you do not take personal offense."

"I don't, and I hope that what I do will bring the press into higher repute with you," Ellen replied. "I also very much appreciate your sharing all this. What you have just told me has been as meaningful as anything I have observed at Huffman Prairie. This is precisely the insight I had hoped to gain for an in-depth story on your work. It is not that I plan to write at length about your family and personal history, but learning about your background is helpful in my gaining a full understanding of how you have arrived at where you are."

Wilbur nodded his agreement.

"It seems to me that your lack of advanced formal education has been more than offset by what you have learned on your own," she said.

"I agree now, and I no longer regret a lack of further education. I last considered pursuing a college course about ten years ago, but I decided I could not afford the cost, and I would not permit my father to finance me. That was about the time I began studying the work of Lilienthal, and you know the rest."

Ellen belatedly realized that she had become so absorbed in listening to Wilbur that she had stopped taking notes. She hoped that she could remember everything they had discussed and reconstruct the conversation in full that evening. She had observed that Wilbur had a habit of staring into space when he discussed his flying machine experiments and when discussing his family, and she assumed this was due to a basic shyness. But when he asked a question, he had turned to face her, as he then did.

"I know you are staying with a great aunt here. Do you have ties with Dayton otherwise?"

"None at all," replied Ellen, pleased that he would take some interest in her background. "My great aunt moved here many years ago with her husband and children. She has been widowed several years, and her children live elsewhere. My family is of old Pittsburgh Presbyterian stock, and few of us have moved from the area. I suppose I have something of a sense of adventure. I wanted to earn my own living and possibly to see something of the world, although Dayton is as far as I have ever been from home."

Wilbur returned to describing his family background. "My father moved around fairly often due to his church responsibilities. I was born in Indiana, and we are basically Hoosiers, although Orville and Katharine were born in Dayton. I was born in April of 1867—I suppose you will need ages for your article—and Orville was born in August of 1871, then Kate three years later. They share the same birthday, incidentally. We first came to Dayton in 1869, when I was two. My father later took up an appointment in Cedar Rapids, Iowa, in 1878 and then came back to Indiana. We lived there until 1884, and that is where I finished my schooling, although we had to leave for Dayton again before I could receive my diploma."

"You are still Midwesterners, I know," she added. "I also consider myself a Midwesterner, being from Western Pennsylvania. Oh, and my birthday is also in April."

She started to make notes again. She also hoped Wilbur would continue talking, especially since it had been on his initiative. She knew that by now she had missed the trolley she had intended to ride, but she was not concerned since she knew another would come in half an hour.

"I am some years older than you, I realize," said Wilbur, "but I have never been beyond the Midwest except for the trips to

North Carolina. Now, I can foresee a trip to Europe to market the flyer in England and France, and possibly elsewhere. I may become something of an adventurer as well."

Wilbur smiled at his own remark, and Ellen smiled in return. *He might have something of a sense of humor with someone outside his family after all*, she thought. She had become increasingly impressed with Wilbur's keen intelligence and scientific mind, and she was particularly pleased that he had become more open in conversation. Her initial fears that the brothers would be reluctant to speak in detail to any reporter, especially a young woman, were completely negated. While she would indeed limit details on their personal and family backgrounds in anything she would write, she found it inspiring that Wilbur, as a young man of limited education and limited financial means, had found such a high purpose in his life. Ellen had become more comfortable in talking with him, even realizing that she admired him. She had mentioned that she would depart in the afternoon of the next day and wanted a final conversation in their shop the next morning. She decided to tell him so.

"You know that I have learned a great deal about aeronautics and about your work specifically during my few days here," she said, "but in addition I have enjoyed the opportunity of getting to know you. Perhaps we do share a few things in common beyond a connection to the newspaper business. I plan to continue a career in journalism, so like you, I have found something I can devote my life to."

"I find that interesting," he replied. "Most young women aspire to become wives and mothers, although Kate appears to have little interest in that direction."

"It is not that I am uninterested in those things," Ellen said, "but I believe there are other things I can do with my life at this time. And I was the first in my family to attend college." She paused and smiled, then continued. "This reminds me of similar conversations I have had with my parents. Actually, I received a proposal of marriage last year, which I declined."

Wilbur nodded but did not respond. Ellen silently rebuked herself for revealing such personal information, which resulted in what she sensed was an awkward silence. She feared that she possibly had gone into too much detail, almost certainly exceeding what would be his interest.

"Well, thank you again for your help today, Mr. Wright," she said, deciding to bring their conversation to a close.

"You're welcome, and please call me Will. You have probably heard that is what others call me. And everyone calls Orville Orv. We try not to be that formal around here."

Ellen felt secretly pleased at his invitation. She also reminded him to call her by her first name.

"I will come by the shop in the morning, Will."

Wilbur returned to help Orville and Charlie close down the site for the day, and Ellen walked to the platform alone to await the next trolley. Realizing that she had accomplished more than she might have expected in the time available to her, Ellen felt confident that she could now write a major article about the brothers, their achievements, and their plans. She was aware that their work had yet to become recognized by the public but hoped that her article might do something to bring that about. She understood, however, that general public recognition would come only with the patent award and a military order, and not just from her article.

The trolley arrived after several minutes, and during the ride into the city, Ellen found her thoughts turning to Wilbur. She felt somewhat puzzled by him. While he was not highly sociable or outgoing, and was almost stiffly formal in his speech and deportment, she still regarded him as an intriguing person, certainly more so than Orville. Wilbur, like Orville, appeared to be a confirmed bachelor, was probably uncomfortable around women, and had emphasized that his primary loyalties were to his family and his work. Yet she was beginning to see more to his nature, perhaps because she wanted to.

* * *

Ellen entered the bicycle shop the next morning to bid farewell to both brothers. "This has been a rewarding trip for me," she began, "especially since you both have been so helpful. I have been thinking, in fact, that I should return to follow up on your progress. I know you have much work remaining, and I think another visit would help, if I can arrange it and if you are agreeable."

Orville was noncommittal on that point, but Wilbur appeared to be more receptive.

"Please notify us of when you would like to return," he said. "We will be undertaking more ambitious flight tests as we move through the summer, so a good time for another visit might be in about three months, perhaps September or October. We should have made significant progress by then, and I hope we will have pushed the flyer to its limits. We may have more to report on the Army and patent matters as well."

He paused, then spoke again. "I do have one request that Orville and I discussed last night. Perhaps you could delay publishing a major article about our work until we have more progress to report. We remain concerned about any premature disclosure of technical details, and our flyer still is not performing up to our expectations. We still need to undertake much further development, as you know. If in fact you do return later, I think your article would be more meaningful if it is published after we have achieved the performance we expect."

"I have been thinking the same thing," she replied, "that I should not publish such a comprehensive story until you have the flyer performing at its full potential, so I will request that of my editor. For now, I just plan to write an article that will emphasize the background to your success with powered flight and describe how you have progressed to this point. But I shall withhold more specific details until after a later visit."

Ellen then bid them goodbye, addressing them by their first names as Wilbur had asked. She returned to Aunt Keys' house and, after a brief conversation, gave her a farewell hug, adding that she hoped she could return soon. She traveled by taxi to

Union Station and had only a brief wait before boarding her train.

As she again observed the countryside passing by during her journey, Ellen found herself feeling satisfaction in the way the assignment had developed and in her tentative accomplishment. She felt very relaxed during the trip, in contrast to the apprehension she had felt before coming to Dayton. She also concluded that she had developed a strong, mutually confident relationship with Wilbur Wright, but she recognized that the most challenging part of her task lay ahead.

Chapter Eight

Ellen

Pittsburgh, Summer 1905

As Ellen stepped off the train at the Pennsylvania Union Station, she saw her parents waiting as she had expected. They welcomed her with great warmth.

"Your little girl has returned unharmed," she told them, with a touch of humor.

Her father spoke first. "This is a milestone for you, I know."

"I'm just glad that you completed the trip safely," said her mother. "I still worried about you, but you appear to be well. Did you have any problems?"

"Things did go well, and my trip was smooth," replied Ellen. "I am eager to tell you everything, but I just want to get home."

Her mother and grandmother had prepared a particularly good dinner that evening, and as they ate, Ellen began filling them in on what she had learned and her progress on the assignment. As the evening progressed, the conversation turned to Aunt Elizabeth Keys.

"She is well, and very alert, but I don't think she will ever travel here," said Ellen. "She feels too old. I think she is prepared to face death when the day comes."

"I expected that would be the case," said her mother. "I had long wanted to arrange for her to come for a visit, but that doesn't appear likely now."

"What did you learn about this flying machine?" asked her

father, admittedly eager to hear more about what she had achieved relating to the purpose of her trip. "Does it really work as those brothers said?"

"It flies," replied Ellen, "and the brothers can control it in the air. They have definitely achieved powered flight, but there are still some operating problems. One thing that bothered me is that the machine has only wooden skids for taking off and landing, and it suffered minor damage on almost every landing. But they were working to control it more effectively in the air. Since they have not attained the level of skill they want to have in flying their machine, they asked me to consider waiting before I report on it in comprehensive detail, and I agreed. They still believe they can perfect the machine and bring it to practical operation this year."

Joseph Hobson continued his questioning. "I'd like to hear something about these brothers. Are they engineers or scientists?"

Ellen had anticipated that her father would pursue that line of inquiry, knowing of his practical frame of mind. Since beginning her own career she had grown closer to him, feeling that she now shared with him the experience of earning a living in the workaday world. With his bald head and expanding girth, Joseph Hobson at fifty-eight had assumed more and more the traditional appearance of a middle-aged businessman. Ellen's mother frequently scolded him for his weight gain, but Ellen felt only increasing affection for him. Since she had matured, she had also gained greater respect for what he had accomplished in life. He had come out of the nearby hills of Western Pennsylvania with few advantages and little education but was determined to make his way in the city. His drive to succeed was manifested by his establishing his own business and, through it, he had been able to provide his children with privileges he had not enjoyed. She thought before phrasing her response.

"No, they are not educated in that sense, but they have gained a store of knowledge from their own study and from contacts with other experimenters in aeronautics. I think they have learned the most from their own experiments, and I suppose I could best describe them as self-taught inventors. They are definitely capable researchers, but their primary occupation so far has been building and selling bicycles."

"Bicycles? What possible connection could there be between bicycles and flying machines?"

"Actually, I have learned that there is some connection. The chain drive to the wheels of a bicycle is similar to their chain drive from the engine to the propellers of the flyer, and the blending of various mechanical components is also similar. I don't understand it fully, but I do know that their expertise in bicycles has been a help to them in aeronautics."

"Did you learn anything about their family?" asked her mother. "Are they married?"

"No, both brothers are bachelors and evidently determined to remain so. They are rather private people, but they did share some details about their family. Both are in their thirties, about four years apart in age, and still live at the family home. They have a younger sister, Katharine, who teaches in the public school system and also lives at the home. She is thirty, about the same age as Richard, and I spoke with her briefly when she visited the shop. Their father is a retired bishop of the Church of the United Brethren, about which I don't know very much. They told me he is quite elderly but that he remains active in church affairs. I know they all look after him as well.

"I suppose some would call the brothers eccentric, but they definitely are possessed of strong character. One thing I learned, for example, is that they would never test their flyer on a Sunday, out of respect for their father. I also determined that it was in their upbringing to be completely honest and truthful about their efforts. That is another reason why I can believe in what they are doing, even though others have been skeptical."

"I gather you admire them, then," said her father.

"I do in many respects, especially the way they work together so closely. They have been partners in everything they have done since they were boys. They started a business together and started work on their flying machine together and have been working continuously on flight for almost ten years. I also learned enough to determine that they have a mutual dependency, and it seems clear that neither could have done what they have working alone. One point I found interesting is that even though they are very close, there are still some significant differences in their personalities. But what I found most unusual is that they are so completely dedicated to their aeronautical experiments that there appears to be nothing more to their lives, outside of their family. I think they are probably difficult to get to know well, and I rather doubt that they have any close friends. I had been told that they had a reputation for shyness as well, and I suppose that is true. It seems they have few contacts beyond their family and those who share their professional interests. I would find it difficult to live that way."

"Then how are they different?"

"First, I found Wilbur, the older brother, to be more helpful to me, and I would judge him to be the more advanced of the two in the scientific sense. Orville is also inventive, but he appears to handle most of the business aspects. I suppose the most sensitive point as it would affect me is that they are both rather distrustful of reporters and the press, and they made certain I knew of their previous unpleasant experiences with news accounts. Both agreed to my visit, of course, but Orville in particular appears to have little patience with reporters. In terms of personality, one difference I noticed is that Orville is very calm and rational, while Wilbur possibly is more nervous or excitable. At the same time, he is more of the public figure and has done most of the writing about their work as well as public speaking."

"And will you return to report on their progress?" her mother asked.

"I asked them if I might return in the fall, and they agreed, at least Wilbur did. I hope Mr. Rutledge will approve also. We all felt that I needed to make a return trip if I am to complete the full story of their aeronautical developments. They will be continuing their experiments through the summer, and Will—Wilbur—felt that they should have the flyer's stability problems solved in perhaps another three or four months. Actually, I think they are somewhat behind their schedule, because of operating problems with the flyer and also their other business and family obligations. I would hope after I make a second trip that I can report that they have perfected their machine, and both brothers thought a further visit would be to their benefit as well. I know that after they perfect the flyer, they plan to produce it as a practical flying machine that others can learn to operate. For myself, I feel fortunate to have gotten this assignment. It is far from what I expected when I began as a reporter, but I want to become more knowledgeable in science and aeronautics. I know I have a long way to go, but I feel I can develop a specialty in reporting developments in science and invention. That might be resisted by those who regard those fields as inappropriate for a female, but that is where I think I should devote my efforts in the future."

Ellen slept soundly that night and enjoyed a relaxing Sunday at home. Her brothers and their wives visited, and later she saw her friend Julia and her husband, John Albright.

* * *

Ellen reported to Mr. Rutledge immediately upon arriving at the *Reporter* building Monday morning. He welcomed her warmly and invited her to sit. She first conveyed Luther Beard's regards to him, and at his invitation, she began her briefing about the major findings of her assignment. Covering much of the same information she had given her family the evening before, she emphasized that the flying machine worked and that the brothers' claims were true.

"I will say again that I feel enthusiastic about this assignment, and I thank you again for giving me the opportunity. I am certain I will complete an interesting article about the brothers and their flying machine. But I must tell you now that I feel a second trip will be necessary to fully cover their developments. The Wright brothers were just beginning to test their new machine when I was there, and there will be much more to report later than there was last week. They have indicated that they would be agreeable to another visit as well."

"That sounds reasonable," Rutledge replied, "and I will keep that possibility open. I am glad that it was a positive experience for you."

After providing Mr. Rutledge with further details of her assignment, Ellen went to Roy Graham's office and greeted him. He returned her greeting with some enthusiasm, saying, "Welcome back, Ellen. I have been eager to hear of your experiences in Ohio."

"They were all positive," she replied. "I think the brothers' work with the flying machine has great possibilities. The most important thing is that they have done what they claim to have done. I now understand much more about how they developed the flyer, and I have seen them fly it. I think it is important for us to remember that what I write will be the first full report on their work to be published in a newspaper. Those few news stories that appeared earlier were very sketchy, and most have been inaccurate. I know I can do much better."

Roy agreed, then filled her in on events in the city room during her absence. She requested that she be permitted to begin work on a report on the Dayton assignment before undertaking new stories, to which he agreed. Afterward, she went to her desk and reviewed the correspondence that had accumulated during her absence and other stories in progress, then turned her attention to organizing her notes. After concentrating on the task for several hours, she found that she was working more meticulously than she had with anything she had written before. She realized, however, that the stress she felt was due to her determination to be even more precise and complete than she had been with any previous stories.

In the days following, Ellen returned to participation in other reporting assignments even as she pushed to complete her story on the Wright brothers. She made sure to gain Roy's approval in stages of what she had written. Mr. Overstreet also approved her efforts with only a few changes. When she submitted the completed draft to Roy, she placed her own name at the top, believing that the time had come for her own byline, especially with such a major story. To her dismay, she found Roy had returned it with a note explaining that the *Reporter* could not permit her to use her own byline. She went immediately to his office.

"Roy," she began, "I thought for this report I should be allowed my own byline. I don't understand why I am not permitted to do so."

"I am sorry," he replied, "and I understand your disappointment, but that is still the policy of this newspaper. There are concerns that a story like this simply would not be accepted by our readers if they knew it had been written by a woman. I know Mr. Rutledge feels that way, and he has been emphatic about it, so I hope you will not speak to him."

"I won't. I suppose this is just something I will have to accept for the time being." She returned to her desk, having decided that nothing was to be gained by launching a diatribe on women's rights, and certainly not at Roy, but she still felt keen resentment.

The full article was published in the *Reporter* early in July, under the byline of a male pseudonym. Her story contained specific information as to her activities, especially with regard to her witnessing of flights. She also summarized progress toward manned flight to date, mentioning Lilienthal, Chanute, and other experimenters, but was more general about aeronautics and with the technical details of the Wright flyer's construction and operation. She devoted special effort to explaining the fundamental differences between Santos-Dumont's airship and the Wrights' heavier-than-air flyer, since she had learned that the sector of the public with any awareness at all of aeronautics tended to confuse the two, regarding any accounts of manned flight as always involving airships or balloons. She did not reveal, however, that she had been restricted by the brothers concerning publication of details of the flyer's design and construction, and instead wrote more on the potential of flight and of the flying machine. Her article also included some brief background information on Wilbur and Orville and recounted their efforts over the past six years. She pointedly delivered a rebuke to skeptics with her documentation that the flights were real and successful, and she concluded with a prediction that the flyer would be practical. She ended with a statement that she planned to cover future flying machine developments, being careful to avoid being gender specific in her personal references.

Ellen felt that her article, when published, was successful, despite its lack of full disclosure on technical details, and she heard many favorable comments. She wrote to the brothers after the article's publication, addressing them jointly and formally, and included copies of her article. She explained to them why she could not use her own byline, but expressed her hope that the situation would change in the future. She closed by thanking them again for their assistance, wishing them continued success, and restating her hopes for another visit. She heard nothing in reply at the time but remained privately satisfied with her accomplishment.

She made certain to emphasize to Theodore Rutledge from time to time her belief that the story of the Wright brothers and their flyer was important and that her continuing efforts on the story could be of benefit to the public as well as enhancing the reputation of the newspaper. Rutledge said that he maintained his interest as well, but he reminded her that this was only one story and that she should give equal attention to other assignments. She agreed, and Ellen returned to reporting principally on stories of local interest. She became aware that the year 1905 was developing as a record year for the steel industry, with investment and output far exceeding any previous year. But she did not write on that subject specifically, as it was the province of business and financial reporters.

Ellen remembered belatedly to visit the Central Carnegie Library, where she located and read the poetry of Paul Laurence Dunbar. Definitely, this would be something she could mention to Orville on her future trip, with the hope that it might induce him to become more favorably disposed toward her.

Ellen had already made the acquaintance of some female reporters of other dailies, and during the summer she was invited into membership of the small Women's Press Club of Pittsburgh. Although membership was limited to full-time newspaper employees, Ellen learned that other writers and literary figures could be given associate memberships, and she benefited from their experiences in addition to learning from other female journalists. She found that she was the youngest member, but she regarded that status, in some ways, as an advantage.

* * *

As September arrived, Ellen requested and received permission from Theodore Rutledge for a second visit to Dayton, contingent upon the Wright brothers' approval. She hoped and expected that progress with their new flyer would lead to sales and production, which in turn would increase the timeliness and importance of her story. She expressed to both Rutledge and her family that since she had become interested in and more knowledgeable on the subject, she knew she could contribute something to public appreciation of the potential and significance of flight.

Afterward, Ellen wrote the brothers.

Dear Messrs. Wright:

I have reached a point where I can make another trip to Dayton. My editor has approved my travel. I believe further observation and reporting by me would be highly beneficial to your objective. Please let me know of a feasible date. As before, I would like to be able to remain four or five days, assuming you would be flying during the time of my visit.

Yours truly,
Ellen Hobson, Miss

Her private hope, of course, was that their reaction to her

article would be favorable and would make them more amenable to her return. She received a reply soon after:

Dear Miss Hobson:

Thank you for your letter. Orville and I would welcome your return to Dayton. We have made several more flights since your visit and have made steady progress. We have still encountered some problems, however. I struck a tree limb while turning for a landing but still brought the flyer in with only minor damage. Then the flyer was heavily damaged in Orv's landing mishap on July 14, and that required extensive repair. But the major point of progress was that we modified and extended the elevator surfaces to give it better stability and control, and we also added some canvas blinders on the rudders to help with airflow during turns. Another thing we did was to curve the propeller blades, which we found gave us greater efficiency. We were finally able to resume testing with our improvements on August 28, and now both of us are making longer flights, with more maneuvering.

I apologize for not thanking you earlier for sending us copies of your article. We received your package about the time we suffered the accident, when we were preoccupied with repairing the damage. But we both found the article to be excellent, and we appreciate that you kept your promises to report accurately and to respect the privacy of our family.

I suggest you plan to return sometime in October. By that time, we should have pushed the capabilities of our flyer to its limits, and the weather should still be favorable. Please advise us of your specific plans. We will try to accommodate your inquiries and will arrange an agreeable date.

Yours truly,
Wilbur Wright

Ellen noted that the letter was signed by Wilbur alone, which pleased her more than she would have dared admit earlier.

She reported the correspondence to Rutledge, who confirmed

that he would authorize expenses for her second trip as soon as she and the brothers had agreed on specific travel dates. Ellen was excited at the prospect of returning to Dayton but debated with herself whether the reason was purely professional or more personal. Wilbur had been very much in her thoughts over the past several weeks, although she could not precisely define the nature of those thoughts. What was clear was that he was on her mind, and she looked forward to seeing him again. But she was highly uncertain as to what end. She fully recognized the Wright family's eccentricities, the brothers' evident distrust of outsiders, their single-minded dedication to their work, and their bachelorhood. She was determined to remain professional, but she could not ignore that a possible conflict with her objectivity might exist.

Chapter Nine

Taking Flight

Huffman Prairie, October 1905

The summer had passed slowly for Ellen, although she had particularly enjoyed her frequent visits with Julia, who maintained her interest in Ellen's involvement with the flight experiments. Now, with the approach of fall, Ellen felt a quickening eagerness. She wrote the Wright brothers in the middle of September, making reference to Wilbur's recent letter and suggesting the first week in October as a time for her return visit. A prompt reply, signed by both and agreeing to her proposed date, further heightened Ellen's anticipation. She informed Theodore Rutledge of her correspondence, and he approved her trip immediately.

Ellen then departed for Dayton on Monday, October 2, after having written her great aunt Keys and asking to stay with her again. The journey itself was uneventful, but Ellen felt impatience with the speed of the train, wanting to be there quickly. Upon her arrival at Union Station, she took a horse-drawn taxi, rather than boarding the trolley, to her great aunt's house. Aunt Elizabeth welcomed her as warmly as before. Ellen spent another pleasant evening bringing her up to date with family news. She also expressed her pleasure in returning to Dayton and her anticipation of writing further on the work of the Wright brothers. This time her great aunt mentioned that she had begun to hear of the flights and that the brothers were increasingly talked of in the community. Ellen retired that evening with a feeling of excitement about her plans for the next day but reminded herself that she had to remain a detached professional.

As she entered the Wright Cycle Company the next morning, Ellen saw that both Wilbur and Orville were there. She was silently relieved that there were no customers present. She greeted Orville first, and made a conscious attempt at warmth in her greeting, but sensed he was as aloof as before.

"I hope you had a pleasant journey here," was all he said in returning her greeting. She replied that she had.

"Hello, Will," she said, turning to Wilbur. She felt a tug of emotion when speaking to him, and she hoped that her face and voice did not betray her. Wilbur, while somewhat more formal than she had hoped, still seemed more welcoming than Orville.

"Welcome back. It is good to see you again," he said. "I trust your great aunt is well." He was pleasant—but did not smile.

Ellen thanked him for his inquiry and replied affirmatively. Orville then stated, "We were pleased with your article. Both Will and I judged it to be far superior to any reporting others have done."

Wilbur nodded his agreement. Ellen felt encouraged by his statement, even though it sounded somewhat forced, and thanked them again. She remembered to mention to Orville that she had located and read a book of poetry by his friend Paul Laurence Dunbar. Orville acknowledged her statement pleasantly, adding that he was increasingly concerned for Dunbar's health, which he said had turned for the worse recently. Ellen responded that she shared his concern.

Although maintaining what she hoped was received as a friendly and relaxed demeanor toward the brothers, Ellen still felt somewhat disappointed that they had not welcomed her return with greater enthusiasm. She had hoped that her successful article would have won their confidence, or at least that of Wilbur. While that appeared to have been the case from their remarks, she could not sense that it was reflected in their greetings to her. She thought, or hoped, that they should have moved beyond such formality by now. But even as they conversed, Ellen silently reminded herself that she was there solely as a reporter. She thought she should initiate a dialogue on their activities.

"If you find this a convenient time, I would like to begin asking a few questions. Could you update me on your progress with testing the flyer?" She directed her question to both brothers.

Both indicated their consent and escorted her to their office. She took out her notebook as Wilbur began to speak. He first provided her with descriptions of their recent flight accomplishments. His main points were that they were approaching where they had wanted to be with the flyer's capabilities, that it was attaining their performance goals, and that they were flying it with greater skill.

"I look forward to witnessing flights again and seeing your progress for myself," Ellen said.

Orville then added his views. "Our major progress has been made over the past month, after we modified the control surfaces. We have progressed both in terms of distance and altitude, and as Will said, we are flying with more skill."

Wilbur then clarified the matters that he regarded as of first importance. "On that point, I believe we have both learned to control the flyer better. Our flying techniques have improved to the point that we no longer suffer any damage on landing. That, to me, is the major difference between where we are now and where we were at the time of your first visit."

Ellen responded that she was pleased to hear their statements. "Have you made progress with your patent application and with the Army?" she asked, again of both.

"Our American patent application is being reviewed, and I believe we will gain the patent soon," replied Wilbur. "We also remain confident that we will eventually gain an Army order, even though we have just received another rejection. This time, we wrote directly to Secretary of War Taft, who is an Ohioan as you probably know, offering our flyer, but the response came through the Army Ordnance Board, and they again assumed that we were requesting financial support for development. We had to interpret that response as an outright rejection, but the major point of annoyance to us was in the way the letter was worded. It indicated that they did not understand that we had already built and tested a flying machine. It also seemed to me that their response bore no relationship to what we had proposed. We will approach the Army again, of course, and with more information, and that should help. But as of now, it appears that they simply are not paying close attention to our proposal. I'm confident we'll eventually get through to the right people, however. I know you understand that with an Army order we will be in a position to offer production models for sale to other customers."

Ellen answered in the affirmative and continued to make notes as he spoke, determined as before to report accurately their views and the specifics of their negotiations.

Wilbur, with the evident approval of Orville, led the conversation. He pointed out that it was helpful to them that the United States did not impose any restrictions on their dealings with foreign governments. They were free to negotiate with the British, French, and others, although he restated that as an American he regarded it as almost unpatriotic to sell the machine abroad before doing so in the United States.

"Have you had further contact with the British?" Ellen asked, referring to their conversations on that matter during her earlier visit.

"We have not," Wilbur replied. "They have not followed up their earlier contact. We think it may be better to wait until we have made more progress before contacting them again."

Orville excused himself to complete certain repairs in the workroom, and Ellen resumed the conversation with Wilbur. Continuing that practice from her first trip made her feel a degree of comfort in one respect. But at the same time, she also felt some apprehension—or a high degree of self-consciousness—in her manner toward him.

She talked with the brothers for the rest of the morning, as Orville later returned to participate, and also reviewed their photographs and test data from the recent flights. Wilbur informed her that they would not be able to fly that day but planned to do so tomorrow. Ellen accordingly departed from the shop by noon, stating that she would see them at Huffman Prairie the next morning, then returned to Aunt Elizabeth's house for lunch. She spent part of the afternoon in her room reviewing and organizing her new notes. She wrote a brief account of the modifications the brothers had made since their crash in July, believing that would expedite completion of her next article. She then determined what further information she would need. Her plan, as before, was to spend the next few days at Huffman Prairie to observe the brothers' continuing flight tests and assess their progress for herself. Aunt Keys appeared pleased to have more time during the day for their conversation.

The next morning, October 4, Ellen rode the Interurban trolley to the Simms Station stop, walked to Huffman Prairie, and met the brothers as before. She saw that they were already at work on flight preparations, and she noticed that several others had arrived at the site. She had not expected so many observers but assumed they all were there by invitation. Wilbur greeted her first and escorted Ellen over to meet his father, who had accompanied his sons to the field that day and was standing near the hangar.

"Miss Hobson, may I introduce my father, Bishop Milton Wright," he stated, with some formality.

Ellen greeted him warmly and was immediately impressed by his courtly manner. He clearly looked the part of a bishop, with his long, gray beard, and was possessed of great dignity. She assumed Wilbur had already explained to him her purpose there.

"I have become highly impressed with what your sons are doing, sir," she said, "and I look forward to writing more about their work."

"I appreciate that," he replied. "All of us in the family believe in what they are doing, but my first concern is and always has been for their safety in the air."

"I understand. That is everyone's concern, but they have

A Romance of Flight

assured me that they have learned to fly the machine safely, and I believe that as well."

Bishop Wright moved to take a seat in a nearby chair, informing Ellen that he planned to return the next day as well. She replied that she looked forward to talking with him further.

Ellen felt almost at home, sitting in the same chair she had used in her first visit and resuming her vantage point at the field, as if she had never left. She saw Charlie Taylor and greeted him, telling him that she hoped they could talk again during those times when he was not needed for flight preparations. He added his welcome at her return and agreed to talk with her whenever he could.

After the necessary preparations, with which Ellen was now familiar, the flight testing began. She also noted that the launch process was unchanged. She observed immediately the extended structure for the elevators that Wilbur had told her about. The first flight of the morning, with Orville at the controls, went smoothly, and Ellen could see that the machine was indeed performing at a higher level than she had observed before. After Orville had landed the flyer, Charlie helped turn the machine around, then approached Ellen and began discussing his background.

"This should be a good time for us to talk," he began. "I will have a few minutes before I must help launch the flyer again, and I'll be happy to tell you about my association with Will and Orv."

"Please do," said Ellen. "I really want to hear it."

"My wife and I moved from Nebraska to Dayton in 1896, more than nine years ago. This was at the suggestion of Bishop Wright, who was acquainted with my wife's family. But actually, it was easy to persuade me that opportunities in a growing industrial city were much greater than in my home state. I was already a skilled machinist, and my first association with Will and Orv was helping them with bicycle repairs. I began buying parts from them for my own work before working for them directly. Then, when they began making and selling their own bicycles in their new shop — this was a little more than three years ago — I went to work for them full-time."

Ellen was more interested in how Charlie had helped them with the flying machine, since he had no special aeronautical expertise. She raised that question directly.

"I understand your reason for asking," he answered. "I started out helping them with the engine, as you know. Neither Orv nor Will had enough mechanical knowledge to build an engine without help, and they still devote most of their time and effort to aerodynamics and control. And of course, Wilbur has done a lot of writing and speaking on aeronautics. So, when they failed to interest an engine manufacturer in the job, they gave me their specifications, and I built the engine on my own. Not that it was perfect from the start, I remind you; we had to do a lot of testing and modification before it was ready to be mounted on the flyer. You probably know also that I built the engines for the second flyer and for this one as well. So that has been my main work. I have helped them in several other areas, but I must admit that I still have no special knowledge of the aeronautical end."

Impressed, Ellen replied that she would explain his contributions in the next articles she planned to write. She had mentioned Charlie only in passing in her first article. He appeared pleased that she would feature him more prominently in future reports.

"Another thing you might want to write about," Charlie continued, "if you haven't already planned to do so, is that they built their own wind tunnel and learned a lot from it."

"They haven't mentioned it, and this is the first I have heard of it. What is a wind tunnel?"

"You asked the right man," he laughed. "It is an enclosed space—basically a long wooden box open at the ends—where you can control air flows and observe them through a window. They would place a wing section in the tunnel, blow smoke through with a fan, and observe from the smoke how air flowed over the wing. That was the major way that they learned how to measure lift for a flying machine. They could adjust the wing surface, then tabulate lift at all angles by measuring the ratio of lift to air pressure. That's how they finally proved that Lilienthal's lift coefficients were wrong. Will and Orv built their first wind tunnel after finishing flight tests with their second glider. I think this was about September of 1901. They decided to work with the wind tunnel because of their frustration with the lift of that glider. The wind tunnel work enabled them to find a better wing design with improved lift for their next model, so it largely answered the remaining questions about lift and control for the powered machines."

"I know that is important, and I will try to understand it better," replied Ellen. "I remember that Wilbur told me that they had refigured the lift computations after their problems with the second glider, but he didn't mention a wind tunnel. In particular, I would like to understand the principle of lift more fully. I read some of Wilbur's writings and have seen his tabulations, but I still don't understand the matter."

"I think you should ask Wilbur for more details. The principles are not all that complicated, and if I can grasp the basic idea, I'm sure you can too, but I think he could do a better job of explaining it. Anyway, I regard that wind tunnel as one of their major accomplishments. I should also mention that they used the wind tunnel to decide the precise design of the wing. They found that a long, narrow wing worked better than anything else that had been tried."

Ellen saw that the brothers were preparing to fly again, which meant that Charlie was needed. She thanked him again for his help.

Ellen spent the rest of the day quietly watching the brothers fly. Flights were indeed smoother and of longer duration than those she had observed in June. The flights she had witnessed on her earlier trip had been very brief, but now they were sustained, and with more maneuverability. That afternoon, Orville flew a record twenty-one miles in thirty-eight minutes in a circuit of Huffman Prairie. Wilbur reconfirmed to her later in the day that their recent flights were the most impressive of any they had yet achieved and that the new machine had been everything they had expected.

Ellen could see that the flights, although still not open to the general public, were much less secret than before, with several observers continuing their presence. She learned that some were prominent local businessmen. Wilbur and Orville thus were able to state to lingering skeptics that reliable witnesses had attested to their flights. More impressive even than the duration of the flights were the complete figure eights they performed regularly, demonstrating convincingly their control of the machine in the air. Ellen joined in the widespread and rising awareness that the brothers Wright were accomplishing something truly extraordinary that autumn at Huffman Prairie.

During the course of the day, Ellen also became aware that among those observing were reporters from other newspapers, and reports of the long flights had gone out over the wire service. She saw that Luther Beard of the *Journal* had joined the group in the afternoon, and she moved to greet him. He acknowledged her immediately.

"Mr. Beard, I'm so happy to see you here. As it happens, this is my second visit to report on the brothers."

"I'm glad to see you again also, Miss Hobson. I must confess that my earlier skepticism was wrong. I now fully believe the claims of the brothers, and my paper will be reporting about them more than before."

At the day's end, Ellen asked Wilbur for his assessment of progress.

"I can state at last that our flyer is a complete success," he said. "I think we have arrived at a point where we can consider ending our tests for this year, perhaps by the end of this month, and Orville agrees. We can then concentrate our efforts on our patent application and on selling a flyer to the Army."

"You must believe you can now overcome the rejections you have received from the War Department," Ellen said.

"I do," replied Wilbur. "I know that we have enough documentation and eyewitness reports to overcome their previous objections, and I am confident we can now gain the attention of people in authority. I also believe it will help that we are ready to deal with the French on license production."

"I believe you will succeed also. It makes sense to me that you have little to prove with further testing now. I'm just happy that I was able to come here in time to see how much you have accomplished."

"I am glad that you are persuaded of the validity of our work."

"I was from the first time I saw the flyer take to the air," replied Ellen quickly. "I was never a skeptic, just uninformed. Charlie has told me some more details of your scientific experiments, and I hope to include that in my reporting as well. He described your work with the wind tunnel and told me more about the principle of lift—things I didn't understand before."

As they talked, Ellen began to reflect on everything she had learned to that point. Of the technical aspects she was indeed absorbing more knowledge, but she still did not have a complete understanding of what the brothers believed to be the future of their invention. Would there be a vast fleet of flying machines across the country? For what purposes would they be used? She knew she needed answers to those questions, and so she brought up the matter directly.

"Will, I must ask you something that I still am not clear about. Orville has said that the flyer would have military value for observation, and I understand that, but what further uses would there be? How would the general public benefit?"

"First of all," he replied, "I believe that with this flyer, others can be taught to fly. What we have learned can be passed on to others. The flyer then can have several commercial uses, including personal transportation. It is capable of carrying a passenger, and we will soon outfit it to do that. We can also give it more power and make it stronger and can also adapt it to carry cargo over long distances. Later, we could build larger flyers to carry several passengers. But the main benefit is that flyers would not be dependent on roads or rails. I am confident that over the next two years we will be producing flyers for both military and commercial uses. I don't claim to be any great visionary about aviation, but I think flying machines will benefit society in that mankind is no longer bound to the surface of the earth. The flyer will also affect our concept of time. We can go more places faster than ever before. I suppose you could say that flyers will make the world smaller."

It had become clearer in Ellen's mind that Wilbur in particular appreciated what powered flight could mean, and she thought he was being too modest in disclaiming himself as a visionary. Theirs was an invention that could change the way people lived, much as the telegraph and telephone had and as the automobile promised to do. She realized that their purpose went far beyond development of a practical flying machine and that they meant to gain its implementation as an instrument of commerce and transportation that would truly advance civilization. She felt pleased with her gains in understanding powered flight since her earlier visit, and she now regarded her knowledge as substantial. She also realized that while Orville was very much the engineer and technician, Wilbur was the true scientist as well as the visionary.

She could sense that Wilbur was waiting to continue the conversation. She ceased taking notes and asked him to tell her more.

"I suppose I hadn't discussed our plans to any great extent before, so I'm glad you brought up the point. I believe Charlie also helped you with the more technical background about our engine. As you know, we are not trained engineers, so we had to learn what we needed on our own." Wilbur then paused and shifted his focus.

"Since I believe we can regard you as a supporter," he said, "I have a further idea, if you are available. From time to time in the past we have invited guests to our home to discuss our work more informally. If you would like to visit this evening, I shall ask Kate to prepare tea."

"That would be delightful, I'm sure." Ellen tried to maintain a pleasant and restrained demeanor in responding to the invitation, although she had difficulty containing her excitement. This was a development she had never anticipated.

"Then perhaps about eight this evening," he suggested, "if that time is convenient."

"That would be perfect."

"I shall ask our brother Lorin and his family to come around also, although they visit frequently anyway."

"I'm sure I would enjoy meeting them."

Wilbur provided specific directions, emphasizing that their home was near the shop, then walked back to the flyer, explaining that he needed to help Orville and Charlie close down operations for the day. Ellen noticed that most observers had already left. She then walked across the field alone toward the trolley platform, feeling nothing less than a sense of exhilaration. Her mild disappointment in Wilbur's less than enthusiastic welcome to her the day before was forgotten.

* * *

As she arrived by taxi at the Wright home that evening, Ellen found it to be a rather ordinary frame house, somewhat smaller and plainer than her own family residence, but appearing to be well-maintained. She was greeted at the door by Katharine, who was polite but reserved as before. Katharine escorted Ellen to the parlor where the brothers and their father sat. After greeting all, Ellen complimented them on the comfort of the home.

"Thank you," said Wilbur. "Orville and I added the porch and some other refinements to the house ourselves a few years back."

Ellen thought that the home indeed presented a picture of simple comfort.

Katharine, maintaining her correct but less than warm attitude toward Ellen, introduced the household maid, a small young woman named Carrie Grumbach. As Carrie brought in the tea service, Katharine explained that she began working for the family as a child. Ellen returned the introduction, then turned her attention to Bishop Wright.

"I know you must be pleased at how much your sons have accomplished in the air," she said.

He acknowledged her statement in what she decided was his characteristic courtly manner, but his subsequent remarks continued to center on his concern for the physical safety of his sons.

Soon after Katharine had served tea, Lorin Wright, who, as Ellen already knew, lived only four blocks away, arrived with his wife and their four children: Milton, Ivonette, Leontine, and little Horace, called Buster. All greeted her graciously. Ellen could discern a Wright family resemblance in Lorin.

As the evening progressed, Ellen sensed that she was not necessarily the focal point of attention as the guest, as the children captured increasing attention from their uncles. That did not bother her, however, as she found herself enjoying the interactions of the Wrights as a family. She had not expected the degree of warmth the brothers demonstrated toward their nieces and nephews, who addressed them as Uncle Will and Uncle Orv. She noticed that both brothers laughed and smiled often when speaking with the children, and eventually Wilbur responded to their entreaties and read them a story. Afterward, Wilbur and Orville asked Lorin if he would watch the bicycle shop while they flew tomorrow, to which he readily agreed.

Orville, while still more reticent than Wilbur, said to Ellen, "Both Lorin and Kate have helped manage the shop when we have been in North Carolina or otherwise occupied." She acknowledged the statement.

Ellen became steadily more impressed by the warmth of the family, from Bishop Wright down to the youngest grandchild. Although, she had been led to expect such closeness, so that it came as no surprise, the reality nonetheless made a strong impression. The evening also presented to her a marked contrast to the sterner, more solemn demeanor that the brothers presented in public.

Ellen deferred asking the questions she had planned, as she felt the brothers wished to devote most of their attention to their family, but Wilbur soon turned his attention back toward her.

"I would like to know about your oldest brother, Reuchlin," she asked. "I know he lives far away."

"Yes," Wilbur replied. "He does not keep in close contact with the family." He provided no reason, and she decided not to pursue further questions on him.

"I hope we haven't bored you with all our attention to our nieces and nephews," he said.

"Not at all," she responded quickly. "I come from a large and active family also, so this all appears quite normal for me."

"We can certainly take time to answer any more questions about our plans that you care to ask."

She thought of several questions that she felt would be appropriate given the occasion.

"Do you know of other serious claimants to powered flight?" Ellen asked of both Wilbur and Orville. "Do you have any new competitors?"

"I am not aware of any serious experimenters in the United States since Langley ended his efforts," said Wilbur. "I know of several efforts in Europe, especially by Santos-Dumont in France, which you know about. But I believe we have a lead of several years over any competitors either here or overseas."

Ellen was satisfied with his answer. Given the relaxed nature of the evening, she decided not to pursue technical questions related to the flyer. Instead, she asked about their views of the work of Santos-Dumont, about how balloons differed in operation from heavier-than-air crafts, and about their plans for carrying a passenger, a matter of increasing interest to her.

After a pleasant visit of almost two hours, Ellen decided to depart, concerned that aunt Keys might worry if she stayed later. She bid all a good evening, expressing gratitude for their hospitality. Will saw her to the door and expressed concern about her finding a taxi late in the evening. Ellen assured him that she would have no problems and in fact found a taxi immediately. She arrived at her great aunt's house some fifteen minutes later. She determined that Aunt Keys had already retired for the night, so she let herself in without waking her. As she settled in her bed, she found that her earlier exhilaration had been replaced by a vague feeling of apprehensiveness, to the extent that she had difficulty falling asleep.

* * *

At Huffman Prairie the next morning, Ellen greeted both brothers by telling them again how much she had enjoyed the evening. She then greeted Bishop Wright, again spending the day there, and spoke further with Charlie Taylor when he was available. She mentioned to him her pleasant visit to the Wright home and restated her interest in learning his views of the brothers. He readily shared his insights and experiences.

"Some of the things I will tell you are along the lines of what others have asked about," he began. "One point I think is worth noting is that while Will and Orv appear very serious to most people, they both possess a sense of humor, and I've heard that they even play practical jokes within the family."

"I learned of those qualities during my visit last evening," said Ellen. "They certainly have a warm and humorous nature when it comes to their family. But please, continue. It is helpful for me to know more about their personalities."

Charlie appeared to think for a moment. "There's another matter people have asked about from time to time. Some who have gotten to know Will and Orv have remarked on the fact that neither has gotten married. When he has been asked, I have heard Will say something to the effect that 'I could not support a wife and a flying machine too.' I think he has used essentially the same response anytime the question has come up about his status." Charlie emitted a short chuckle after he spoke.

Ellen could not be sure that he had not pointed the remark at her.

"On the other hand," he continued, "Will is always cautioning Orv to beware of young women."

Ellen considered that remark to be in a more light-hearted vein and laughed softly.

"I have heard that Orv possibly proposed marriage to a young woman some ten or twelve years ago," he continued, "but I don't know any details, and that was well before I knew the brothers. Will may have had a friendship with a young lady some time ago as well. I have heard some vague talk of it. But as far as I know, there have never been any hints of romance by either since, and I seriously doubt that you would get either of them to comment on such matters. I certainly don't ask them, and it does seem highly unlikely to me that they could have carried forward to success with the machine if either had been married. They are that single-minded in their dedication."

"I appreciate that," responded Ellen quickly, "and that confirms my impression as well. I simply wanted to gain as much background information on them as possible, although I certainly wouldn't include anything that personal in the story."

"It's probably better that you don't," laughed Charlie. "I can't imagine anything that would displease them more than seeing something like that in print. I would also guess that if you did so, that would end their cooperation with you."

"I agree. It is rather obvious that they are private individuals, and I respect that. And you're right, I would never ask them questions of that nature."

Charlie hesitated for a moment, then spoke again. "You know, while people may joke about Will and Orv becoming old bachelors, I think, in Wilbur's case, the truth is that he is just a little woman-shy. He is actually articulate and is a decent public speaker, as you know, but tends to be a little withdrawn around women. In fact, I would say he has talked to you more than he has to any other female in my memory."

Ellen tried to conceal some slight embarrassment, and she hoped that her face did not flush. She quickly asked, "What about Orville?"

"I think Orv probably just is not very sociable. My sense is that he is far more likely to remain a bachelor than Will is. But the most important thing to understand about both of them, I think, is the Wright family. I believe that both their father and their sister expect them to remain unmarried and to continue as partners in this venture from now on. There just seems to be some kind of unspoken understanding that that is what life holds for them. Again, I am trusting that you will use some discretion with what I have said."

Ellen confirmed the point and decided to end that line of discussion. She then turned to another matter that had been unclear to her, but had bothered her increasingly, and that was the division of activity between the brothers. She felt that the answer might become another matter requiring some discretion in reporting.

"Perhaps you could help me clarify something else I have wondered about," she began. "Both refer to their work in joint terms, always 'we' and almost never 'I'. But I have begun to sense that Wilbur is the senior partner, and that he has provided the real technical genius behind their success. I think reviewing his technical papers just reinforces my point. I have learned something about the principles of flight, enough to know that they can be comprehended by someone without any special expertise, as Wilbur and you have told me. That is why I feel I can make such a statement. As we have discussed, I would not write anything to that effect. I'm sure that it would be highly sensitive with the brothers, and I don't want to risk losing their cooperation, but I raise that question with you. Am I correct?"

Charlie considered his answer. "I won't confirm your view, but I won't disagree either. I know that Wilbur alone invented the wing-warping system, and as you know, that was the key to controlling the flyer in the air. I have come to recognize what an accomplishment that was—possibly their greatest single accomplishment. For my part, I regard it as particularly impressive that Wilbur devised the specifications for the engine on his own. Just as a contrast, and I don't think he had any detailed knowledge of its design, he also determined that a large and heavy engine probably was the major factor that made Langley's aerodrome fail in its flight attempts."

Ellen understood that Charlie, while not saying so explicitly, had effectively confirmed what she had supposed. But she knew that she should not write anything that would imply that Wilbur was the senior or more inventive partner in any published article.

"I have to say again," said Charlie, "that I hope you won't repeat anything I have told you about these matters to either of them. I've probably said more already than they would have wanted me to, and I am loyal to them. I hope you understand that."

"I do, and I shall honor your request. But what you told me has been of more help than you know. You've been a friend on this, Charlie."

Charlie excused himself to help with the preparations. Ellen again observed quietly, then moved to engage Wilbur in more conversation during the times when he was not preparing to fly. She had already concluded that his initial remoteness or aloofness toward her was not so much due to any natural shyness, but that he had instead purposefully placed a wall up to protect himself from any semblance of intimacy with someone outside the family. She had already decided that had explained his rather formal greeting at the beginning of her visit. But she also felt that, just possibly, the wall was now cracking. She thought Charlie was right, that Wilbur probably had talked to her more than he had to any woman in recent years, and that gave her a tentative feeling of accomplishment.

Flight tests were smooth and fully successful as they had been the day before, culminating in a record-setting endurance flight by Wilbur. He flew twenty-four and one-half miles, making twenty-nine rounds of the field, and before fifteen witnesses, including Ellen. Ellen again simply enjoyed observing, rather than attempting to gain any further technical understanding or reporting insights. She had seen the firsthand reports in the Dayton newspapers, and she knew that at last the people of Dayton were aware of what was being accomplished at Huffman Prairie.

At the end of the day, Wilbur, appearing tired, approached her.

"I know we have discussed this before, but I ask again that you exercise some discretion in reporting on my family. I'm glad that you have met my family, of course, but we all have a high regard for our privacy."

"You can count on me to respect that," she replied, "and you know that I did so in my first article. My interest in your family and in your individual backgrounds has been entirely in an effort to more fully understand your motivation and how you have made the progress you have with aeronautics and the flying machine. It was very enjoyable for me to have the opportunity of visiting your family at your home. That only reinforces my determination to write a more substantive story on your work than anyone has accomplished before."

"I suppose the most crucial thing you should understand about Orville and me, and I believe you already do, is that our work on the flying machine is the most important thing in our lives. This has been our great obsession for the past six or seven years."

Wilbur looked away as he considered his next sentence, and Ellen could tell that this was a moment of utmost seriousness for him.

"Every other consideration has become subordinate to our work. My first priority always has been my partnership with my brother, and the same applies to him with regard to me. We have that understanding to support each other without limit. My family also expects things to remain that way. I'm not sure about what Charlie may have told you, but the nature of my work and my family duty require that my life remain the way it is."

That had been precisely what Charlie had told her, although Ellen quickly responded that she and Charlie had discussed primarily technical matters. She nonetheless wanted to think that Wilbur indeed felt more comfortable around her, as manifested by what he had just said. She flattered herself that his increasing openness was her personal achievement, especially given what she had been told originally to expect about the brothers' discomfort around women. Despite that progress, she began to realize that she had become strongly drawn to him on a personal level.

She questioned in her mind whether she could succeed in remaining objective in anything she wrote, given the direction of her thoughts. Further, she was concerned that Wilbur might sense her growing feelings for him and was troubled by the possibility that he would react negatively to it. Was he discreetly trying to head off any emotional scene or foolish declarations by her? She knew there could be no mistaking Wilbur's determination to maintain his established position in life, a position that definitely did not include any room for her.

Rather than ask any more questions, she thanked him again for his help and bid him good evening. She left the field alone and returned to the city on the trolley.

That evening, Ellen sat quietly before the fireplace in the company of her great aunt. She kept her thoughts to herself, not feeling able to share them with Aunt Keys. But in attempting to clarify her feelings, she knew by all that was rational that she should not feel as she did. She was a young woman on her first major independent reporting assignment. Wilbur Wright was a somewhat shy, even eccentric, bachelor completely dedicated to aeronautics and to his family. Yet she could not banish thoughts of him from her mind, and the idea of leaving Dayton, and returning to Pittsburgh and to her life there, had become something she dreaded. Feelings that she had regarded as ambivalent during the summer now were unmistakable. She had not anticipated such a situation emerging from this assignment and attributed such feelings to her own emotional weakness. She silently rebuked herself for being so foolish but simultaneously resigned herself to the fact that she could not will her feelings to change.

After staring into the fire for an extended time, Ellen forced herself back to reality, knowing that she could not stay on further, that she must return to Pittsburgh and to her life there. Yet her brief time in Dayton over two visits seemed to her almost a separate lifetime.

* * *

As October 6 dawned, the realization that it would be her last day there weighed heavily on Ellen as she prepared to depart. When she arrived at Huffman Prairie, she greeted Will and Orv, then took her usual chair. She again spent the morning quietly observing their flights. Bishop Wright had not come that day, but there were numerous observers as before. She exchanged only pleasantries with Charlie and spoke only occasionally to the brothers, asking few questions of either. As they paused for lunch, she approached them and forced herself to make her departure announcement.

"This seems to have been such a short visit for me, but I feel I have largely completed my work here," she began. "I know I have learned more than I would ever have thought possible earlier, and the time has come for me to leave. I shall depart tomorrow morning."

"I am glad that you have found your assignment worthwhile," replied Wilbur, without elaboration.

"I also recognize that what you are doing could help us and also help the field of aeronautics," said Orville, in what Ellen regarded again as a rather forced manner.

"I will continue to observe your flights for the remainder of the day. If I have missed anything significant for my reporting, it will give me a chance to fill in any gaps." She struggled to control her voice, fearing it would crack with emotion, and was satisfied that she had completed her statement with an even tone. Both acknowledged her statement pleasantly, but neither demonstrated any further reaction. She returned to her chair.

After eating her lunch, Ellen passed her last afternoon at Huffman Prairie as she had expected, making notes of her observations and on any further thoughts as they occurred. She felt almost lost among the many other observers but decided that that was probably to her benefit. She did speak with other reporters and observers from time to time, and she also spoke to Charlie, although not on matters of substance. Neither Orville nor Wilbur appeared to pay particular attention to her during the afternoon, although she had a few questions remaining that she wanted to ask.

Their flight experiments operated smoothly for the remainder of the day. Both Orville and Wilbur commented to her during a break that they were satisfied they had learned to control and maneuver the machine reliably and that they had brought it to the point of practical operation. Afterward, Orville piloted the flyer on another flight of some fifteen minutes. As the afternoon shadows began to lengthen, Will approached and informed her that Orville's flight would be the last for the day. Ellen noticed that other observers were departing the field. Wilbur then returned to help Orville and Charlie detach the tail section and push the flyer into the hangar. She felt herself sink into a feeling of depression as she prepared to leave, but her spirits rose when Wilbur again walked toward her.

"We will be leaving the field soon, and I realize this may be one of your last chances to ask questions, so is there any further information I could give you?"

"Yes," she answered quickly. "I do have several things to ask about your business plans."

As they began to talk, Orville and Charlie walked toward them.

"I think we've finished for the day, Will," said Orville. "Are you ready? There will be a trolley along in a few minutes."

"You go ahead," he replied. "I'll stay behind and lock up, and I will make a last check around the field for any supplies or equipment that should be in the hangar. Ellen also has several questions to ask me about our plans, so we will catch the next trolley after you."

Orville gave Wilbur a quizzical look but accepted his statement without further comment, and he and Charlie departed. After seeing them off, Wilbur strolled around the test site for a few minutes, with Ellen accompanying him, occasionally picking up small parts and supplies he found on the ground. In the distance, they saw the trolley arrive and come to a stop, then depart with Orville and Charlie aboard. Wilbur, as he had said he would, checked all equipment and supplies inside the hangar, then locked it. He stood near the door facing Ellen and began to speak more about their plans.

"I don't know if we have made it clear, but since our tests with this flyer have now accomplished everything we had hoped, we have a practical flying machine. I anticipate we will conduct flying tests for only another month at most, and after we end flying, we can concentrate on winning a patent and on commercial matters."

"I suppose that wasn't entirely clear to me," replied Ellen, even though it was, "but I see now that since there are only two of you, you have to do everything yourselves. I know that Charlie and your family have been very helpful too."

"Precisely. And it will have to remain with us until we have received the patent and have succeeded with Army negotiations."

She decided at that moment to introduce a subject she had not discussed before.

"I do have another question, or point," she said, "and I hope you will not think I am out of order by asking it. While I understand your concerns about a lack of patent protection, and that the Army might appropriate your ideas without credit, it still seems that your overall secrecy and restrictions on reporting may have been counterproductive. You might find that if you become somewhat more open, it will actually help you, especially since you are ahead of anyone else in the field."

"I know," replied Wilbur, "and I think you may have a point. Ultimately, we will have to end our restrictions in order to market our flyer. But how and when we will do that are difficult questions. The main concern I have had is that just holding a patent still would not protect us fully. Others could still make use of our work without credit. We would have legal recourse, but infringement could be difficult to prove. That is why we have tried to maintain secrecy on the details. Regardless of whatever else may happen, we must maintain control of our invention."

"Again, I can understand your concerns, and I know that it would be difficult to change. I was just thinking what might be the most effective policy for you."

A Romance of Flight

Wilbur acknowledged her statement. He paused, appearing lost in thought for a moment. "Well, shall we leave?" he asked.

Ellen nodded her agreement. They walked toward the trolley stop, exchanging only pleasantries about the good flying weather they had enjoyed. They had remained at the field for perhaps only fifteen minutes after the earlier trolley had departed, so their wait was extended. Two other men came up to the platform. As they sat waiting, Wilbur said little, beginning what for Ellen was an awkward silence. She attempted to start a conversation.

"Tell me what you feel while you are in the air. What are you thinking about during flight?"

"I have to spend most of my time and attention on the controls, of course," he replied. "I do like the wind rushing past my face. I have little time for sightseeing, unfortunately, but it is spectacular to see the ground from a high altitude."

He offered little more.

The next trolley, with only two other passengers aboard, arrived on schedule. They boarded and took seats opposite each other, and the two men followed. Ellen had hoped Wilbur would continue conversing, but he remained quiet for the duration of the ride, even staring into space as she had observed him doing habitually. She began to wonder if she had offended him after all by questioning their policies on restricting information. He said no more until they approached the city center and Ellen's stop. As the trolley slowed, Ellen indicated to him that it was her stop and rose to get off. Wilbur acknowledged her statement, then said quickly, "I can get off with you here for a moment, if you don't mind. I want to make sure you are clear about our schedule."

"I think I am," said Ellen, relieved that he appeared willing to speak again, "but I would be pleased to talk further, if it will not cause you to be late for dinner."

"That will be no problem."

They stepped off after the trolley drew to a stop and walked a short distance from the nearly empty platform. The year was moving further into autumn, and darkness was approaching rapidly. No other persons were nearby. As the trolley departed, Ellen turned to Wilbur and spoke first.

"I know that you and Orville will now focus on gaining the patent and landing the Army order, but do you in fact have a firm schedule for those things?"

"No, and I still can't forecast how long they will take, but we hope to succeed within six months. We will be quite busy at any rate. More people are learning about our work, and that carries both advantages and disadvantages. Unless we can accomplish both tasks soon, we will never gain full recognition for what we have done. There is always the possibility that others could jump ahead of us in the future, although I don't regard that as much of a threat at this point."

"You can be sure that I will be following your progress even after I have written and published my articles."

Neither said anything more for a moment. Ellen again attempted to fill the silence.

"It is gracious of you to extend your day to help me the way you have," she said. "I just hope it will not cause you too great a delay in getting a trolley to your home."

"It will not," he replied quickly. "Trolleys still run every half hour into the evening." Again, there seemed to Ellen to be an awkward pause.

Wilbur spoke again. "Can you think of anything else you want to ask?"

Ellen replied in the negative but felt a sadness approaching dread that her last chance for a private conversation with him was ending.

Wilbur looked back to the trolley platform. "Well, if you should think of more questions, you may ask them tomorrow at the shop. You will still come by before you depart, won't you?"

Ellen hesitated before answering yes. She wondered then if she should just walk away now, but Wilbur made no move to return to the platform. She felt tears welling and did not look directly at him.

He spoke again, staring into the distance. "So, I'm sure you look forward to returning to Pittsburgh."

"My visits here have been very meaningful," replied Ellen, her voice almost breaking. "I know I should look forward to returning, but instead I now find myself reluctant to leave."

Wilbur seemed puzzled. "Why should you not wish to return? It is your home, your family is there, and your job is there."

"But you are here."

It was almost as if she heard herself say the damning words without willing it. She felt she had lost her breath.

Ellen had turned away from Wilbur but forced herself to look back at him. He looked startled. Fighting back tears, and struggling to maintain her composure, she began to apologize. "I . . . should not have said that. I only meant that I have grown to feel great interest in and involvement with your work. I . . . Well, it is better that I go."

She began to walk toward the trolley track, beyond which was the street leading to her great aunt's home.

"No!" said Wilbur, with an urgency in his voice. He stepped in front of her and grasped her shoulders with his hands. He gazed at her directly as he spoke. "My life for thirty-eight years has been nothing but family and work in partnership with my brother. We are involved in something we believe will change the world. I have never thought there would be anything else. But now, you have come into my life, and made me question everything. It is something I . . . have never dealt with before."

Ellen did not respond, feeling almost in shock. Attempting to collect her thoughts, she could not quite believe that Wilbur had meant that she could be of importance to him, although such a meaning should have been unmistakable. On the other hand, she knew that she could no longer conceal her feelings, however foolish she previously had regarded them to be. After what seemed to her as a prolonged silence, she began to speak.

"I know only that whatever I feel is less important than your work and your family. The last thing I would wish to do is cause problems for you and impede your work. I will leave tomorrow, and that will be that."

Wilbur hesitated, then spoke. "As you are reluctant to leave, I am reluctant to see you leave. That is what I have been debating for the past hour, whether I should tell you so."

"I do understand now, and that means more to me than anything I could ever have imagined. When I return home, I will still think only of you, but I recognize your circumstances. If I should become a . . . a part of your life, it would cause a rift with your family and could even destroy your partnership with Orville."

"You are probably right about my family," he responded, with a tone of resignation in his voice. "And Orville is Orville." He began to turn away again. "I still want you to know that I have felt . . . that you have, that is, brought a change in me that I could not ever have imagined before."

He paused, then spoke again. "But I don't understand how someone like you could hold any personal feelings for me. After all, I am just a shopkeeper, basically a bicycle mechanic. I am approaching middle age, have lost most of my hair, and still live with my family. My obsession in life is flying machines. What is there for you?"

"You are a very special and accomplished person, Will," she replied. "That is what I have come to . . . to admire . . . about you. If knowing me has made you realize that there is much more to your life, and more to you as a person, then maybe I have served a useful purpose. Incidentally, my oldest brother is several years younger than you and is starting to lose his hair also. So that is hardly anything you should worry about."

"I just didn't let myself consider before that we could mean anything to each other," he replied. "But I have found much to . . . admire . . . about you as well."

He paused again, apparently collecting his thoughts. Ellen understood that he could not use the word love. Nor, for that matter, could she.

"Perhaps we could write to each other from time to time," she said.

He nodded in agreement. "You will still come by in the morning?"

"Yes."

"You know," said Wilbur, as they parted, "I have never withheld anything from Orville before, but I will not tell him of this conversation."

Ellen did not reply, but she began the walk to her great aunt's house. She did not look back.

* * *

Ellen had not slept well but still felt relatively refreshed as she set out for the bicycle shop the next morning. She arrived at midmorning and found both Wilbur and Orville present. She steeled herself against her emotions as she addressed them jointly, not looking directly at Wilbur.

"My train is scheduled to depart at noon, so I thought I should come at this time to say goodbye. Once again, I appreciate all your help to me on this visit, and I look forward to writing your story very much. I will ask you to please convey my regards to your father, to Katharine, and to Lorin and his family. I enjoyed becoming acquainted with them also. And again, I especially appreciated your hospitality in opening your home to me."

Both acknowledged her statement, but neither said anything specifically. She extended her hand to Orville first. She felt that Wilbur's handshake was uncertain. She began to back away slightly as she continued her farewell.

"I will send copies of my new articles to you when they are published, of course, but that may be a month or more away. I will continue to follow all reports on your progress, and I hope I will have the opportunity to write and publish more articles on aeronautics, to build on what I have learned here."

"We shall look forward to reading your articles," said Orville, in what Ellen regarded as yet another forced attempt at pleasantness.

"I'm sure that whatever you write will help us," added Wilbur. "But if you find that you need more information, by all means, contact us again."

"Thank you," replied Ellen, "but I'm sure I have more than enough. I do hope we can correspond at some point, but I don't anticipate the need for a return trip."

Neither offered a response.

"Well, I know you are busy," she stated to both, "and I must return to my great aunt's house to pack. I will say again that I believe you are on the threshold of great accomplishment and recognition."

She wanted to say more, but decided not to.

Orville nodded, but said nothing.

Wilbur's face was also masked, but he spoke. "We wish you a pleasant journey," he said.

Ellen forced a smile, then turned and left the shop, holding back tears. She boarded a streetcar to the city center, changing to the southbound car to return to her great aunt's house.

***

After finishing her packing, Ellen sat quietly in the parlor. Elizabeth Keys commented on her grandniece's melancholy expression. "You look so blue, my dear," she said. "I thought you would be excited to be returning home."

"It is not that I am unhappy to return home, Aunt Keys, but I suppose this has been an exhausting or draining assignment in some ways. Perhaps I am just tired. I hope I can relax on the train, and I'm sure I will feel better after a few days at home."

She then rose, kissed her great aunt goodbye, knowing that it might well be the last time she would see her. She hailed a taxi at the street and proceeded to Union Station.

***

Ellen sat in the crowded waiting room of Union Station, sinking steadily into what she could regard only as a state of melancholia, when she heard her train announcement. With a quiet sigh, she rose, picked up her luggage, and walked toward the boarding platform. As she found her car and saw the conductor, she gradually became aware, through the throng of people hurrying in various directions, of a figure at the edge of the platform looking toward her. Denying recognition at first, she then realized beyond doubt that it was Wilbur. As their eyes met, he began to walk rapidly toward her. Oblivious to any possible stares from others, Ellen dropped her bag and rushed toward him. They met in an embrace, she with tears in her eyes.

"I will see you," said Wilbur. "I will work out a way, and I will write."

"Please make it soon," replied Ellen, her heart pounding. "I couldn't bear not seeing you again now."

"I knew when you were leaving, and I found a convenient excuse to come here since we needed additional supplies from the hardware store. I feel lucky that I made it in time. I will come to Pittsburgh somehow. I don't like deceiving my family, most of all Orville, but I did so last night when he raised questions about you. In fact, it was almost confrontational, but I cut the conversation short. If he asks any more questions, I will still deny any personal feelings, but I know now that I do not wish to face life without you. I have many more things I want to say, but I know you must leave now."

"At least I can return with a lighter heart," replied Ellen. She kissed him quickly on the cheek, then turned toward the train. Wilbur helped her with her bag as she reached the car door and met the conductor. She boarded, feeling joy as well as the wrench of separation. The whistle blew, and the train began to move before she could find her seat. She looked out a window to see Wilbur looking up at her. She managed a smile and a weak wave.

The trip was smooth, and the weather was clear, but Ellen ignored the scenery as the train sped through the countryside. Her thoughts were entirely about Will and Huffman Prairie.

Chapter Ten

Journalism

Pittsburgh, 1905–1906

Ellen's train arrived at the Pennsylvania Railroad Union Station on schedule. As she stepped out onto the platform, Ellen saw her parents waiting. She moved across the platform toward them almost at a run and hugged both with such enthusiasm that they seemed surprised.

"I'm glad your train was on time, so I suppose you had a pleasant journey," said her mother as they traveled home. "Was your visit as productive as you expected?"

"The train was fine, and I did have a productive visit," Ellen replied, as they traveled home. "Everything went as I had hoped, and I have so much new information that it will take me some time to organize it all. I also understand much better how the machine flies, and with that understanding, I can write a more complete story of the brothers and their flyer."

"It appears that you are as encouraged as you were after the first trip," said her father.

"Even more so. I really think I have accomplished something worthwhile, and I've become involved with a field that could determine my future as a reporter."

After arriving at home, Ellen's enthusiasm about the success of her assignment continued to be reflected in her every remark. She spoke warmly of her great aunt Elizabeth as before but focused chiefly on her reporting experience.

A Romance of Flight

"How did you get along with those brothers this time?" asked her father, as they sat in the parlor. "I know you said you had success with getting their cooperation last time, but did things go as smoothly this trip as before?"

Although she had anticipated a question of that nature, Ellen still felt her skin flush at hearing it. Her mind raced to process all its implications. She knew that she must try to respond with some detachment, and she spoke positively of both Wright brothers.

"Yes, I have gotten to know them better, and I believe that I forged a good working relationship. I emphasized to both that my reporting could benefit their efforts, and I think they were persuaded of that."

"What about the younger brother? I've forgotten his name, but you had said before that he appeared to be the less interested of the two in working with a reporter."

"That is Orville. He was still rather aloof, but I learned that that is basically his nature. Fortunately Wilbur, the older brother, more than offset any reticence on Orville's part. He is a somewhat reserved individual, but he still provided the help I needed. I also received a great deal of background information from Charlie Taylor, their machinist. He has worked with them for four years and is quite talkative by nature. He understood why they were quite guarded about their privacy and helped by advising me about what I should and shouldn't ask the brothers."

She continued to discipline herself to appear objective, not wishing to betray any emotion at the mention of Wilbur's name. The conversation during dinner turned more to family matters, which Ellen felt was of greater interest for her parents and grandmother as well as more comfortable for her. She paid special attention to her grandmother Ryan by sharing news of her sister.

Although relaxed at the end of the evening, Ellen could hardly sleep that night, even in the warm familiarity of her own bed. She turned over in her mind the question of what she should tell her parents about Wilbur, if anything. She decided she should wait until she could talk with him again.

* * *

Upon entering the *Reporter* building on Monday morning, Ellen reported directly to Theodore Rutledge as she had after her first trip. He welcomed her with a degree of enthusiasm that mildly surprised her and invited her to sit and tell him of her experience at that moment. She did so and began her report.

"Mr. Rutledge, I feel even more strongly than before that I have found a story of great significance, and I thank you again for giving me the opportunity. This second trip has made all the difference."

"I am happy to hear that," he replied. "I hope you can do as well with your new articles about these birdmen, if that is the right term, as you did with your first."

"I know I will. I can write with a far greater depth of understanding than I had three months ago, and I really believe this is a story the public should appreciate. I think I had a particular accomplishment in that I made the brothers feel somewhat more comfortable with having their story printed. As you know, both are inclined toward secrecy, and they still have their suspicions of reporters and the press. I can understand that to a degree, but I know I persuaded them that it would be to their benefit if they permitted more detailed reporting on their work. And because of that, I can do more in telling their story than others have so far.

"I have also decided that I would like to continue following aeronautical developments, if that is agreeable with you. Inevitably there will be others who will experiment with powered flight, and I would like to be able to compare their efforts with those of the Wright brothers. It seems logical that eventually I should expand into reporting on science, industry, and invention as a professional specialty. Once again, I know there may be those who question a woman working in those fields, but I can do it."

"I believe you can also, and I will give it consideration," replied Rutledge, "but I would like to assess the public reaction to your new articles about the Wright boys first. I remind you as well that you will still be covering city news and other local developments."

"I understand, of course. It is just that I have found a field that I can become particularly dedicated to. As always, I will continue to pursue any stories that you and Roy assign me, but I would like to follow the progress of the Wright brothers while doing so."

Ellen was encouraged that Rutledge seemed supportive of her plans. She did not, of course, tell him of the more personal reason for her desire to follow up on the assignment, but afterwards she worried that her undisguised excitement about the experience might cause him to raise that question in his mind. To lessen that possibility, she had already decided that she would try always to speak of the brothers jointly, and that if she spoke of Wilbur specifically, she would do so with detachment, as she had with her family. She was acutely aware that it would serve only to reinforce existing negative views of female reporters if it became known that she had developed a personal relationship with someone she had been assigned to report on.

After leaving Rutledge, Ellen went to Roy Graham's office and greeted him. He also welcomed Ellen back warmly, a matter of some relief to her, as she had feared that Roy had not held the same level of interest in or support for her assignment as had Mr. Rutledge. He listened with interest as she summarized her trip, which was generally similar to what she had told Rutledge, and congratulated her on the apparent success of her assignment. He then briefed her on happenings in the city room during her absence. After thanking him, Ellen went to her desk and began to review her personal correspondence and other news stories in progress.

Josh Raymond and another reporter came by her desk, welcomed her back, and inquired about her experience. She regarded their words as encouraging indicators of her growing acceptance in the office, and Ellen acknowledged their interest graciously. She then turned to the task of organizing her notes and writing the series of articles on the Wright brothers and their flyer. As the day passed, she found the task becoming progressively more difficult; she could not separate thoughts of Wilbur from her writing efforts. Additionally, she found it difficult to write about the brothers as equal partners. She knew that would be necessary, however, as she could not convey in print anything of her personal view that Wilbur was the true genius behind powered flight.

During the course of the week, although required to devote some time to helping with other news stories, Ellen succeeded in shaping the first article into final form. She still provided only general details of the flyer's construction and operation, maintaining the restrictions that Wilbur and Orville had asked, though disclosing somewhat more than she had in her earlier story. But she wrote many more details of her observations of the new flight tests, including specific facts on the flyer's greatly increased performance capabilities, and accounts of the long flights and figure eight maneuvers. She submitted her final draft to Mr. Overstreet, who immediately raised questions about the scope of its coverage. Ellen responded by outlining her plans for the remaining two articles and how the series would result in a comprehensive story. She was relieved when Mr. Overstreet eventually approved her plans and her writing style, and he passed the first article with few changes.

* * *

Ellen received a letter from Wilbur at her office some two weeks after her return from Dayton—and before her first article had even appeared in print. She opened it eagerly.

Dear Ellen:

It seems almost needless to state that I have thought of little else but you since your departure. For the first time in my life, I have had difficulty concentrating on my work. I hope you are not afflicted to the same degree.

I will not dwell on my personal feelings, since there are several important professional matters about which I should inform you. Incidentally, Octave Chanute visited us just after you left and observed several flights, and I'm sorry you did not get a chance to meet him. The major news, however, is that Orville and I decided to suspend flying on October 16, rather earlier than we had planned. We had become concerned by the appearance of more reporters with cameras at Huffman Prairie, and we still cannot permit photographs. After we ended our flights, we decided to disassemble the flyer and place it in storage. We then turned the field back to the Huffman family as agreed, but they promptly demolished the hangar we had built for the flyer. That left me with a twinge of regret.

We made great progress in more than fifty flights with our new flyer, as you know, and we have achieved the performance we wanted. We are now confident that we can train others to operate the flyer, and we will begin doing so next year after we receive our patent. I take the view that there is another immediate benefit to ending our flight experiments for the time being in that we are now able to turn our full attention to patents, licensing, and marketing. I have written letters to aero clubs in Great Britain, France, and Germany, describing our progress with the flyer, and we hope that will stimulate further interest in those countries. We are also working on several technical improvements, including a better and more powerful engine. Based on our progress this year, I believe that we will overcome the second rejection by the Army and gain an order sometime in the next year.

There is another matter that should be of special interest to you: Orville and I have finally agreed that our insistence on secrecy and control of details has been counterproductive. Consequently, we plan to invite more publicity soon, as you recommended. I thought you would be happy to know that, and I will keep you informed.

I promise that I will find a way to travel to Pittsburgh soon. I know you would like to reply, but perhaps it is best that you don't for the time being. I am not ready to have a confrontation with Orville about receiving a personal letter from you. I will deal with my family later.

With love,
Will

Ellen was so overcome that she brushed away tears as she

finished the letter. She would of course have been pleased at anything Wilbur had chosen to write, but she was especially gratified that he regarded her as a partner in his endeavors by discussing his business plans. She knew that a direct reply to him would raise suspicions within the Wright family, so she reluctantly accepted Wilbur's advice and refrained from writing him. She also maintained silence on the matter to her own family, as difficult as it was, but she wanted to discuss with Wilbur their further plans before revealing her feelings to her parents.

The first article in Ellen's series, again under the pseudonymous male byline, appeared in the *Reporter* near the end of October. By that time, she had almost completed her second article, in which she expressed her view that the Wright brothers were on the brink of major recognition and emphasized that they were not aerial showmen but serious experimenters who had developed a practical flying machine, succeeding where so many had failed. It was published in mid-November. In her third and final article, appearing early in December, Ellen reported in detail the brothers' progress toward an American patent, foreign interest, potential interest by the Army, and the flyer's possible applications. She concluded with statements about the brothers' views on the broader future of aviation.

Ellen had learned from news service reports of the founding of the Aero Club of America, on November 30, 1905. She incorporated that news into her final article, including her view that the event reflected the increasing importance and acceptance of powered flight.

* * *

Her articles attracted widespread interest from the *Reporter*'s readership, which Rutledge felt had enhanced the paper's standing. They also gained for Ellen increased respect among the staff, who recognized the series as her accomplishment even though published under another byline. Although pleased with the many positive responses from the public, she also heard from the usual skeptics who cast doubt on the reality of the flights. She could only guess how much more vehement the doubters would have been had they realized that the reporter was a woman. She even developed a grudging respect for the policy that prohibited her using her own byline for this story. While still angered and frustrated by the skeptics, she was determined to endure the criticisms and to continue her efforts. That was one lesson Ellen had learned from the brothers Wright.

After her series had been published, Ellen sent copies to Wilbur and Orville, along with a cover letter addressing them jointly. She again referred to the false byline and explained her approach to the content of the articles. She did not write anything of a more personal nature, nor did she refer to Wilbur's private letter. The brothers soon replied with a brief letter, signed jointly, formally thanking her for her efforts and expressing pleasure with the articles.

Ellen received another letter from Wilbur just before Christmas.

Dear Ellen:

The first and almost the only thing I want to express is my intense desire to see you. Of course, I wish you and your family happiness during the holiday season.

Orville has accused me of seeming distracted over the past several weeks, but my explanation was that I felt somewhat let down with the ending of flight tests for the year, and that is true as far as it goes. There has been a potentially significant business development I can tell you about: a French government delegation just visited us in Dayton to discuss the flyer. They expressed interest but still appeared to me to be indecisive and reluctant to act, so this has led to more frustration for us. We have also just received an official letter from the British declining to order a flyer, so we remain stymied in the matter of sales. I still believe both contacts have potential, and I am not discouraged for the longer term.

Incidentally, we are aware of the founding of the Aero Club of America that you mentioned, and we have written them a letter describing our work as well. I hope this will benefit us in the future also.

Now, I have devised a plan by which you can write me without arousing suspicions from Orville. I have made an agreement with Charlie Taylor, without providing any elaborate explanations, that if he should receive any letters addressed to me in his care, he should immediately convey them to me privately. I am enclosing Charlie's home address, and you may henceforth write me in his care. I believe I can trust his discretion.
With much love,
Will

Ellen was pleased and relieved at Wilbur's plan. She agreed with Wilbur that they could trust Charlie's discretion. She did not know if Wilbur had told him that any such letters would be from her, but she suspected that Charlie had guessed or discerned his feelings, as well as hers.

Ellen enjoyed a happy Christmas with her family.

* * *

In her short life, Ellen could not recall looking forward to a new year with such enthusiasm and optimism, and indeed, as the year 1906 dawned, there would be numerous events that would impact significantly her future and the futures of the Wright brothers. In a letter in mid-January, Wilbur asked Ellen to locate and read an article appearing in the January 13 issue of *Scientific American* that expressed skepticism about their flight claims. He had just written an indignant rebuke to the journal, accusing them of failing to investigate the matter sufficiently, and wanted her to watch for its publication. On a more positive note, Wilbur mentioned that Amos Root had published an update on their flights of the last year in his beekeeping journal. Ellen replied to him, in care of Charlie Taylor as they had arranged.

Dear Will:
I just wanted to tell you quickly that I will read and study the Scientific American *article. I also remind you that I have been*

the subject of some skepticism about my reporting, so we will have to withstand negativism together.

There is much more that I could say, but I will delay for now, and just await further progress.

With love,
Ellen

Ellen found the *Scientific American* article, entitled "The Wright Aeroplane and Its Fabled Performances," and discovered that its skeptical comments were in the form of a response to the letter the brothers had written to French contacts about their flights of September and October. She could readily understand Wilbur's unhappiness with the article. She also obtained a copy of Amos Root's *Gleanings in Bee Culture* and read his updated and positive story.

In his next letter, in February, Wilbur mentioned that he and Orville had suffered a personal blow with the untimely death of their friend and Orville's high school classmate, Paul Laurence Dunbar, on February 9. Ellen then learned through wire service reports that Professor Samuel P. Langley of the Smithsonian, the most notable aeronautical experimenter after the Wright brothers, had died on February 27. He was aged seventy-two, with his powered flying machine experiments a failure. In her reply to Wilbur, she expressed her sorrow at the death of Dunbar and also related her awareness of Langley's passing.

Events moved ahead in Dayton, as Wilbur related, reflecting the goals and modified policies of the brothers. Of immediate significance, the brothers made a public announcement on March 2, attended by the press, of their recent flights and the progress they had made. On that same occasion, Wilbur magnanimously paid public tribute to Langley as an inspiration to their efforts.

Wilbur reported their flight announcement to Ellen in a letter the following week, adding to her that in his view their powered flight accomplishments were becoming more widely recognized by the public. Ellen thereupon wrote a brief story on the announcement for the *Reporter*. At the close of that same letter, Wilbur said that he could at last plan to travel to Pittsburgh, in connection with a trip to Washington. He could not forecast a specific date but hoped it would be later that month. Ellen responded immediately, telling him how proud she was of their rising recognition and that she would count the days until his arrival.

* * *

While impatient for Wilbur's visit, Ellen devoted her full attention to what she regarded as more routine reporting duties. The days again seemed to pass slowly for her even as she thought constantly of Wilbur.

One afternoon late in March, as Pittsburgh was beginning to receive the first portents of spring, Ellen was typing a story at her desk when Roy Graham approached her.

"There is a Mr. Wright here to see you, Ellen."

Ellen's heart leaped, but she hoped she had suppressed any visible reaction, reminding herself to remain calm and appear professional. Earlier, she had mentioned to Roy that the Wright brothers might be visiting Pittsburgh soon. She did not immediately look around for Wilbur but replied to Roy in an even tone. "Good. Please show him to my desk."

Roy moved to do so, while Ellen, with forced casualness, rose and turned to meet Wilbur. He walked across the city room toward her, escorted by Roy. She noticed immediately that he was dressed in a suit and carried a bowler hat, appearing rather more elegant than she had ever seen him before. They shook hands and greeted each other cordially but formally.

"I'm so happy you could come, Mr. Wright," said Ellen. "How was your trip?"

"Very good, thank you. I've never visited Pittsburgh before, so I am happy to have the opportunity at last."

"Then I hope you can remain long enough to see something of the city."

"I hope I can manage to do so. I plan to stay overnight, but I must continue on to Washington tomorrow morning. Pressing business."

Turning to Roy Graham, Ellen said, "I'm sure you are aware that Mr. Wright is one of the brothers whose aeronautical experiments I have reported on."

Graham replied pleasantly that he was so aware.

"I would like to interview Mr. Wright about his and his brother's progress since I visited Dayton last fall," she continued. "Do you suppose I could use Mr. Rutledge's office? I believe he is out this afternoon, and it is so noisy in the city room."

"I don't see why not," replied Roy, "and I must agree that things are rather noisy today. I hope I will see you again, Mr. Wright."

Wilbur nodded and returned the pleasantry as Graham returned to his office. Ellen pulled a file from her desk drawer and took it along with her notebook, then escorted Wilbur to Rutledge's private office, closed the door, and closed the shades on the window. She dropped the file and notebook on the desk and rushed into his arms. They kissed passionately.

"I don't need to tell you that I have lived for this moment, just to be with you," she said, after kissing him again. "But how did you manage to leave without revealing that you planned to come here?"

"I have a legitimate reason to be in Washington, to inquire about our patent application, and I also wanted to confer with Army officials. I simply told Orville that I would need to spend two or three days in Washington but didn't say that I would be traveling through Pittsburgh, of course. It has amounted to another instance in which I did not lie but didn't tell the whole truth either."

Ellen decided that explanation did not need any comment from her, and she turned to other matters.

"With all that has happened, I've almost forgotten about your bicycle business. I hope you are still prospering with it."

"Business is steady, although it always slows in the winter.

And it is a matter of importance, since we still need the income to support development of our flyer. We have yet to earn a dollar from the flyer, as you know."

Wilbur paused, then spoke again. "Ellen, I've been wanting to tell you about my conversation with Orville when you left in October. It was after dinner at home that he raised the question about your leaving, which he already knew, and which I confirmed, of course. He offered the opinion that it was well that you were leaving, since he felt you had designs on me, as he put it. Then he accused me of having more than a purely professional interest in you.

"I was a little shocked by Orville's attitude. I denied his accusation, of course, and again defended you as a capable reporter who could be of enormous help to us and to our work. I told him I was confident you would write thoroughly and accurately about our work, which would go a long way to offsetting the distortions and errors that have been printed in the past. I told him further he had no reason to suspect your motives, and that your presence at Huffman Prairie certainly had not been any impediment to our experiments. Orville said he didn't doubt your seriousness as a reporter, but he also felt I had been looking at you as well, and that Kate had said the same thing. The only thing I said in response was that he had nothing to be concerned about, that there were no such distractions, and that I hoped he would be pleasant to you when you came by the next morning. Orville said he was glad I recognized that family and work came first, and that we could put this behind us. I told him there was nothing to put behind us and bid him good night.

Wilbur paused, as if to catch his breath. "Orville and I have disagreed about many things over time, but we had never had such a conversation of that nature before."

"He hasn't brought it up again?"

"No, and I'm relieved at that. Maybe my words were effective."

A Romance of Flight

Wilbur and Ellen continued their conversation, with Wilbur updating her on his activities since his last letter. They reported on their respective families. Ellen suggested that they should talk further while strolling out of doors, where she could point out some attractions of the city as well. Wilbur favored the idea.

Ellen returned her file and notebook to her desk, then approached Roy Graham and said, "I would like to escort Mr. Wright to the central business district and give him a brief tour. I hope to be back in an hour or so."

Roy indicated his approval. Ellen put on her coat, as it was still cool outside. She and Wilbur walked directly to the Allegheny River and began to stroll along the river walk.

"I see no reason to conceal my love for you, Will," said Ellen. "We should not have to defend or explain ourselves to anyone."

"Ellen, you know this is the year Orville and I have been working toward. We should get our patent soon, and we should also gain foreign production agreements. Then I believe we will win an Army order. If we can accomplish those things, we are on our way, and then I know I can begin talking more seriously to you."

"One matter could become an obstacle," said Ellen. "If we publicly declared our feelings for each other, my entire reporting effort might be regarded with suspicion by Mr. Rutledge and Roy Graham. We would have to devise some way of answering any criticism on that point."

Wilbur listened, then spoke again. "I knew from our last day together at Huffman Prairie that I wanted to marry you, but worries about my family's reaction just overwhelmed me, and I also feared that I might have been misreading your feelings. But knowing now that you feel the same way, I believe we can work together to overcome any obstacles. I expect Orville and Katharine would be opposed to the idea even if all our plans for the flyer are realized, and possibly my father would be as well. I'm afraid they would regard my intention to marry as disloyalty toward them. But if we can work through all these business and legal matters, I feel that I will have earned enough independence to do what I want. I now think we can look toward next year as the time when we can marry. I am not a man of means, but we can begin earning a substantial sum off our invention soon, and that will be vital."

"I am not concerned about money," replied Ellen. "You know that. I only want what you want, and I know that we now care enough for each other to overcome all obstacles. Incidentally, if what you have just said was a marriage proposal, I accept."

Wilbur smiled, as did she.

"I suppose it was," he replied, "and I regret I did not make it more formally. I strongly believe that I should speak to your father before we make more specific plans, however."

"I agree. That was always the way I thought it should be, and I have not mentioned anything about us to my family either."

"I believe we can get to that point soon, and that is what keeps me going. It must seem absurd to you that a man my age cannot discuss such matters freely with his own family, but that is the reality. Most of all, I do not want to do anything that would cause a breach with Orville. We have been so close all our lives. We even maintain a joint bank account."

He thought for a moment, then continued, "I know only that the five months we have been apart have seemed like an eternity to me. There are numerous pressures and problems with our work, and you know about them, but the real obstacle keeping me from you is my family. That is still what worries me most. Before you came into my life, I had agreed with them that I would never have any business pursuing a romance, and I said so. I know you must think my family situation is unusual, even eccentric, and I suppose that is true, but we cannot ignore it. You remember that I told you Orville had raised the question of my personal feelings for you before you left last October, and how I gave a misleading answer. Well, my response must have satisfied him, since he hasn't raised the question again. It still troubles me in that I had never done anything like that before, but I did not feel in a position to confront anyone in my family at the time, certainly not Orville. Among other things, he certainly would have brought up our priorities with the patent and contractual matters. And in truth, those things must take precedence over any personal considerations."

"We can deal with your family, Will. Others have dealt with similar challenges. I only want to be of help to you, and I can be. It also occurs to me that we have never had a chance for a real courtship, although I don't have any regrets. But we have a future together, and I think you should tell your family. Then I shall tell my family also."

"Perhaps you should wait longer. I still have to decide how I should deal with my family, and there is our business in Washington to attend to. I will write you about how I see our situation after I return home."

"I don't think my family would be opposed to you," said Ellen, "although they don't know anything, and I agree that we should be able to present specific plans to them before I do anything on my own."

"I suppose that is the wise course to take. But do you think it would be possible for me to meet your parents while I am here?"

"It is possible, of course, but I would rather wait for another occasion, after our plans are more definite."

Wilbur indicated his agreement. As they walked, Ellen asked him to pay particular attention to the incline railways running up Mount Washington, one feature of the city that she enjoyed. Wilbur responded that he would like to ride a car up the incline on a future trip. They continued to stroll along the river. The weather was clear and pleasant for an early spring day. Wilbur had become silent. Ellen could see that he was deep in thought and that he was troubled. She decided to remain quiet until Wilbur broke his silence.

"I must tell you again that regardless of my feelings for you, our work must come first. It is not that your life is any less important than mine, and I know it is unfair for me to expect you to remain in the background while I carry through with these urgent tasks, but that is what I hope you will agree to do."

"I already knew that would be the case, and it does nothing to alter my feelings for you. I will wait if I have to, but I say again that all I want to do is help you. I also want you to know that this has changed my life as much as it has yours. Before knowing you, I could never have imagined that I would be doing anything other than continuing to work as a city reporter."

"The fact that you are there to support me only makes me more determined to carry our plans forward, whatever the obstacles," he said. "The fact that you would change your life for me means more than anything that has ever happened to me."

Ellen reminded Wilbur that she needed to return to her office. He had registered in a hotel near the Union Station, and as they parted, he invited Ellen to join him for dinner that evening.

* * *

When Ellen arrived home at the end of the workday, she informed her mother that she would not have dinner at home but would return downtown to dine with a friend. Her real purpose in returning home, however, was to secure a small photograph of herself mounted in a gilt frame and displayed on a dresser in her room. She wrapped the photograph, taken just after her graduation from college, in plain white paper and tied it with ribbon. Returning downtown by streetcar, she met Wilbur in the lobby of his hotel, and they dined in the hotel restaurant. That evening they decided to simply enjoy being in each other's company and not discuss the challenges they faced. Ellen decided, however, to speak of their feelings again.

"Will, it seems that everything has happened so fast. I still do not know when or how I came to mean anything to you, and it seems we have not had an opportunity to discuss that. I will tell you that I began to have feelings for you during my first trip to Dayton. I tried to deny them at first, but I soon admitted to myself that the real reason I wanted to make the second trip was you."

"You are right that we have not really discussed this before, and I want to as well. I began to develop an attraction to you during your first visit also. I think we connected somehow during those first few days, but I felt strongly inhibited from doing or saying anything. I thought it impossible that a young woman like you could ever hold any feelings for me, and that it would be foolish of me to think otherwise. I wanted very much for you to return, of course, but when you did, I still felt that I had to remain at some distance. Otherwise, I felt I would indeed play the fool."

"I suppose we can almost laugh at ourselves now, since that describes almost exactly the way I was feeling. And I will tell you something else: I never planned to confess my feelings to you. But that evening at the trolley platform, they just seemed to overwhelm me."

"I know," he replied, "and that is when I knew I could no longer remain silent either. I am glad you said something; otherwise, I don't know what would have happened. Maybe nothing would have happened, and we would both have been poorer for that."

With that short exchange, Ellen felt greater happiness than she had ever felt. At the conclusion of the meal, she spoke again.

"I have something I want to give you, Will. I know your birthday is next month, and since I cannot be with you then, you may consider this an early birthday gift."

She handed him the wrapped parcel.

"May I open it now?" he asked.

"I want you to. I only hope it pleases you."

Wilbur unwrapped the picture, and Ellen could see that he was deeply affected by the gesture.

"I have to admit that this is the first time in my life that I have received such a gift."

Ellen almost gave way to tears. "I just hope you will keep it near you always," she said, touching his hand across the table.

"I shall never let it out of my possession, but of course I can't display it openly at home, at least not yet. I'll send you something for your birthday as well. I did remember that your birthday is close to mine. I had already planned to do so, but now I will turn my attention to it right away, as soon as I return from Washington."

Wilbur departed the next morning. Ellen accompanied him to the station to bid him goodbye. His parting statement was that he was determined to return to Pittsburgh as soon as possible, but he could not forecast the next time he could get away. They embraced without regard to any stares from onlookers. Ellen gave way to soft tears as he boarded his train.

* * *

Wilbur, as promised, sent a package to Ellen in time for her birthday, again addressing it to her at the *Reporter*. It was a photograph of him standing beside the flyer at Huffman Prairie.

Ellen replied to him immediately.

Dear Will:
Nothing you could have given me could have pleased me more than this. It signifies everything I love about you. I know you trust me and that you regard me as a partner in your quest.
Until we can see each other again.
With love,
Ellen

* * *

As the Wright brothers continued their efforts with the Army and the Patent Office, the pace of international aeronautical activity also increased. France in particular was a focal point of development. Articles about powered flight were appearing more frequently in the press, and the brothers were indeed becoming better known to the public. But the Army still appeared uninterested. More encouraging to Wilbur, a new article in *Scientific American* appearing in the issue of April 7 accepted the Wrights' claims about powered flight, effectively countering the skepticism of the January article. He wrote Ellen of his pleasure at the evident vindication. She was delighted to learn of the development, of course.

As Wilbur had forecast, the brothers succeeded the next

month, after several frustrations and more than three years of effort, in gaining their US patent. Issued on May 22, the patent, while based on their application for their 1902 glider, still extended to and covered their powered machine. Ellen immediately wrote a brief story on the patent award for the *Reporter*. She then wrote the brothers jointly, telling them of her awareness of their accomplishment, that she had written a story on the award, and offering her congratulations.

* * *

Another event that spring, which Wilbur reported promptly to Ellen, was to carry more ominous portents for the future of the Wright brothers. The upstate New York motorcyclist, engine maker, and budding aviator, Glenn Curtiss, had contacted them by letter around the time of their patent award. Curtiss asked them if they would be interested in an engine of his design and informed them of his own interest in aeronautical development. The brothers replied that they would not be interested in his engine at the time but asked him to keep in touch.

Before the Curtiss contact, Wilbur had written Ellen of the visit to Dayton by a representative of a French business syndicate, following soon after the initial inquiry by a French Army officer. Since Wilbur had gained the impression from the December visit that the French government had appeared reluctant to act, he felt encouraged by this subsequent contact. The officer, a Captain Ferdinand Ferber, had said at the time that a private syndicate might be more decisive. In addition, the syndicate's American representative, Arnold Fordyce, had visited Dayton accompanied by Commandant Bonel, Chief of French Army Engineers, and proposed to the brothers that it would buy and present a Wright flyer to the French government not later than August 1. The brothers responded that they would ask a price of one million francs, or some $200,000, for the delivery of a flyer, including spare parts and training of pilots.

Wilbur thought that the syndicate's interest lay with the future commercial benefits that might accrue to them as a result of the transaction, an outcome of which he would not disapprove. The plan included the negotiation of a French production license. He felt in addition that a deal with the French especially would lead to widespread interest from other European powers. Wilbur informed Ellen of his views immediately.

A subsequent letter from Wilbur carried more disappointing news. He informed Ellen that despite their intensive negotiations, financial disagreements and numerous demands for specification changes had led the French to cancel the deal on April 5. He had learned one reason for the difficulties leading to the cancellation was that the French thought that the Wright machine could be duplicated by French experimenters, making such an import and licensing agreement unnecessary. Wilbur told Ellen he was dismayed at the setback, but he reiterated his determination to forge ahead.

The brothers were able to keep the $5,000 deposit held in escrow against the French contract, but that was little consolation to them at the time. At the conclusion of his letter, Wilbur stated he and Orville had mutually realized that, as anticipated, they would need to travel to Europe to negotiate sales and licensing agreements personally.

* * *

Ellen wrote Wilbur again in June.

Dear Will:
 I am intensely interested in your progress, and I am confident you will overcome lingering difficulties.
 I fervently hope you can devise some way to come to Pittsburgh this summer.
 Until then, you remain constantly in my thoughts.
 Love,
 Ellen

Despite her wishes, however, the pressures of the French syndicate negotiations, dealings with the Army, and attention to normal business precluded any extended travel by either Wilbur or Orville during that time. Ellen then offered to travel to Dayton on some pretext, but Wilbur discouraged the idea, believing that it would only lead to complications. He promised instead that he would travel to Pittsburgh later in the year. They continued to correspond often, with Wilbur instituting the practice of enclosing drafts of articles he was writing. She assisted whenever she could with his writing style, her skills complementing his mastery of the technical aspects of aviation and his detailed descriptions of their machine.

Ellen reported in her next letter to Wilbur that she was finding it difficult to resist telling her family about him. Her parents were happy with her progress as a journalist, but they still expressed to her occasionally their wishes that she would marry and become a homemaker.

During that summer, Ellen learned from Julia Albright that Walter Carrington had married. She felt no particular interest in or emotion at the news.

Ellen's stature as a reporter began to rise despite her having only two years' experience. She became increasingly active in general news coverage, as she had been largely able to move away from coverage of women's news. She participated in reporting from the local perspective the sensational crime in which the millionaire Harry Thaw of Pittsburgh shot the famed architect Stanford White at Madison Square Gardens in New York on June 25, over White's attentions to Thaw's young wife, Evelyn Nesbit. The story was headline news in Pittsburgh for months. The case pioneered the insanity defense and eventually ended in a mistrial the next year. She was also assigned to report on the impact of President Roosevelt's Pure Food & Drug and Meat Inspection Acts, both of which were passed on June 30, 1906. She acquired a strong interest in that landmark legislation, and she developed stories on how the average family would benefit. But general city news stories continued to constitute the majority of her assignments. Of some disappointment to Ellen was that no new stories pertaining to science and invention came to her attention, and none were assigned.

* * *

In a later letter to Ellen that summer, Wilbur affirmed his confidence in their future but emphasized that he was very busy with business matters. He continued to share detailed information on all flyer developments with her. Wilbur related that Octave Chanute had pressured them to fly again sometime that year, as much to quiet remaining skeptics as anything else.

He also explained that, while he and Orville were not unalterably opposed to further flying, they had decided against any testing or aerial exhibitions at the time, feeling that they should give priority to negotiating the several foreign license production agreements. In addition, they were intensively pursuing further patents and advanced engine development.

Wilbur later informed Ellen that he and Orville had met Glenn Curtiss for the first time when he visited Dayton in September, and they had readily shared information with him on their flyer, including photographs. Their policy toward other experimenters—which they had made progressively less restrictive with the granting of a patent—was that they were willing to share their knowledge and information for research purposes, so long as commercial use and profit-making activities were excluded. Curtiss continued to assure them that his emphasis was on engines.

In addition to what she learned from Wilbur, Ellen followed aeronautical developments from all news sources. She learned that Alberto Santos-Dumont had made a successful flight in a heavier-than-air flyer, of his design, on October 23. The feat was met with great acclaim in France and was also heavily publicized in America. In his next letter to Ellen, Wilbur told her that he had learned that Santos-Dumont's flight was only some two hundred feet in distance, comparable to their first efforts at Kitty Hawk, and that the craft had not demonstrated any maneuverability. He was not concerned that the flight posed any potential threat to their lead, but he was annoyed at Santos-Dumont's public claims to be the first to succeed with powered flight. He felt, however, that there was a benefit in that the publicity accorded Santos-Dumont served to increase public recognition of the Wright brothers as well.

Ellen learned subsequently that Santos-Dumont had made a longer straight-line flight in November, but that flight still did not appear to advance the field. A further favorable development for the Wright brothers was that Sherman Morse, a reporter for the *New York Herald*, had interviewed both brothers at their home and published a major article on their work in November. Ellen had seen the article as soon as Wilbur had.

Early in December, Wilbur and Orville, with Octave Chanute, traveled to New York to attend the annual Auto Show. Thereafter the brothers traveled to Coatesville, Pennsylvania, to confer with George Spratt, a young acquaintance of Chanute who had earlier observed their gliding experiments at Kitty Hawk. Spratt had medical training, and Chanute had recommended him to the brothers as a possible provider of medical treatment if they were injured in connection with their flights. They then continued to Washington on business matters. Before the trip, Wilbur had sent a brief letter to Ellen stating that his return from Washington might be his best opportunity for some time to see her. The brothers proceeded to attend to their business in Washington, and Orville returned to Dayton on December 13. Wilbur remained for two days for further consultations, then traveled to Pittsburgh and Ellen.

Ellen was working at her desk when Roy Graham informed her of a telephone call. There was only one telephone for reporters, and she answered with some apprehension due to the lack of privacy it offered.

Wilbur spoke. "Ellen, I have arrived. I hope we can meet soon. Are you free to talk now?"

Ellen was excited at the sound of Wilbur's voice, but she remained outwardly calm, mindful of the possibility of being overheard.

"Somewhat," she replied. "I will try to meet you. Where do you suggest?"

"I suggest the lobby of my hotel, the same as last time."

"I will try to be there within the hour."

Ellen explained to Roy that the call was from a possible news source with regard to a story who had requested that they meet outside the *Reporter* building—all true as far as it went. She requested his permission to speak with the individual. Graham agreed without asking for further details.

After working for a respectable period at her desk, Ellen donned her coat and left. As she saw Wilbur, her heart leaped, but they greeted each other with formal restraint in the busy hotel lobby. As before, their time together was brief and intense, since he could spend only a matter of hours in the city before returning to Dayton. They walked again along the Allegheny River, ignoring the chill. After Wilbur had detailed to her his activities in Washington, they began to speak of other matters.

"These past nine months without seeing you have been very frustrating for me," said Wilbur. "I know I tend to talk only of my problems, so tell me how your year has gone. Are you still happy with your position?"

"Yes. I have continued to make progress, and I enjoy the work most of the time. I have found Mr. Rutledge to be a man of integrity. He is certainly no crusader, nor am I, but he does not believe in or practice 'yellow journalism.' He is also committed to accuracy, so that makes my work environment more comfortable. There is always competition to discover attention-getting stories, of course, but we try to stick to the facts while pursuing the story. Another thing I am pleased about is that I have become better accepted by the older reporters. I think my articles about you and Orville and the fact that you are gaining further recognition have helped me in that. So, I am happy with my position, as far as it goes, but I would give it all up in an instant if you ask me to come to Dayton to be with you."

"As much as I want that also, I think it would be a mistake for both of us. I ask you again to wait until we overcome the hurdles we now face. We are involved in negotiating another agreement with the French, but if past experience is any guide, concluding it will be exceedingly difficult. Then there is still the Army matter before us. I am glad that the Army and French interests coincided, but it does increase our workload. Our major accomplishment is that we have the patent, and I think we can now deal more confidently with the Army."

"I realize all that, and I shall do as you think best, of course," she replied. "But I have a question for you, Will. Are you happy? With all the progress you have made this year, have you gained any satisfaction or sense of fulfillment about the way things are going?"

"When I think about the overall picture, I really can't say that I am happy. Even though we have received our patent, and as important as that was, it seems that obstacles keep appearing, making it more difficult for us to achieve what we have worked for. In some respects, I think Orville and I were both happier in our flying pursuits in the years leading up to the time when you came into my life, when we were on the threshold of our major achievement. I don't mean for that to sound like my present frustrations have anything to do with you, but there is that coincidence."

"I can understand what you are saying, but for my part, I believe that everything will turn around for you in the coming year. I know you will obtain an order from the Army and that foreign production will get underway. You cannot fail now, and you will gain the success you deserve. Then the future is ours."

"I hope you are right."

Ellen presented Wilbur with a small Christmas gift, a pocket watch, knowing that he could carry it inconspicuously. She was pleased that he had thought in the same manner and gave her a small gold locket. Once again she felt great sadness when they parted, but that emotion was partially offset by her optimism for the coming year.

In a letter to Ellen dated New Year's Eve, Wilbur described what he regarded as another major development: he and Orville had just received a new purchase option from the French syndicate, dated December 27. He regarded this as especially important considering that their first contract had been cancelled. They were prepared to reduce their price, and he was confident that a new order would give them a sound basis for a business of producing flyers. As a result, he also felt more optimistic than at any time over the past year. Ellen felt particularly pleased at this development, and at the upbeat tone of his letter, after he had seemed so downcast the last time they had been together. She told him of her happiness and encouragement at the brighter prospects.

Chapter Eleven

Travels in Europe, Delays in Pittsburgh

Pittsburgh, Paris, Dayton, 1907

Ellen had enjoyed the holiday season just past, but she thought constantly of Wilbur even while in the company of her family and friends. Only a few days of the new year had elapsed before she received a letter from him. While Ellen had expected a letter, she was still greatly pleased at its arrival. She opened it eagerly and began reading.

> Dear Ellen:
>
> I have some exciting news to report. Orville and I have just been contacted by a man named Charles R. Flint from New York. I have learned that he is well-known as an investor and promoter and has become interested in our work and its market potential. He does business as Charles R. Flint and Company, and possesses a wide circle of business and financial contacts. Chanute knows him as well. Already Flint has offered to pay a substantial fee for the right to represent us exclusively in all international—including French—market rights. He has invited us to New York to meet with him, and we will be seeking legal assistance on the matter while there. As I will be traveling with Orville, I cannot stop in Pittsburgh this time. I don't need to tell you how much I regret that, but it appears that this contact could lead to a highly

beneficial business relationship, and we certainly could use some help in foreign markets. I don't know yet if we will sign an agreement with Flint, but the prospects appear favorable.

You will be foremost in my thoughts while I am in New York, of course. I expect that the major sticking point in negotiations, as before, will be that of an actual flight demonstration for potential customers. I hope we can reach some kind of compromise. Flint already has suggested that we undertake a European trip sometime during the year, both to conduct flight demonstrations and to negotiate directly with governments and investors. I know that will be necessary at some point.

This matter has moved to the top of our priorities. I shall let you know our schedule when I have arranged it, and I just hope you see that this step is essential, even though it means a further delay in our being together.

Love,
Will

Ellen's reaction was as Wilbur had anticipated. She wrote a brief response to him, addressing it in care of Charlie Taylor as always, expressing her encouragement at the Flint development and wishing them a successful trip. She could not help feeling somewhat dejected at another delay in their plans, although she did not tell him so specifically.

Wilbur wrote Ellen again in March, after his return from New York, reporting that they had concluded a contract with Flint. He then informed her that he and Orville also had just completed a new licensing agreement with the French manufacturing syndicate, particularly important since the collapse of the earlier proposal. But his major news was that they would indeed be undertaking an extended trip to Europe to fulfill the French patent and licensing arrangements and to negotiate such agreements in other countries. He stressed that their difficulties both with the Army and the British had made the successful implementation of the French agreement an even stronger priority. Further arrangements and appointments in France and elsewhere were also needed. Wilbur told her that he would be departing first, with Orville joining him there later. He acknowledged that Ellen would be distressed at his extended absence, but he asked that she understand its priority.

From his letter, Ellen understood his priorities. She replied that she was indeed distressed, but she also assured him of her continuing and full support.

* * *

From a subsequent letter from Wilbur, Ellen learned that they had endeavored to building a completely new flyer, their fourth, for the European tour. The new machine was fitted with their improved engine of thirty-five horsepower and promised further improved flight performance. In recognition of the need for better takeoff and landing capability, they equipped the new flyer with wheels to replace the wooden skids. Thus, they would be free from the launch derrick and rail they had used at Huffman Prairie. The brothers made arrangements to ship all of the components to France in crates, where they would then reassemble the new flyer on location. Despite the many practical difficulties involved with the shipment, both recognized that if they were required to conduct flight demonstrations, their flyer had to be available then and there.

After completing arrangements in Dayton for the European trip, for which his expenses would be paid by Flint, Wilbur departed for New York on May 16. Since he was traveling alone, he stopped in Pittsburgh, but as before, his visit was necessarily brief. Ellen met him in the lobby of his hotel at the end of her workday, and they dined together at the hotel dining room as they had before. Despite their delight in each other's company, the mood of the conversation turned somber.

"You know I understand why you must make this trip," said Ellen, "but I shall still miss you and worry for your safety over there."

"You shouldn't worry on that account. All the arrangements

are made, and Orville will join me about a month after my arrival. We have a lot of work to do, and I feel certain we will be so busy that the time will pass quickly."

"I hope so. But as selfish as it may seem, I still deplore the length of time you will be away. I am afraid it will pass slowly for me."

"I understand your feelings, but we both realized it would have to be this way, at least until Orville and I can complete the legal agreements and get European production underway. I am so sorry this delays our plans."

As the evening concluded, Ellen was again almost tearful as she began to anticipate the impact of the long time they would be apart.

Wilbur attempted to console her. "I keep thinking of how difficult this will be for us both," he said, "but the scope of our endeavors has become so broad that it now appears that we will have to wait longer than either of us expected. Our major business frustration is that we are still behind schedule with respect to the Army and commercial orders. That is what makes success in Europe so critical for us. I just beg of you to be patient. It will come our way eventually."

"You know that I support you wholeheartedly," she replied. "I know I have to wait, and I will wait until you have completed your business in Europe. I am also reconciled to the fact that we cannot plan to marry this year, but next year should be ours."

"I agree. We may be behind schedule, but we will make it up and get to where we need to be. What we are doing now will determine ultimate success or failure for us."

Then, shifting his train of thought, he said, "You know, we have been together, at least in spirit, for almost two years, and I can't begin to describe the impact you have had on my life. In most respects, I feel I am the luckiest man in the world. I know our circumstances are unconventional, but I am more determined than ever to make a future for us—as we both want. If I am as successful on this trip as I expect, I plan to tell my family about you when I return."

A Romance of Flight

"I only know that while I feel frustrated now," she said, "I think we have stood the test of time with regard to love. I am convinced beyond any doubt that we should be together."

They parted that evening with a mutual feeling of closeness, even a spiritual bond, stronger than ever.

Ellen bid Wilbur a tearful goodbye at the Pennsylvania Railroad Union Station the next morning.

***

Ellen felt she was with Wilbur in spirit as he embarked for Europe on the RMS *Campania* on May 18. Always writing by hand when traveling, he composed and mailed a letter to her when he arrived at Liverpool. He described his experiences on the liner, including that he had kept largely to himself during the voyage, planning his activities and reading. He then traveled to London, where he was met by Flint's European associate Hart O. Berg, who was based in Paris and had traveled from there. Wilbur had been warned by Flint that Berg was skeptical of his and Orville's aeronautical experiments and had doubted their claims for powered flight. Nevertheless, Berg was there to assist Wilbur, and they traveled together to France, where they began to carry out an extensive itinerary, visiting several countries in connection with sales and licensing efforts. Ellen received another letter from Wilbur early in June, describing his experiences at the beginning of his European tour.

Dear Ellen:

Needless to state, I miss you constantly and hope the days will pass quickly here. I expected problems in conducting business in Europe, but fortunately, I have persuaded Hart Berg here of our flyer's capabilities and of the value of our work. I had been told he would be skeptical, but now he is very actively assisting me. He has experience in negotiating with the French and cautioned me of the difficulties, and he has also helped me with the problems of negotiating a British order.

He definitely can help in the organization of a European Wright Company, but the best news to me is that Berg now appreciates my abilities as a businessman, so he does not feel it necessary to conduct all the negotiations himself. I think now that I can handle negotiations alone in the future. I understand the principles of negotiation and have learned something of corporate organization, but it has been useful to have Berg with me. His advice has helped me avoid some mistakes, I'm certain.

I would never admit this to anyone else, but I fight a daily battle to concentrate on business tasks when all I want to do is think of you. Perhaps things will go faster once Orville arrives. Please know that I am well and making progress.

With love,
Will

* * *

Ellen knew that Orville would leave Dayton, which he did on July 13, and joined Wilbur in Paris on July 28. A later letter from Wilbur informed Ellen of difficulties they experienced in Paris. All components for their new flyer had been crated and shipped across the Atlantic to Paris, and the shipment arrived on schedule early in August. Slow mail and poor cable communications before Orville's arrival had not benefited their endeavors, however, and led to misunderstandings and strained relations between the brothers. Since Wilbur stayed behind to deal with the Army, he reported that Orville was having the better time traveling in Europe. He also became concerned that Wilbur was pursuing negotiations and making agreements without his specific approval. But after his arrival, Orville quickly understood the difficulties Wilbur had been facing and learned that he had not in fact negotiated anything unilaterally. Both brothers then inspected the flyer shipment and determined that the crates were undamaged and that all was in place. Ellen felt relieved that misunderstandings had been cleared up quickly.

Somewhat later, Ellen learned from Wilbur of the conversation between the brothers regarding their efforts. He reconstructed the exchange in a letter. "Will," said Orville, after they had completed their inspection, "I think I now understand better what you have faced here. My main concern was that you would lock us into something that I might not agree with. But it appears you have been using sound judgment all along."

Wilbur explained to her that he and Orville understood that they were always a team, even if they were geographically apart. He then reported that Orville understood immediately how things were in France and told him again how very glad he was to have him there.

They continued working together as closely as they had in Dayton. Charlie Taylor then joined the brothers in France early in August to help with the flying exhibitions.

Wilbur continued with detailed letters to Ellen, the single activity he concealed from Orville, keeping her fully informed of his activities, including the difficulties. Not all of his correspondence pertained to business, however, as Wilbur also described with enthusiasm his experience of the glories of Paris, having visited its museums and historical sites and having seen many architectural wonders. In a lighter vein, he reported buying a new suit of clothes, at Berg's insistence, to make himself more presentable for social occasions.

Wilbur had returned to London and then had traveled to Berlin in advance of Orville's arrival, initiating talks with the British and German governments. The Germans in particular were skeptical but expressed an interest in buying flyers if they were permitted to witness a demonstration. In Paris, Wilbur also found time to investigate the progress of Santos-Dumont and reconfirmed his earlier view that the Brazilian's work was no threat to their lead. Further, Santos-Dumont, although having successfully tested a flying machine, or aeroplane, had returned to concentrating on airship developments.

Of most significance, the brothers had conducted negotiations with the War Department for a flyer order up to the time of

Wilbur's departure but received their third rejection at the end of July, after both were in Europe. After learning of the rejection, Wilbur wrote Ellen that he had come to expect such setbacks in dealing with the Army but that he still remained optimistic for the longer term. He felt especially encouraged when he learned that the Army Signal Corps had established an Aviation Section on August 1, even if still primarily oriented toward balloons. One major negotiating obstacle, that Wilbur had acknowledged earlier, extended from their expectation that the Army should simply take their word on the capabilities of their flyer without an actual demonstration. But Wilbur found a point of optimism when he discovered through his contacts in France that Lieutenant Frank P. Lahm, son of an American businessman and Aero Club member living in Paris, had been posted to the Signal Corps and believed fully in the Wrights' flight claims. Thus, they could count on his support in dealing with the Signal Corps.

Ellen received another letter from Wilbur later in August.

Dear Ellen:

Things are progressing very slowly, but there are still positive signs. Some events have unfolded that have made me reconsider what we decided before coming here. I must concede that Orville and I might have been mistaken in not resuming flight tests earlier in the United States, as Chanute advised us to do. Flint also had made a suggestion that we make a flight over Jamestown, Virginia, on April 26, before I departed for Europe, as part of the ceremony commemorating the Three Hundredth Anniversary of the first permanent English settlement. The problem for us was that such a flight would have required floats for water takeoffs and landings. Orville and I had experimented with such a hydroaeroplane on the Great Miami River, but we could not get the flyer modified in time for the Jamestown event, so we abandoned the idea.

We continue to be highly active with the other business and legal aspects of our work, however, as well as improving our flyer. I followed reports of other aeronautical developments in particular, as we were aware that other aeronautical experimenters were reporting progress both in the United States and Europe. In that regard, I think the publicity we have enjoyed in France may help to spur Army interest in the flyer. My major concern is not loss of our lead to others but that we still lack actual sales of the flyer, either to military or civil buyers.

I hope Berg will help us achieve a breakthrough with the French, but don't be surprised if it is slow to develop. I am sorry to dwell so much on business, but I know that you would want to know those details.

I fervently hope I can return to you by October.

With love,

Will

* * *

In a subsequent letter, Wilbur informed Ellen of his problems as well as progress. French negotiations had been slow. Even with Berg's help, they dragged on through the summer, as many obstacles and territorial battles presented themselves. Wilbur became increasingly concerned that failure to establish a company in France would weaken them in discussions with the Germans; German military maneuvers had prevented any serious discussions with the government from progressing before September. The German government, aware that the French had not negotiated any purchase or licensing agreement, eventually declined to order any flyers as well.

Ellen continued to write to Wilbur in Europe, addressing him directly before Orville left, then in care of Charlie Taylor after his arrival. She tried always to be encouraging in her replies when she sensed that he felt discouraged or frustrated. Additionally, during the long months of Wilbur's absence, Ellen read everything she could find, from wire service reports to stories in large newspapers, about his fortunes in Europe. His activities, as well as Orville's after his arrival, were covered extensively by the press.

Despite her support of the trip, Ellen found herself feeling increasingly depressed at Wilbur's prolonged absence. The two years she had known him were easily the most significant of her life, but the time they had been together could be measured in days. The word *sacrifice* gained an even stronger meaning for her, as she felt that she—and not Wilbur—was making the major sacrifice. She knew that he could not abandon his current efforts and his vision for the aeroplane to be with her, and indeed should not, even though she would have given up everything else in her life to be with him. She continued to apply herself at work and participated in reporting several significant news events. She ensured that the activities of the Wright brothers received full coverage in the *Reporter*, including writing brief accounts on her own. She sought and received authorization to ensure that stories directly from other sources were printed.

Ellen had little personal life. Questions still came periodically from family and friends about her prospects of marrying and raising a family, which she was always careful to shrug off. She frequently responded that she primarily enjoyed being an aunt, since her brothers now had two children each. Julia and John Albright, expecting their first child soon, had occasionally offered to introduce her to suitable young men, but Ellen always declined. Ellen debated whether to confide in Julia about Wilbur, but she decided against the idea for the time, believing she should not do so before informing her family.

One day during the summer, Ellen's father called her at the *Reporter* and asked her to join him for a late lunch, an invitation he had not made before even though their offices were only a few blocks apart. She happily accepted. They met at a nearby restaurant.

"I had meant to do this long before now," he said as they were seated, "but I didn't want to appear to be too protective or intrusive. I always thought I should maintain some professional distance between us, but you are three years along in your career now, and I see no reason why we can't talk during the workday from time to time."

A Romance of Flight

Ellen acknowledged his opening statement but sensed that he wanted to discuss something of importance with her, especially since she knew he seldom went out to lunch. She decided to allow him to develop the conversation. He began by asking her how she was enjoying her job.

"I am getting along well," she said. "I have recently been given a larger office area in a better location. I think I am well supported by Mr. Rutledge and by Roy Graham, for which I remain grateful, and you know that I recently gained a raise in salary. Do you think it is time that I should move into an apartment and live on my own?"

"No, that is not an issue for your mother and me at all. It is just that we are always concerned for your happiness. I am glad that you are doing well as a reporter, and we are proud of you, but we also sense that you do not appear to be especially happy. If you are having a particular problem, we would like to help. Is there something we can do?"

"I know you would prefer that I marry and become a homemaker and mother. But I'm only twenty-five. There is plenty of time."

"We realize that also, but you appear to have no interest in meeting a suitable young man. What are you waiting for?"

Ellen was not surprised to learn that the real subject her father wanted to discuss concerned her plans in that direction, but she nevertheless began to feel defensive. She did not know how to respond to that line of questioning when she had pledged to Wilbur to conceal her feelings for the time.

"I am happy enough. You have no reason to worry about me. Perhaps I will have more to say on that subject in a few months."

She almost smiled at her own remark but tried not to allow any facial expression to betray her feelings. At the conclusion of the meal, she thought that her father was reassured, although sensing that he still felt puzzled to some degree. As they parted, Ellen felt slightly guilty at not disclosing the most important matter in her life, but that—she thought—would change soon.

As she walked back to her office, Ellen reflected briefly on what her life would be like if she had not experienced the accidental, certainly unintentional, act of falling in love with Wilbur Wright. Unquestionably her life would be much less complicated if she had formed an attachment with a local young man with an established occupation rather than someone who was developing a world-changing invention. She soon brought herself back to reality, knowing that however complicated matters might appear, she would not have altered events as they had unfolded if she could.

Conditions continued to improve for her professionally. With her larger office space came a rolltop desk and a new typewriter. Ellen felt the regard of Theodore Rutledge and Roy Graham reflected in the fact that they had hired another young female reporter recently and that she had been asked to assist in her training. Most of the older male reporters who had been scornful or hostile toward her initially now were more congenial, and she knew she had won at least their professional respect. There was in general a fairly high job mobility in the newspaper profession, as reporters frequently changed employers, and that had affected the *Reporter* as well. As a result, Ellen had advanced rapidly in seniority. Rutledge had even mentioned the possibility of allowing her to write under her own byline soon, and she knew that experienced female reporters with other Pittsburgh papers had been permitted the privilege.

Ellen felt strong civic pride in the fact that Allegheny County was experiencing such strong growth, with a population approaching one million. After a long struggle, the adjoining city of Allegheny finally merged into Pittsburgh, bringing the city's population almost to 700,000, making it the sixth largest in the country. Ellen always enjoyed walking by the city's tallest skyscraper, the Frick Building, of twenty-one stories. She aspired to make it to the top floor someday. Automobiles were rapidly becoming more commonplace, and the city had overcome the damage of a major flood. Another area of progress was that the water system was in the process of becoming filtered, and Ellen wrote a story on that coming development and the benefits it would bring. She felt all the signs of technical development would help the *Reporter* as well as enhance her career prospects. But she remembered that her future was not in her home city.

While she remained busy with other assignments, her personal priority was to write further stories on aeronautics and on the Wright brothers, including continuing coverage of their activities in Europe. Her work supplemented and coincided with the broad press coverage and growing recognition of the brothers. Her correspondence with Wilbur, while not known by others at the *Reporter,* helped her to report more authoritatively. With her rising stature in the profession, at least locally, Ellen had begun to receive more challenging assignments, including stories on science and industry.

Ellen found one story, even though not her direct responsibility, particularly challenging. She had followed developments in the stock market crash of March 14, spurred by the collapse of several major banks, and attempted to understand the implications. Then in October, a further financial panic, stemming from the stock speculations of a bank owner that resulted in a run on several banks, led to new bank failures and had threatened the broader banking system and the entire economy. The stock market fell precipitously. She had not participated in reporting on the earlier crisis, but she then became involved by assisting the *Reporter's* financial editor in writing on the new developments. She gained in the process a better understanding of complex market forces, including learning how the financier J. P. Morgan, acting in concert with other wealthy and powerful individuals, had stabilized the banking system and prevented further panic. She also gained some understanding of how the national banking system worked and the impact of bank runs. She had even observed runs on banks in Pittsburgh, as the panic had spread rapidly across the country.

Ellen was particularly impressed by the accounts of how one hundred and twenty-five bankers and other influential men had been locked in the Morgan Library in New York until they could agree on financing arrangements to restore public confidence in troubled banks and brokerage houses. She also recognized, however, that strong action through such a cabal of wealthy individuals ran sharply counter to President Roosevelt's trustbusting policies and his suspicions of "malefactors of great wealth." In the aftermath, Morgan was credited by many with saving the country, but he was accused in other quarters of acting against the public interest to enrich himself and his associates by purchasing threatened assets at distress prices. Regardless of the disparity of views, the panic disappeared almost overnight, and the economy stabilized. Although she had learned much, Ellen decided that business and financial reporting would best be left to others.

In quieter moments, Ellen reflected on and appreciated the close bonds she possessed with her family in addition to her professional progress. She remained confident in the love of Wilbur, but despite what she had told her father, she indeed did not feel happy. The dominant fact of her life continued to be Wilbur's absence. With her increased salary, she could have indeed afforded to take an apartment on her own, but she felt it best to continue living at home for the time. She also resolved to always affect a cheerful demeanor while at home with her parents, feeling that would lessen their worries. She lived with the hope that in the coming months her situation would change permanently.

* * *

In mid-November, Ellen received the letter that she had longed for: Wilbur's announcement that he was coming home.

"I am scheduled to arrive in New York on November 22," it began.

"As usual, I will have to exercise some discretion in my schedule with respect to you, even though I will not be traveling with Orville. I will need to go to Washington first to deal with the Army, but I will come to Pittsburgh as soon as I can free myself to do so.

"We accomplished as much as we reasonably could in Europe, but overall I would have to regard the experience as frustrating. We still have much to do there, but for now I am simply happy to be returning home and seeing you."

Wilbur proceeded according to his schedule but could not leave Washington until December 4. He then traveled directly to Pittsburgh, where Ellen had an emotional reunion with him at the Pennsylvania Railroad Union Station. She thought he looked well, attired in a new suit he had bought in Paris. Their joy in being reunited momentarily superseded all the difficulties he had experienced in Europe. They began walking near the river, despite the near-freezing weather.

"Tell me more of your experiences in Europe," she began. "I know we have so much to talk about, but that is what I want to hear first."

He started to summarize his activities before leaving France, but then he interrupted himself to ask Ellen how she had gotten along over the past months.

"I have continued to work on several stories, and I would say I'm doing very well with the *Reporter*. I even became involved with covering the financial panic about two months ago. I'm sure there was extensive coverage in Europe. But I still want to hear more about your trip."

Wilbur seemed almost reluctant to discuss business but began to do so at her insistence.

"As I have told you, we definitely made progress overall. I think our business prospects have improved, but I would still have to regard the six months I spent in Europe—and the almost five months Orville spent—as largely a waste. Flint means well, I'm certain, and Hart Berg was a great help, but it appears that his efforts were a failure as well. Our agreement with the French broke down again, this time largely over our demand for a long period of exclusivity in marketing rights. And there were disputes among potential investors within the syndicate. We also failed to conclude any deals with either the British or the Germans, as you know. The Germans were interested but would not sign a contract without an actual flight demonstration. We considered forming a German subsidiary company, but that did not go through either. I think the Germans reconsidered their priority after learning the French had not signed with us. I was and still am particularly concerned about control of foreign ventures anyway. I think what Orv and I must do now is remain in Dayton and build several flyers in order to have them available for purchasers."

"Did you conduct any flying demonstrations?" asked Ellen. "I gained the impression from your letters that you had not."

"We didn't. As you know, we had our new flyer shipped to Europe specifically for demonstrations, and we equipped it with several improvements to make it more marketable. But we never flew it or even had it uncrated and assembled. Orville and I jointly decided not to fly without a firm contract somewhere. So, we left the flyer in storage for future use.

"The major point in our favor is that our work still is far in advance of what Santos-Dumont and any of the French, including Henri Farman, have done. We simply didn't accomplish what we had hoped this year in the business sense, but we are still well-positioned to succeed in the next few months. This is the major point that affects our future, and if things develop as I hope, I will feel in a position to speak to your father. I promise you I will do whatever is necessary. Also, I have become more encouraged recently about the Army. I believe that we are making real progress toward an order at last. I spoke with some Army officials in New York when I returned, and I sensed some renewed interest in Washington as well. One thing Orville and I have decided is to resume flight testing next year. We never intended to suspend flying for two years, of course, but that is the way things have worked out. We need to be ready to demonstrate our flyer to the Army, among other things."

"I also believe that you will succeed with the Army, and soon," said Ellen, "and I know new flight tests will help. I have learned that while many people are now aware of powered flight, they still tend to regard it as a novelty, and of course there are still the skeptics who will have to see it with their own eyes before they believe it. The Army order will finally convince the skeptics of your accomplishment."

"That is the way we see it," replied Wilbur. Then, changing the subject, he said, "Ellen, I appreciate your concerns for our business success, but I would still rather talk about us. Please join me for dinner. I hope you will have the time."

"I will, but I should return to my office. I've probably taken more time away from work than I should have."

They parted, to meet again in the early evening. They dined at Wilbur's hotel, and Ellen told him more of her recent activities.

"I want you to know that I had another opportunity to report on the aeronautical field. I participated in coverage of the great balloon race from St. Louis to Asbury Park, New Jersey, for the James Gordon Bennett Cup. The race was completed on October 24, but you probably know something about it already. I will try to write more about your European tour for my newspaper as well."

"Yes, I was aware of the big race, and it was interesting, but I strongly believe that our work with heavier-than-air crafts will make balloons and airships obsolete. I am glad that you are continuing to report on aviation developments, though."

"Incidentally, the balloon race was the first story which I was allowed to publish under my own byline, and that was an important step for me. I do feel that I am becoming successful in my profession, but I will resign my job and travel with you and do whatever I can to help. All you have to do is ask me."

"I still would have to veto that idea," he replied firmly. "As much as I want you with me, it would severely complicate matters, especially at this crucial time. Orville would be certain to be opposed, and this is a time when we strongly need to work together. I will say again that I am optimistic that we will succeed next year. Once we are over the Army and European hurdles, I know we can marry, regardless of any opposition from my family."

Wilbur departed the next morning, December 6, arriving in Dayton that afternoon.

* * *

Little more than a week after Wilbur's departure, a telegram came from Dayton informing the Hobson family of the death of Elizabeth Keys. Ellen was particularly saddened at the news, having grown to regard her great aunt as having been a particularly significant part of her life as a result of her trips to Dayton, but she also realized that she would be traveling there to attend the funeral. It was agreed within the family that neither of her brothers should take time from their jobs to attend, and Ellen made the journey with her parents and her increasingly infirm grandmother Ryan. She respected that her grandmother, while grieving, accepted the loss as inevitable. Ellen functioned as a guide for her family, having made the trip twice before, but upon arriving at the Keys house, she in turn had to be introduced to her mother's cousins and their families. She had decided not to contact Wilbur beforehand but instead called him at the shop after her arrival when she had a quiet moment. Ellen was relieved that he, rather than Orville, answered the telephone, and she quickly suggested that they meet after the funeral. Wilbur agreed and added that he had read of her great aunt's death. He said that he and Orville planned to pay their respects by attending the funeral and burial service if she was agreeable, which of course she was.

The funeral was held at the First Presbyterian Church in the central city. The sanctuary was far from full, and at the conclusion of the service, Ellen saw Wilbur and Orville departing from a rear pew, but she decided not to speak to them at that time. The burial service was in the same Woodland Cemetery overlooking the city where, Ellen knew, Wilbur and Orville's mother Susan Wright was buried. There Elizabeth Keys was interred next to her husband. After the brief graveside service, Ellen greeted both Wilbur and Orville and brought them to her family for formal introductions.

"I would like you to meet my mother and father, and my

grandmother, Mrs. Ryan," Ellen said to both. Turning to her family, she said, "You already know that Wilbur and Orville Wright are the brothers who invented the flying machine I reported on two years ago and have followed developments on since then. They have recently returned from a trip to Europe where they negotiated sales of their machine to foreign governments."

Wilbur returned the greeting first. "I am pleased to meet you all," he said. "I regret only that it is on such a sad occasion. Please accept our condolences on your loss." He looked directly at Ellen's grandmother as he spoke.

"We felt that we should pay our respects also," added Orville, "in part due to our gratitude for your granddaughter's help to us."

Grandmother Ryan acknowledged their sentiments graciously.

Ellen's father began exchanging pleasantries with both, asking questions about their current business plans and future development of the flying machine. Ellen was careful to give equal attention to Orville, hoping she had succeeded in hiding from her parents anything of her feelings for Wilbur, although she wondered if they suspected. She also became concerned that Orville, while outwardly pleasant, appeared suspicious anytime she spoke directly to Wilbur.

Ellen had decided already to make a request to both. "Since I am here," she said, "I would like to visit your mother's grave, if you are agreeable. I know it must be nearby."

"It is," said Wilbur. "It is just a short walk. We can be there in a minute." Orville nodded his agreement as well.

Ellen expressed appreciation to them for the gesture, then informed her parents and grandmother that she would join them later. She walked with Orville and Wilbur the short distance up the hill to the site, marked only by a simple gravestone. She found herself genuinely moved by the experience, and she lingered reverently at the site.

The three walked down the hill and soon caught up to the funeral party at the cemetery entrance. As they approached, Wilbur, walking slightly behind Orville, surreptitiously pressed a note into Ellen's hand, which she quickly placed in her purse without reading. Both brothers then bid goodbye to her family and left on their own. Ellen returned to the Keys home with her family and other relatives. When she was alone, she read the note, in which Wilbur outlined plans for them to meet later that afternoon at a city park near the Great Miami River.

Ellen, of course, stole away for the meeting, using the pretense that she wanted to walk along the river once again as she had during her earlier visits to Dayton. Wilbur was waiting for her near the Third Street Bridge.

"I feel like a foolish schoolboy, having to meet furtively like this," he said in greeting, "and I am forty."

Ellen could relate to his anguish over the situation. She had worried herself about meeting him in a more public place, since Wilbur was now well-known in Dayton.

"You know," he continued, "I had what I could have called a friendship with a young lady, or a girlfriend, when I was in my early twenties, but since then I had given up all thoughts in that direction. Over time, I suppose that is one reason why my family came to believe that Orville and I should remain unmarried. On one level, it seems ridiculous that I should feel so constrained by family and business obligations, with my being both mature and having no legal encumbrances. I feel I have as much right to seek happiness as any man."

"You do, and I feel the same about myself," replied Ellen. "I accept that your work is most important, and you know that all I want is to help you. Really, all you have to worry about is your family's reaction, and I think you can win them over. I can't believe that they would be as rigidly opposed to our marriage as you think. I know they have specifically defined roles for you and Orville in life, but they can change, as you have. My parents may be somewhat shocked as well, but I know I can overcome that."

"My family is not my enemy," said Wilbur. "I feel great loyalty to all my family, of course, as well as a sense of duty to them. It is just that our situation is something that has never been anticipated by any of us." He uttered a small laugh at the thought.

"I still would find it hard to believe that they would deny you a chance for happiness. After all, your older brothers married and had families."

"I promise I will work it out, but it will take more time. I say again that Orv and I must first complete these things we have been working for, otherwise there will never be a bright future for us. If we should fail now, some in my family might blame you. I can't permit that."

"So, you will not tell them about us yet?"

"I'm afraid not. Let us work through our European and Army negotiations first. I know this means further delay, but I believe it is best for our future if we remain quiet for now."

"Then I will not tell my family either," said Ellen. "I will wait until you think it is the right time."

Ellen extracted a promise from Wilbur that he would not wait long before coming to Pittsburgh again. They then parted with mutual expressions of hope for the coming year. She walked quickly back to the house, fearing that her family would question a prolonged absence.

The family returned to Pittsburgh the next morning, and Ellen felt a strong sense of closeness with them, having made the trip together. Ellen resumed her normal work routine the next day. Soon, however, she was assigned to help cover the great mine explosion in Jacobs Creek, Pennsylvania, on December 19, in which 239 were killed.

Wilbur wrote a brief letter to Ellen at the end of the year, describing the Wright family Christmas dinner at his brother Lorin's home and expressing his wish for her enjoyment of the holidays.

Chapter Twelve

Kitty Hawk, Success, Family

Pittsburgh, Dayton, Washington, Kitty Hawk, 1908

After the isolation and frustration she had been feeling over the past several months, Ellen regarded the new year as holding great promise for her, both professionally and personally. But she reminded herself that she had welcomed the last two years with optimism also, only to have her plans postponed. She still strongly believed the delays that she and Wilbur had encountered during that time would be overcome at last. Of primary importance, she was confident that the business frustrations of the brothers would end, and that confidence enabled her to approach her job each day with renewed enthusiasm.

Ellen was privately concerned that Wilbur and Orville had not conducted any flight tests for more than two years

They still led in the aeronautical field, however, as no other American experimenters had yet succeeded with powered and controlled flight. The brothers had not rested on their accomplishment and continued to make improvements to their flyer. Their new thirty-five horsepower engine promised higher performance and greater reliability than before. With the resumption of testing, they expected to make long-distance flights, and with a high degree of safety.

But while they were recognized as the leaders in powered

flight, at least in America, others were becoming active. It was publicly known that Glenn Curtiss was developing a flyer under the auspices of the Aerial Experiment Association, known as the AEA, at his shop in western New York. The AEA had been founded on October 1, 1907, under the sponsorship of Alexander Graham Bell, who experimented in aeronautics among other endeavors, and several prominent men of science were associated. Its primary purpose was to provide financial support for Curtiss's designs and experiments, and the associates increasingly publicized their activities, in contrast to the relative secrecy of the Wright brothers.

Periodic reports reached the brothers that others less well known and not as advanced were at work also, including a Dr. W. W. Christmas in Virginia who was pursuing development of a powered flyer of his own design. In Santa Ana, California, unknown to Wilbur and Orville at the time, and unknown to Ellen, for that matter, a young man named Glenn Martin, only twenty-two years old, had been inspired by their work and had begun experimenting with flight. He was undertaking the construction of a flyer of his design and planned to test it himself. European activity was also gaining momentum. In France, Henri Farman and the Voisin brothers in particular supplemented the efforts of Santos-Dumont, who had returned to the development of dirigibles. By 1908, France appeared to have embraced aviation more enthusiastically than any other country, and some French experimenters did not accept the superiority of the Wright flyer over their machines.

Wilbur, in his first letter of the year to Ellen, expressed, among other matters, that he thought the French leadership claims were ironic in that their interest had originated with Chanute during his trip there in 1903, during which he had first described the Wright glider experiments. In Wilbur's view, the claimed French superiority was based on his and Orville's early research rather than attained through independent effort. He continued to emphasize to her that while neither he nor Orville held any fear of competitors, they remained adamant that any new flying machines must be based on original work. Ellen knew already that the brothers were quite prepared to take legal action against any experimenters who made use of the Wright patent without credit and compensation to them.

One event that angered both, as Ellen soon learned, was the publication of an article in the February edition of *McClure's Magazine*, in which a reporter who had never interviewed either brother wrote a story representing as if he had done so, expressing it in the first person. Once again their old distrust of the press was brought to the forefront of their considerations.

* * *

On the military front, the success that the brothers wished for—and that Ellen had fervently wished for them—appeared to be at hand. The quickening of interest in the flying machine by the War Department that Wilbur had sensed was confirmed. The Signal Corps had, on December 23, 1907, issued a formal specification for a heavier-than-air machine for its new Aviation Section, accompanied by invitations to bid. The heavier-than-air craft would supplement the Army's employment of balloons for observation. The goal that Orville had described to Ellen at their first meeting was to be fulfilled. The Signal Corps specification attracted wide interest and many bids, but that of the Wright brothers was easily the most credible. Further, they had sharply reduced their bid price from their previous proposals. They won the competition and received the order on February 10, 1908, for a flyer at a basic price of $25,000, which included the training of three Signal Corps pilots. The contract also provided for bonuses to be paid for exceeding the specified speed performance of forty miles per hour.

For Wilbur and Orville, the Army order was the culmination of more than three years of effort and represented the triumph of their perseverance as well as of the flyer's technical merits. Equally important for their future, a renegotiated contract with the French business syndicate for formation of a Wright company in France finally was completed and signed on March 3. The contract again was contingent upon a satisfactory flight demonstration, to which the brothers finally agreed. Wilbur immediately conveyed his views on all these developments to Ellen. Responding in a letter through Charlie Taylor, she expressed her great pride in and enthusiasm for their success.

* * *

Wilbur traveled alone to New York on March 15, remaining until March 20 to deal with business matters. He again delayed his return to Dayton to visit Ellen in Pittsburgh, although only for a few hours. She met him at the Pennsylvania Railroad Union Station as before, and he embraced her with great enthusiasm. She sensed immediately that he was more optimistic than she had ever remembered. Wilbur stored his luggage, and they walked along the Allegheny River as they talked.

"Ellen, we are now on the point of achieving everything we have worked for over the past five years. You know the problems we had with the military order, but we finally won the attention of the War Department, as I was confident we would all along. We're now ready to start building the flyer for the Signal Corps and to resume our own testing. We need to get more flying experience not only to train Army pilots but also to carry out demonstrations during the European tour. On that point, I must tell you that we have decided to return to Kitty Hawk, and the flying weather should improve for us to start there next month. At last everything seems to be going the way we want."

"That sounds wonderful. When do you plan to leave?"

"I will likely leave Dayton on April 6, which means I should arrive there on the eighth. I'll work to get the camp in order, then Orville will see to shipping the flyer before he comes. This is our third flyer, incidentally, the same one you saw at Huffman Prairie. We have already brought it up to current standards, with upright seating and control levers, and we have also installed our new engine and made other improvements. We will reassemble the flyer at the camp as we did before, and I hope to secure help from men at the Life-Saving Station again."

"Will the flyer have wheels as well?" she asked.

"No," he replied. "We thought we would not need to change from skids since we will still be operating on soft sand."

"Do you think I could visit you at Kitty Hawk? I would love to watch you fly again. And I don't think it is of any use to try to hide our feelings from Orville any longer."

"I shall deal with Orville, and soon. I want you to visit, of course, but I remind you that the location is very remote. You will have to stay in the town of Kitty Hawk, which is, as you know, about four miles' distance from the Kill Devil Hills."

"I will ask Mr. Rutledge for the assignment and for support for the trip. I can certainly justify the assignment as a legitimate story, especially in light of your order from the Army."

"The other point, as I'm sure you realize, is that I will need to go to France again to fulfill our contract there. I will have to conduct the flying demonstrations and then help organize production. I may be away for several months."

"I did expect that," she replied, "and I shall miss you intensely, but I suppose what keeps me going is knowing that once it is completed, you will be more settled."

"That is my expectation as well. When I return I shall speak to my family. Then I believe we can make firm plans."

They devoted their remaining time together to discussing their plans. As the time drew near for him to return to the railroad terminal, Wilbur said, "I will say again that I want to marry you, and as soon as I can, after we complete our business in Europe and with the Army. I will stay in Europe only as long as it takes to finish essential business."

"I know. I will follow your progress every day that I can, and if I can help you from here, I will."

"My train is due to leave in less than an hour, so we must start back now. Unfortunately, I won't arrive home until late in the evening."

A Romance of Flight

"Perhaps you can nap on the train, then," Ellen offered.

She waited with Wilbur until the train was called. They embraced and bid each other goodbye, but this time without the degree of sorrow they had felt before, knowing they would see each other again soon at Kitty Hawk.

* * *

With frequent communication, Ellen knew Wilbur's Kitty Hawk schedule. He wrote her that he immediately found conditions at their Kill Devil Hills camp to be in disarray. Their old campsite had been almost obliterated by stormy weather and shifting sands, and he worked intensively to bring it up to usable condition. Wilbur stayed temporarily at the Life-Saving Station while he hired a crew of local workers, and with their help he constructed a more elaborate camp with larger buildings. He then notified Orville, who arrived at Kitty Hawk with the crated flyer on the twenty-fifth of the month.

Before Wilbur had left for Kitty Hawk and his preparations there, the brothers had begun construction of the Army machine at their shop in Dayton, relying on Charlie Taylor as well as additional workers for the task. That project proceeded smoothly, but all did not go well with the reassembly of the flyer at Kitty Hawk. The brothers encountered several delays, some due to the modifications required to carry a passenger, and were unable to resume flying until May 6. After testing was underway, however, the flyer showed improved capabilities from the start. Wilbur suffered a crackup in an early landing but was not seriously injured, and after repairs, testing continued smoothly. The brothers made ten flights on May 8, following with more on succeeding days. Wilbur carried as his first passenger Charles Furnas, a young mechanic who had accompanied him from Dayton, on May 14, although in that accomplishment the brothers later learned that they trailed Henri Farman in France, who carried the first aerial passenger in his Voisin flyer on March 21. Furnas also flew with Orville later.

Wilbur faced a challenge in finding time to write Ellen and

keep her updated, and to post the letter without Orville observing, but managed to do so.

One event that Wilbur conveyed to Ellen was that, soon after they had resumed flying, reporters from several cities learned of the new experiments and converged on Kitty Hawk. But many of the resulting published stories still contained errors and exaggerations, serving only to increase the brothers' annoyance with the press. By that time, however, they had generally accepted the reality of reporters and press coverage. Possibly of greater importance was that the press finally regarded the Wright brothers as newsworthy; there was a general public awareness of their work and of the reality of powered flight. Photos of the Wright flyer in the air were published that summer in *Collier's Magazine*, effectively ending any remaining attempts at restrictions on details of their design. Publisher Robert Collier was an enthusiast about aeronautics and subsequently became a friend and supporter of the brothers. Octave Chanute also wrote a brief article for the *Independent* describing the Wrights' achievements in the new tests, which was published in June. Additionally, reports of the new Kitty Hawk tests were published in *Scientific American* in the summer issue. With greater awareness of their successes, Orville and Wilbur found themselves becoming considerable celebrities. They had never sought such a status, of course, and both found themselves feeling somewhat uncomfortable at the attention they attracted. While not present, Ellen could appreciate their celebrity status through public reports.

* * *

Ellen became increasingly eager to be there in person, and Theodore Rutledge approved her request to report on the Wright brothers' new flight tests. He authorized travel expenses to North Carolina. Alerted by Wilbur that flight testing would be delayed due to the camp reconstruction and flyer reassembly, she did not depart for Kitty Hawk until May 6. The train journey, requiring her to change trains in Washington, was of course new territory for her. Ellen had no time to tour the city, but she could see several landmarks and the Washington Monument from a distance. She traveled from there through Virginia to Elizabeth City, where she found accommodations for the night. Following Wilbur's instructions, she traveled the next day by motorboat across Albemarle Sound to the village of Nags Head, south of Kitty Hawk. He had warned her that the boat trip would take five hours, but she found herself less than fully prepared for such a duration, and she was greatly relieved when the boat finally docked at the Nags Head landing.

She saw Wilbur waiting at the dock as he had promised. He helped her out of the boat, and they greeted each other formally, but with handshakes. Both realized that since he was now well known, he was likely to be recognized by passersby and possibly reporters, and neither wanted to deal with any publicity resulting from being observed in an embrace.

As they rode into Kitty Hawk, Ellen said, "I know you will have little time for me, but I will be content just to be in your presence again for a few days. It will be reward enough for me to observe your flight tests as I did at Huffman Prairie."

"I appreciate that. Both Orv and I are a little nervous about these tests, since they are the first flights either of us had flown in almost three years. It always seems that whatever we are doing is critical to our futures, and that certainly is true this time."

Ellen took a room in a boarding house that Wilbur had arranged for her in the village, while he returned to the camp. After resting and recuperating from the stress of her boat trip, Ellen walked about Kitty Hawk to gain a feel for the environment and the people. While she could not regard the village as charming, she appreciated that the rugged construction of houses and other structures was necessary to withstand the frequently stormy weather. She became especially interested in the Outer Banks dialect of the citizens, which sounded almost Elizabethan to her. She learned later that the brogue had developed most likely due to the area's isolation. Ellen found that she also enjoyed the ocean breezes and the smell of sea air—a new experience, as it was the first time she had been to the seashore.

The next morning, Ellen paid a villager for a wagon ride to Kill Devil Hills. She sought out Orville upon her arrival at the campsite, making certain to congratulate him on his and Wilbur's mounting record of success. He acknowledged her comments evenly. She exchanged further pleasantries when he was not immediately occupied and also conversed with reporters from other newspapers from time to time. She selected a spot to quietly observe flights and to make notes.

The flight tests she observed during her visit all proceeded smoothly. Ellen had almost no private time with Wilbur, and she returned alone to Kitty Hawk at the end of each day. He had told her that he could not see her in the evenings, as he felt he should remain with Orville and their crew. She had expected that, however, and remained content just to observe flight tests during the day and be at Kill Devil Hills. Ellen planned to stay only three days to observe and informed Wilbur of her schedule. She emphasized that she felt confident they were well on their way to accomplishing what they had intended. On the day of her departure, Wilbur accompanied her to Nags Head and the motorboat dock.

"I keep telling you how I regret the time we must be apart," he said, "but I know you understand."

"And you know that I support you in this and all that you do," she replied.

"I'm afraid that the entire tour will take six months and implementing the French contract is only a part of that; I must also convince the Europeans that our flyer is more advanced than anything developed there. Orville will remain in Dayton to complete the Army flyer and to train pilots, so it will be easy for you to write me in Europe. We will certainly keep in close touch."

They talked further at the dock before it was time for Ellen to board. Ellen dreaded the long and uncomfortable boat trip ahead of her, but she did not say so to Wilbur.

"When I leave here, I will have to return directly to Dayton," said Wilbur, "since I need to help with the Army machine and to complete my preparations for Europe. I must tell you that another problem we are now facing is that we are under serious financial pressure. Our expenses with the flyer have been mounting over the years, with no return, and we don't earn that much with our bicycle business. That alone makes this European trip all the more critical. Unfortunately, I will not be able to stop in Pittsburgh on my way to New York this time, so this will have to be my goodbye for Europe as well. But the good news is that if we accomplish all that I expect, and the flyer is produced both in Europe and for the Army, I should have made enough money and be well enough established in business that I can proceed with marrying you regardless of any family opposition."

He had never sounded so definite to Ellen before, and despite her sadness at his extended absence, she was ecstatic. She kissed him, disregarding any possible stares from onlookers, then quickly boarded the motorboat. As the boat departed, she looked back at Wilbur, waving goodbye as long as he was in sight. The realization that it would be many months before they were together again weighing heavily on her.

* * *

Through her continuing correspondence with Wilbur, Ellen could keep close track of the brothers' reactions to other aeronautical developments and experimenters. Even as they concentrated on their flying, they received confirmation, sometime after the fact, that Dr. Christmas had become the second man to fly a powered flying machine in the United States, on March 8, actually beating Curtiss and the AEA. The AEA then accomplished its first successful powered flight on March 12, with Curtiss's Red Wing design, on the ice of Lake Keuka in upstate New York. The Curtiss machine was piloted by Casey Baldwin, a member of the AEA. Lorin Wright had traveled to Lake Keuka on behalf of his brothers to secretly observe the tests for evidence of patent infringement. Upon learning details of that flight from Lorin, Orville and Wilbur concluded that Curtiss had made use of information they had supplied earlier to Lieutenant Thomas Selfridge, a young Army officer detached to the AEA. Selfridge had made inquiries to them about certain technical details, which they had cheerfully supplied on the understanding that the work of the AEA was purely scientific and not commercial. Later, the publicity surrounding the AEA tests raised further concerns with the brothers about possible infringement of their patent, but they decided not to take action at the time. In a letter to Ellen from Kitty Hawk, Wilbur mentioned that he had become concerned over patent infringement as soon as he learned of the first flights of Curtiss's machine.

As they continued to follow developments, which Wilbur reported in detail to Ellen, they learned that the Red Wing was destroyed in a crash on March 17, but with no injuries, and that the next Curtiss design, the White Wing, had flown for the first time on May 18. When the brothers saw a magazine advertisement by the AEA offering the White Wing for sale, they were alarmed in that it further indicated patent infringement by Curtiss, but again they took no action. The advertisement later was found to be fictitious, but that discovery did little to allay their suspicions that infringement had occurred. Curtiss next built a new and improved design named the June Bug, which he flew himself on June 21. Then the major event for the AEA came on July 4, when Curtiss demonstrated the June Bug. Coming on Independence Day, in the presence of government observers, it became the first officially witnessed flight in the United States. Curtiss had emerged as a potentially powerful competitor.

* * *

Wilbur remained at Kitty Hawk until the end of May. He and Orville were fully satisfied with the capabilities of the modified flyer, highlighted by their first passenger-carrying flights. One matter that had disturbed Ellen privately was that the brothers again left their flyer at Kitty Hawk, although taking the engine. She knew they cared little for preserving their work, being more oriented toward future developments, but she worried that the flyer would be left to the mercy of vandals and the elements.

Ellen knew that Orville had remained in Dayton for most of April to supervise construction of the military flyer, and that he returned there in advance of Wilbur to oversee its completion. Reinforced by the success of their new tests at Kill Devil Hills, the brothers delivered the Army flyer on August 20, ahead of schedule. The event was accompanied by extensive publicity and further exemplified the accelerating progress and public acceptance of the reality of aviation. The Army flyer incorporated all the improvements of their experimental models, including the thirty-five horsepower engine and upgraded controls, with the pilot sitting upright and operating all controls by levers. It was also fitted with a wheeled undercarriage rather than the wooden skids with which Wilbur and Orville had flown up to that point. The brothers still had not formed a company for the business of building flying machines, but they had increased hiring of new employees as their activities increased.

* * *

Ellen wrote stories about the success of the new Kill Devil Hills tests and also reported on Wilbur's plans for his European tour. She followed with a report on the delivery of the Army flyer. Finally being permitted to report under her own byline, she took satisfaction in being able to reveal that she had been the journalist who had first reported on the Wright brothers' experiments in Dayton. She did not hear any negative reaction to that disclosure and was gratified in the reputation she had earned in the field. Compliments on the quality of her reportage became routine. She also took satisfaction in that she was one of the youngest women reporters to have gained her own byline, a fact she had learned through membership in the Women's Press Club.

Soon after Wilbur had departed for Europe, Ellen wrote Charlie Taylor, who had never traveled to Kitty Hawk, telling him of her experiences there and again expressing gratitude for all his help in the past. In his reply, he thanked her for her support but then confided to her that he was beginning to worry that his heretofore prominent role with the Wright brothers was being gradually diminished with the addition of so many new employees. Ellen was concerned upon hearing his report, feeling great loyalty to Charlie not only for his earlier help but for his discretion in helping her maintain contact with Wilbur. She replied, again thanking Charlie for his friendship and expressing sympathy for his feelings. But she was undecided if she should convey his concerns to Wilbur.

Ellen at first accepted Wilbur's long absence with equanimity, understanding the trip's necessity and feeling great pride in his success. But as the year moved into summer, and feeling the emptiness of his absence, Ellen again began to feel increasingly isolated and to experience lingering doubts about their future. The doubts and depression seemed to her much stronger than what she had experienced the year before.

She did not doubt Wilbur's love nor the sincerity of his intentions, but she remained acutely aware that the certain objections of his family would present the most serious obstacle for them. Her new doubts, however, arose more from her concern that the major problem might lie with Wilbur, not his family, and Ellen wondered if he realistically could carry through with his commitment to her given the multiple pressures on him. She feared that he still would not be able to resolve in his mind what he would regard as a conflict involving her, his family and their expectations, and his obsession with flying machines. She recalled Charlie Taylor's early comment about Wilbur—that his reply to those who asked was that he did not have time for a wife and a flying machine—and wondered if it ultimately might be the reality.

In addition, Ellen was increasingly aware of the passage of time since they had met. She had largely defined her life around the times when she was with Wilbur, but that had involved only two occasions in 1906, three times in 1907, and twice in 1908, and never for more than three or four days on each occasion. Now, at

A Romance of Flight

age twenty-six, and knowing Wilbur to be fifteen years older, she increasingly dwelt on these matters during the long months of his European trip. He wrote frequently, but his attention did not completely eliminate her concerns. Her parents also remarked occasionally on her evident melancholia. Her dedication to her job remained undiminished, and she pursued a variety of reporting assignments, but she always made certain that she covered Wilbur's European activities regularly.

One major development of which Wilbur wrote was that, after the successes of their new Kitty Hawk tests and delivery of the Army flyer, they had decided to close their bicycle business permanently, freeing them at last to devote their efforts entirely to aviation. Receiving payment for the Army flyer had relieved their financial pressures. Ellen replied promptly, giving her support for their decision to close the business. Wilbur also told her that the City of Dayton wanted to confer some official honor on its native sons, but that he and Orville declined at the time, citing the press of business.

Despite her continuing doubts and worries, or perhaps in part because of them, Ellen decided at the end of the summer, after reading Wilbur's latest letter, to speak to her parents. Among other things, she thought that disclosing what her life had been about for that time might help her better deal with her private feelings, and she decided to proceed without specifically informing Wilbur. One evening after dinner, and after her grandmother had retired, Ellen informed her parents that she had something she wanted to tell them and asked them to join her in the parlor. Taking a deep breath, trying to control her anxiety, she began.

"I have decided to tell you something that I have been withholding for almost three years. It is not that I wished to deceive you, but once you have heard me out, I hope you will understand why I have not spoken before now. I know you want only the best for me, and I have always appreciated that.

"Now, what I have to tell you extends from my two trips to Dayton three years ago to report on the flying experiments of the

Wright brothers. Although neither of us planned or expected anything like this, in our brief time together, Wilbur Wright and I came to mean everything to each other. We both realized that we had bonded at a personal level. Since then, we have continued to write and to see each other when we could. In addition to the time I introduced him to you at Aunt Keys' funeral, he has visited Pittsburgh three times to see me in connection with his business trips to New York and Washington, and of course, I saw him recently at Kitty Hawk. He has also written frequently from Europe. We have kept our feelings and plans to ourselves until now, because he was worried that his family would not react favorably. I know there is an age difference between us, but neither of us feels it. He wants to marry me, but there are the serious pressures of business as well as the certain opposition from his family, and he is exceptionally loyal to his family. I must admit that I have been feeling discouraged by all the delays and the problems we face, but when we parted at Kitty Hawk, we agreed that our feelings for each other will overcome all obstacles. I know he will work to persuade his family, and I can only ask that you will support me."

Both her parents looked distressed, but they said nothing at that moment. Feeling some relief at finally expressing what she had wanted to say for almost three years, Ellen continued. "The reason I have not said anything before now has been due to the peculiarities of his family, and I must try to explain that situation to you before anything else. I wanted to tell you about Will long before, but he asked me to delay because of his family concerns, and I have respected that. Both he and Orville had regarded themselves as confirmed bachelors totally dedicated to their work, and their family has viewed them in the same way. Will said he never gave any thought to marriage until I came into his life. For myself, I came to admire him, then to love him, not for the important work he is doing, but for the person he is. Orville is his partner and closest associate, but he is a difficult personality, and he would be certain to oppose his brother's marriage. I am certain Orville will never marry, and it appears to be the stance of his family that Wilbur should not either.

"There are definitely some peculiarities to his family, as I said, and they have troubled Wilbur as they have me. But because of his loyalty and sense of duty to them, he has been strongly inhibited from doing anything that they could regard as defiance of them or their values. For that reason, he still has not told his family of his feelings for me. The main thing he feels essential is to attain business and financial success, which is what makes his European trip and production of the flyer so vital. He and Orville will also organize a company in Dayton soon. With those things accomplished, he at least could take away the objections of his family that his marriage would constitute interference with their business obligations, and he would also feel much more independent. I think so as well, and I hope you will see things the same way."

In addition to feeling relieved, Ellen felt almost serene after she had finally told her story. She sensed that her parents were troubled by her disclosure, but she hoped that in the end they would be understanding.

Her mother spoke first. "I must confess that I am not wholly surprised," she said. "I could sense some feeling between you and Wilbur at Aunt Elizabeth's funeral last year. And I suspected when you said you were going for a walk that evening that you might have been meeting him."

Ellen nodded.

"If this man is of good character, and he can make you happy, we have no reason to be opposed," said her father. "I would not regard the age difference as a significant barrier."

"We never have," said Ellen. "When we are together, we just relate as human beings, and we seem to be natural partners. And as you state, he is definitely a man of character. I know that his being bald on top doesn't make him look youthful, but he really is a young man."

Looking directly at her father, and with a smile, she said, "You really couldn't object on that ground."

"I can't, and I don't. Neither does your mother." He stroked his bald pate in acknowledgement.

"What are your immediate plans?" asked her mother.

"Nothing will happen until his return from Europe, of course, and that may not be until the end of the year. But after he returns, he has promised me he will speak to his family."

"I suppose," said her father, "that this flying machine invention could earn them a considerable fortune over the next few years."

"It could," Ellen replied, "and he has mentioned the profit potential, but that was never his main goal. They want to be successful in the business, of course, but Will is more dedicated to what the flying machine could accomplish, how it could advance civilization and change the way people live. Money was never my concern either. I only want to help him, and I already have in many respects."

"I suppose it will take us some time to absorb all this," said her mother. "What you have told us answers many questions we had about your life over the last two or three years, and certainly it explains why you weren't interested in meeting any eligible young men."

"I know, and as I said, I did not like deceiving you, but I hope you understand now. This has its complications, and it is a situation I could never have imagined before. Neither of us wanted to wait this long, of course, but Will knew it would have been almost impossible to make firm plans in the midst of all their business and contract pressures and problems. For us to have moved forward before now would really have incensed his family. But he and Orville have made enough progress that he feels the time is drawing closer. For my part, I will ask you not to discuss this outside the household. I would not want anyone at the newspaper to know yet."

"We shall respect your wishes, of course," said her father.

Her parents ended the discussion by reiterating that they believed she was mature enough to know her mind and that they would support her in any way they could. Ellen retired that evening feeling that an enormous burden had been lifted from her. She also reminded herself of her good fortune in the parents she had. Now, in spite of the frustrations and doubts she had been feeling, she could wait for Wilbur's return with more confidence in the future.

She wrote Wilbur soon thereafter to recount her conversation with her parents. She then visited her friend Julia and told her essentially what she had just told her parents.

"Ellen, I must say that I am astonished," Julia said, "but at least what you have said helps me to understand you better. It also explains many questions I had about you over the past two or three years."

"I know, and I just hope that you understand why I have withheld all this until now."

"I suppose I do, but it will still take some time to absorb. I will tell you that I support you as well. You certainly aren't foolish by nature, and I know this is serious because it has gone on for so long."

"I would have confided in you if circumstances had been other than what they were, and I thank you now for your understanding."

Ellen stayed longer, in part to spend time with Julia's small son.

Some two weeks later, she received a reply from Wilbur, in which he not only stated his support for her decision to speak with her parents, but asked her to convey his regards to them and to tell her father of his intention to speak to him formally upon his return from Europe.

Ellen continued to be challenged by her journalistic duties, reporting on several interesting news developments during Wilbur's absence. It was a time of several political corruption scandals in Pittsburgh, and she participated in that coverage. Also, the city celebrated its sesquicentennial, being founded in 1758, and Ellen wrote articles in commemoration of that event, some independently and some in collaboration with others.

Chapter Thirteen

Recognition, Confrontation

Dayton, Europe, Washington, Pittsburgh, 1908-1909

Ellen was gratified that Wilbur was able to keep her fully informed of his activities and plans, despite the usual necessity for discretion in writing and posting letters. With a tight schedule, and able to spend only two days at home between his return from Kitty Hawk and his scheduled departure for New York, he was still able to write to her. He described how his time in Dayton had been largely devoted to his extensive travel preparations. After saying goodbye to his family, he boarded the train to New York, telling Ellen that he might not be able to write often, but would catch up.

Once Wilbur was able to do so, he wrote her of his trip and further adventures. He had crossed the Atlantic again by passenger liner, arriving in Paris on May 29, where he immediately undertook a busy and varied schedule. He spent several weeks dealing with contacts in Paris before beginning his planned European exhibition tour and recounted to Ellen his difficulties there. As July arrived, Wilbur's attention was on the flyer, where it had remained stored from the year before. After uncrating the components and completing reassembly, Wilbur wrote to Orville sharply criticizing him over the manner in which the flyer had been packed for shipping originally, another manifestation of his anxiety over anything involving their flyer. But after further correspondence with Orville, his initial anger subsided as both eventually understood the inherent problems of maintaining effective communication across the ocean. He was happy to tell Ellen that those matters were resolved.

Wilbur had selected the racecourse at Le Mans outside Paris as the site of his flying demonstrations. He attracted the interest and support of the French firm M. Bollee and Company at Le Mans, which proved invaluable. While making a preliminary test of the flyer, however, he suffered a serious burn on his arm from falling against the engine. The burn took some time to heal, but he was able to begin his public flying exhibitions on August 8 with no lingering effects from the injury. When he took to the air, Wilbur was pleased that the flyer performed perfectly, and he promptly reported his early flying results to Orville. His demonstrations were widely and favorably covered in the French press. Ellen was pleased, both with Wilbur's progress and with his diligence with keeping her well-informed.

Wilbur continued to write Ellen regularly. Among other matters, he discussed the Chanute situation with her, as well as his continuing patent infringement concerns. All earlier tensions between the brothers were forgotten, and Wilbur was particularly concerned with Orville's upcoming demonstrations with the Army flyer. Of growing concern to both brothers was the evident patent infringement by the AEA, stemming directly from the advertisement they had seen offering its aeroplane for sale. Yet another disturbing development was that Octave Chanute had begun to criticize the brothers over the prices they had charged the French. Despite his intensive preparations for his aerial demonstrations and business negotiations, Wilbur kept Ellen informed of all business matters as well. His next letter described how he had been alerted that the French were likely to be skeptical of his demonstrations, but that the success of his first flight at Le Mans dispelled any doubts. His flights became highly publicized throughout Europe and in America, and he gained strong personal recognition as well. He told Ellen that he felt he was personally popular with the French public, but that perhaps he was something of an enigma, as he always remained rather reserved and businesslike, even on social occasions. He continued his demonstrations not only for the French but also for officials from Germany, Italy, Russia, and other nations. He was received in the highest levels of government and society, and he dined with princes and prime ministers. The social events also were covered extensively in the American press.

The brothers maintained their business agreement with Charles Flint, but Wilbur increasingly pursued appointments and negotiations on his own, feeling a declining need to be represented by others. He continued to write Ellen of matters beyond their concerns for their future, telling her that he had to shop for new formal clothing in order to be properly attired for formal occasions, something with which he had no experience.

One subsequent letter particularly pleased Ellen, as she had not expected the nature of its contents. It began:

Dear Ellen:

Things are still moving at a breakneck pace. One thing I want to share is that I have made many new friends here, and some have offered to introduce me to women. I suppose it is flattering to be regarded as an eligible bachelor, but I have always declined, without explanation. I have never informed anyone I am committed to another.

I have many things to tell you about my flights and about business developments, but will save those for when I have more time.

With love,
Will

A Romance of Flight

Ellen was delighted at his news, particularly of his account of his social activities, but her major reaction was that she felt more reassured of his devotion to their future after the doubts she had been feeling.

In her reply, Ellen reported that her parents continued to express support for her and their plans. Wilbur replied with his intention to speak to his family upon his return, and if that meeting went well, he would come to Pittsburgh to ask her father formally for her hand.

Ellen followed news reports closely of his demonstrations in France, and of the delivery of the Wright flyer to the US Army. Delivery of the first military heavier-than-air flying machine, combined with the strong European interest in aviation, left little room for official skepticism about the reality of powered flight on either continent. Literally thousands of people had witnessed flight on both sides of the Atlantic. Ample skepticism remained, of course, over its practical value, both in military and civil circles. But as a result of their successes, the Wright brothers had become famous on two continents. They were equal celebrities, and Wilbur's activities were reported almost on a daily basis in American newspapers.

He was able to send another letter during the middle of the negotiations, and to further update her on his activities. At a banquet in his honor on November 19, Wilbur expressed high optimism about the future of aviation. Further, and to him, far more important, he was achieving solid results in Europe, enabling him to forget the frustrations of his trip the previous year. After several false starts, he had negotiated a British licensing agreement with the Short Brothers manufacturing firm of Northern Ireland. Implementation proceeded smoothly, and production of the Wright Model B by Short Brothers for the British market was to begin in 1909. Ellen was especially excited at the news.

* * *

As she followed Wilbur's exploits in Europe, including those reports in her own newspaper from the Associated Press, Ellen felt not only more pride than ever in him, but she increasingly enjoyed the respect she had earned in the eyes of the news fraternity. Her reportorial efforts on flight had been validated, both for her and for the *Reporter*. One day early in September, Roy Graham mentioned the point specifically.

"Ellen, I must confess that when Mr. Rutledge first gave you the assignment to report on the Wright brothers three years ago, I had my doubts. But I have come to realize that this was indeed an important story. I'm glad that you pursued it, and it has undoubtedly benefited the paper. We were the only newspaper in Pittsburgh to report on the Wright brothers at the time, and one of the first in the country."

"I appreciate what you are saying, Roy. I didn't know what I was getting into at the time, of course, but you are so right. I am glad that I had the opportunity to be one of the first to report the full story, and of course I am happy the brothers have become successful. But most of all, I am grateful to Mr. Rutledge for having the foresight to think that this could be an important story."

"I know you reported on their new flights at Kitty Hawk, but have you kept in touch with the brothers otherwise?"

Ellen felt some breath escape at hearing the question, but she responded evenly, "Not very often, but I hope to talk with both again after Wilbur Wright returns from his European tour. I'm afraid they may have some trouble allowing me the time, since it appears that they are major celebrities now."

"Well, again," said Roy, "I just wanted you to know that I admire what you have done and are continuing to do on the subject."

He returned to his office. Ellen thought for a minute with gratitude about what a good friend Roy had been throughout her entire experience at the *Reporter*.

Little more than a week after that conversation, Roy approached Ellen with a concerned, even distressed, look on his face.

"Ellen, I thought I should bring this to you at once, before you saw it elsewhere." He handed her a wire service report. She felt her heart almost stop as she read the news, that Orville had suffered a crash of the Army flyer at Fort Myer, Virginia, on September 17, during a routine test flight demonstration. His passenger, Lieutenant Thomas E. Selfridge, only twenty-six, had been killed. The tragedy had been witnessed by some two thousand spectators.

Ellen knew that Orville had begun his tests only two weeks before, soon after Wilbur had begun flying in France, and that six days later he had carried as his first passenger Lieutenant Frank Lahm, their early supporter. She also knew that Orville had distrusted Selfridge due to his association with Glenn Curtiss but was still required to train him due to their contract obligations and due to his position as an Army officer. As she read further into the report, Ellen learned that the crash was caused by a cracked propeller blade. The cracked blade had caused a structural vibration of such force that the flyer became unstable and went out of control. Orville was seriously injured and was hospitalized, but Selfridge died on impact.

Fighting to maintain her composure, Ellen thanked Roy for bringing her the report and said that she was indeed distressed at the news. She told him she would like to be assigned to report on the tragedy and write a story, to which he agreed. She felt herself bitterly regretting that she had not insisted on being in Washington and in Fort Myer, just across the Potomac, to cover the tests in person, especially since she knew that their largest competitor in Pittsburgh, the *Gazette Times*, had sent a reporter for that purpose. She began a letter to Wilbur immediately. She felt certain that Wilbur had been informed already by telegraph through the transatlantic cable, but she knew that he would want her personal letter of condolence and concern. She knew also that she must write Charlie Taylor, who had accompanied Orville to Washington to help with the tests and would have been present the day of the crash. Ellen feared that, among other concerns, the

Army might cancel the order and that legal difficulties for the brothers would follow.

After three agonizing weeks due to slow shipborne mail transport, Ellen received Wilbur's lengthy reply to her letter. He began by stating, as she had expected, that he was grieved by the tragedy and deeply concerned about its impact on the Army contract and on their futures. He also blamed himself, feeling that he had made a mistake in leaving Orville there to face the task alone, especially with regard to the pressures of dealing with spectators and reporters. Wilbur then told her that he had suspended his own flying for a week on the news and was considering suspending the remainder of his exhibition schedule and returning to the United States. Ellen, in her reply, discouraged that idea. She urged him instead to remain and complete his schedule and reminded him that there was nothing he could do in the United States to help at the time. She later learned that he had already decided to continue in Europe, even if reluctantly. In his next letter, he told her that despite the tragedy and his own intensive schedule, he still thought constantly of her and counted the days until his return.

In the meantime, Ellen received a letter from Charlie Taylor and learned from him that Katharine had left her teaching position to be with Orville at his hospital in Washington—news that gave Ellen a feeling of great relief. Also, with Orville recovering, Wilbur planned to remain in France until the end of the year, and he continued his status as a celebrity as well as a prizewinner with his flight exhibitions. The French public was enthusiastic, and the success of the Wright machine had eliminated all doubt as to its superiority over others. The French also were impressed that Wilbur maintained his refusal to fly on Sundays, as his father had asked.

On October 6, he carried a passenger aloft for more than one hour over the Le Mans field, satisfying a requirement of the French syndicate holding the patent and licensing rights. The agreement then was signed, and the Wright brothers received a payment of $100,000. On the next day, October 7, Mrs. Hart Berg, wife of their business associate, became the first woman air passenger, a distinction to which Ellen had once aspired. France thereafter offered to confer on Wilbur the Legion of Honor, but he refused that and all honors in which Orville did not share equally.

William Howard Taft had been elected as Theodore Roosevelt's successor, in a resounding victory over William Jennings Bryan, on November 3. The Wright brothers as well as Ellen's father applauded the victory. Of more immediate impact on the brothers, their Army contract was preserved after an investigation determined that the crash was not due to a design flaw. Ellen's early concerns that lawsuits or other actions against Wilbur and Orville might follow proved unfounded, as the accident was not held against them. The Army ordered a replacement flyer and planned to resume testing after it was delivered.

By the end of his four-month exhibition schedule, in early December, Wilbur had made more than one hundred flights, totaling more than twenty-five hours in the air, and had carried a passenger on numerous occasions. He told Ellen more about his plans in his next letter.

Dear Ellen:

I had hoped and planned to return home by Christmas, but now I feel compelled to remain longer and compete for the Michelin Prize, scheduled for the last day of the year. It also appears that it will be necessary for me—and for Orville, if he is well enough—to travel to Italy to negotiate Italian rights and to train two pilots there. The Italian Club of Aviators has asked us to train pilots, and they will want to purchase our flyer as well.

All I can tell you now is that I will return as soon as I can. I need your support now more than ever.

Love,
Will

Ellen was deeply disappointed that he would not be back by the end of the year, but in her response, she pledged her continuing support. Wilbur succeeded in capturing the Michelin Prize, with a flight of seventy-seven miles in freezing weather.

Ellen informed her family of Wilbur's delay, telling them that she felt it was her duty as well as her desire to continue to support his added endeavors. They were concerned, but they restated their support for her. But she felt dejected that she would not be able to see him at Christmas. It was Wilbur's only Christmas away from home in his life.

* * *

Despite all of Wilbur's success in Europe and the continuing confidence of the Army, Ellen still felt frustrated and apprehensive as the year 1909 arrived. She had already accepted that she was unlikely ever to be first in Wilbur's life and again reminded herself that their plans had been delayed more than once. Wilbur sent her a New Year's Day greeting restating his commitment to their future, but that did not completely reassure her. Her dominant wish was for Wilbur's early return, but on January 12 she learned he was joined in France by Orville, recuperated, although still suffering some limitations from his injuries, and by Katharine. Katharine planned to devote herself to helping her brothers, including traveling with them through the remainder of their tour.

In his next letter to Ellen, Wilbur described how Katharine was enjoying the attention she received as sister to the two famous aviators and in the process had become something of a celebrity herself. She learned from other reports that Katharine had in fact charmed the public and was being credited with actively assisting her brothers in development of the flyer. Ellen could not help feeling some slight jealousy at not being there with Wilbur as his wife, but she accepted that she loved someone who was now a public figure, and a popular one at that. She knew that she would have to remain in the background for the time being, even though it served only to make her life more complicated. Her parents followed news of Wilbur's activities as closely as she did, and they

A Romance of Flight

discussed his exploits with her often. Ellen continued her established pattern of life in Pittsburgh, even as she continued to deal with her loneliness and feelings of isolation. No news stories other than Wilbur's tour held particular fascination for her, but she pursued diligently whatever she was assigned.

In February, another event caused Ellen to feel greater pride for the brothers than ever. Although still in Europe, Wilbur and Orville received an official commendation from the US Congress for their accomplishments. Political skepticism about the military potential of powered flying machines was no longer a significant factor, as reflected in the prompt appropriation for the replacement flyer. In France, Wilbur moved to a field at Pau, south of Paris, where he began the training of two French pilots. More celebrities, including the British and Spanish kings, observed his flights. Orville and Katharine joined him there, and Katharine flew as a passenger.

After some two months at Pau, Wilbur carried through with his Italian plans by traveling to Rome on April 1, again followed by Orville and Katharine. When their training duties were completed, the brothers sold their demonstrator flyer to Italy as planned, then, with their sister, sailed for the United States. Wilbur and Orville urgently needed to be in Dayton to guarantee the delivery of the Army replacement flyer on schedule. All looked forward to returning home, of course, although Wilbur had not yet told his brother and sister of the additional reason he was eager to return.

Ellen was aware of their arrival date in New York: May 11. The brothers were surprised, even overwhelmed, at finding themselves publicly welcomed as heroes. Reporters and photographers met them as they walked down the gangplank, and crowds closed in for a look at the famed flyers. Wilbur had been abroad a full year, and while that had been far longer than he had planned or desired, he wrote to her of his special satisfaction at his and Orville's accomplishments on both sides of the Atlantic. After a decade of struggle, their achievements finally were appreciated by the public, and their exhibition earnings and business agreements had made them prosperous as well. When he was able to gain a little time for privacy, he wrote Ellen of the events.

Ellen also followed closely the news reports of the brothers. In part due to their celebrity status, there was rising public fascination over the fact that neither brother was married, much as there had been earlier with Wilbur in Paris. Both were regarded as eligible, if rather eccentric, bachelors. They received many questions from the press about their aeronautical achievements and business plans, to which they responded fully, but when asked any questions about their marital status or any plans related thereto, neither would comment. They arrived home on May 13, where they were again met with great public acclaim. Wilbur wrote that they were especially relieved to find their father in good spirits.

Ellen knew that the time had come for Wilbur to speak to his family about her, and after relaxing at home for several days, Wilbur told her he decided he could delay no longer. He told Ellen he was mentally preparing himself to reveal his plans with Ellen to his family, then wrote of his specific plans. He promised to tell her in detail how events evolved. More than a week later Ellen received his letter.

Dear Ellen,

I am sitting in my room as I write, as I have just revealed my plans to my family. I'll try to reconstruct the conversation as best I can remember. This evening, I asked Orville, Katharine, and my father to join me in the parlor after dinner. I sat down across from them, fighting the rising tension I felt, and spoke. I first told them of how I had enjoyed being home after so long a time, and that, now that I have had a chance to catch up, the time had come to discuss the future. I said I had a personal matter of great importance to discuss with all of them, and as the people closest to me, I hoped they would be understanding.

No one responded at the time, but I could tell they were listening. I took a deep breath and proceeded. I recall my exact words.

A Romance of Flight

"I have been totally dedicated, as has Orville, to our work with flight, especially over the past seven or eight years. I have had very little of what you could call a personal life. But there has been something more to my life over the last four years, something that I never expected to happen, and it is now time to tell you.

"I have continued private contact with Ellen Hobson since her second visit here as a reporter. To come to the point, I wish to marry her. We are planning to do so this year. Ellen and I have delayed making firm plans because she recognized the priority of our commitments with the Army, with the patent, and of course with our work in Europe. We have now accomplished those things. We have also begun to earn a great deal of money and have achieved a degree of financial security as a family. But I am not getting any younger, and I am ready to build a life for myself. I hope you will not oppose me in this. Being apart from Ellen this past year has only strengthened my determination. I ask you to believe that her support throughout our efforts has been of immeasurable value to me."

Unfortunately, the reactions of both Orville and Katharine were almost as I feared: their faces appeared frozen, clouded over with concern, but neither said anything. My father responded first in this way:

"Will, I have no doubt that you have feelings for this young woman, but you have no business contemplating marriage at this time, and at your age."

I said that I respected his opinion, but felt I had fulfilled all my obligations to my family, as I always have, and now, with the success of the flyer, it is time to look to my personal happiness. I stressed that I had earned that right at this stage of my life, and I could find that happiness with you.

Orville, who appeared to be barely containing his anger, spoke next. He called me foolish, stating that there was no way we could continue our work if I had a wife to look after. He said I had betrayed him by keeping our relationship a secret from him. He appeared to me to be agitated to the point of almost being out of control. He appeared to me to be agitated to the point of almost being out of control.

Katharine also objected, first by reminding me of my duties to his family. She then agreed with everything Orv had said, calling me foolish, going so far as to say, "We could never look at you the same again.'"

I had considered all those points, of course, and I replied to them as a group. I replied to them as a group, explaining our reasoning for keeping this private. I commended you for being so patient and understanding from the beginning. I reminded them that through all of this, I have never let any private feelings interfere with work, that it always comes first. I tried to reason with them. I told them that you and I could have gone through with our plans two or three years ago but we didn't because of my obligations. I explained that you could become a part of this family and that I didn't see any conflict there. I told them, "I didn't expect any of you to welcome what I am telling you with enthusiasm, but I think you should take more time to reflect on the matter rather than simply opposing me."

I had previously decided not to disclose precisely how I had maintained contact with you. I didn't want to involve Charlie Taylor at the time, and I felt somewhat relieved that Orville had not raised that question. But there was no progress from that point. Orville in particular remained angry, and Katharine was cold. Father appeared bewildered. I asked them again for understanding, then told them I would go to his room for the evening.

This brings me to the end of this letter. I must tell you that I feel crestfallen, given the way my announcement was received. The fact remains that my father, Katharine, and especially Orville are adamantly opposed to the idea of my marriage. I thought I presented things in a completely reasonable manner, but the discussion still turned into a confrontation. I suppose it was unrealistic for me to think that I could bring them around to at least tolerating my plans.

I will continue to try to gain a degree of acceptance from them, *but there is no question that they are going to be extremely difficult. I told them of your help to me over the past four years and how I felt that you should become a part of the family.*

I will see you as soon as I can complete the upcoming business with the Army. I look forward to seeing you, of course, and I hope that a full year apart has not changed your feelings in any way. Probably you should not reply immediately, since I intend to be there as soon as possible.

Love as always,
Will

Ellen was distressed when she read the letter, but she decided to inform her parents without delay.

"I am very disappointed to tell you that things did not go well for Will in his discussions with his family," she said. "They all seemed rather angry with him and are strongly opposed to any marriage. They may be hostile to me as well. He had warned me that things might be difficult, and they were, but I simply don't understand their rigidity in all this. The whole matter now rests on whether he will be willing to disregard or even abandon his family for me. That wouldn't be easy for him, of course, but for my part I don't see why he should have to make such a choice in the first place. He has been the dutiful son and brother all his life.

"I am still determined that we will have a future, and I am going to tell him that we should go ahead and plan to marry regardless. I hope you will see things the same way."

"I'm afraid I don't understand his family either," said her mother. "It's not like anything I have ever experienced, but we will still support you in doing whatever you feel is necessary."

"We just want you to be happy," added her father, in a subdued tone.

Despite lingering tensions from the confrontation, Orville and Wilbur continued to communicate fully on all business matters and on development of the flyer. In his next letter to Ellen, Wilbur still conveyed the impression that he was dispirited.

Dear Ellen:

I suppose things have returned to an appearance of normalcy here. At least Orville and I are continuing to work together. But he has mentioned that he is suspicious that we might proceed to marry in spite of the family's opposition, and he is emphatic that such a course would end our partnership and endanger all that we have accomplished. I told Orville that that was the last thing I wanted to have happen, and I practically begged him to be more open-minded and to show respect for you as well. I saw no indication that he was moved. Katharine also seems cold to the idea, but she offers nothing specific in opposition.

I still plan to see you as soon as I can, regardless of my family, and I will keep you informed of all developments as always.

With love,
Will

Wilbur wrote soon after.

Dear Ellen:

Orville and I accepted an invitation to visit the White House and President Taft on June 10, where he presented us with special medals. On our return to Dayton, a great celebration in our honor was held at the county fairgrounds, with Father himself delivering the invocation. Soon after, we were awarded the Congressional Gold Medal, presented on June 18, along with several local awards. We had to travel again, as we had to be at Fort Myer on June 20 to complete preparations for the delivery of their replacement Army flyer. We completed the replacement machine, largely by our employees, later that month. We delivered the flyer to Fort Myer, and Orville restarted flight testing on June 29. The Signal Corps officially accepted on August 2. Orville continued with the training of three Signal Corps officers as pilots.

I know that is a great deal of information to absorb, but I know you would want to know.

Love,
Will

A Romance of Flight

Ellen continued to follow aeronautical developments, which were increasing in frequency on both sides of the Atlantic. Louis Bleriot accomplished a major milestone when he precariously but successfully crossed the English Channel in his Model 11 monoplane on July 25. Bleriot had met Wilbur in France, and in fact he had employed the Wright control system on his flyer. Upon hearing the news, Wilbur remarked to Orville that, while Bleriot's achievement was noteworthy, he could have done the same earlier had he wished, since he had made flights of over two hours. In fact, he had considered competing for the feat, but he decided it was not important enough to delay his return home.

Ellen had followed every detail of Wilbur's activities since his return and had written most of the coverage of the Wright brothers appearing in the *Reporter*. She still found it difficult to generate enthusiasm for other assignments, but one exception was her review of the performance of Isadora Duncan, goddess of the dance, at the Nixon Theater that summer. She had not requested the assignment but found it rewarding, especially since she had seldom attended the theater. She continued to keep her parents informed of developments with the Wright family, stating that she expected Wilbur to visit her as soon as he was free. She hoped that she could then confirm their plans.

Wilbur wrote to Ellen that he had declared to Orville he would depart Washington before the official Army acceptance of the flyer. Further, he told Orville of his specific plans for the first time. He included his plan to stop in Pittsburgh, to which Orville had made a caustic response. Having informed Ellen, he arrived on August 1 for his reunion. Ellen was waiting for him at the Pennsylvania Railroad Union Station. It had been over a year since they had seen each other, but when Ellen saw him she realized in that instant—whatever her previous doubts or discouragement—that her love was lasting. She ran to him, and they embraced intensely. They walked together to Wilbur's hotel, where she waited for him to register, and then strolled around the city, enjoying the warm summer weather. Ellen knew Wilbur was equally overjoyed to see her, and he told her so. But he appeared to be very serious from the first moment and barely smiled.

They talked continuously, however, with Wilbur recounting his confrontation with his family and their hostile reaction to their plans. But Ellen felt that something more was troubling him.

"Will, I know the past year has been filled with major events, and not all of them have been good. There was the tragedy at Fort Myer, and I know your family is opposed to our plans. But I sense there is something more bothering you. Please tell me."

"As usual, you are right," he replied. "I didn't plan to bring this up, but since you can tell something is on my mind, I will do so."

He took a deep breath and continued. "While in France last fall, I was named as correspondent in a divorce suit brought by a Lieutenant Goujarde of the French Army. He alleged I had an affair with his wife. The allegation was published in French newspapers back in January."

"I admit that I had seen some sketchy reports that made their way to the States," Ellen said, "but I refused to give them any credence. But I will ask you now for the record, was there anything to it?"

Wilbur hesitated. "No," he said. "I had met the couple, but that was all. It was just a consequence of my being something of a celebrity, I think. I was afraid that something would be reported in the newspapers here, and I learned that it was. Even the *Dayton Herald* carried the story, with a big headline on June 8, just before we went to Washington. I don't need to tell you how much I resented that. Anyway, the press eventually retracted the story, and I hope it is over with now. I'm just sorry if you had any doubts."

"I had none. You know that what you say is good enough for me. For now, I am only concerned that you seem so disturbed over the matter. I don't see that this should be a problem for us."

"Nor do I, but the story did follow me home and just represents to me another danger of the press. Orville and I always wanted recognition, of course, and now we have it, then this kind of story appears. Sometimes it makes me wonder if it was all worth it."

"You surely can't question whether it was worth it. You can't possibly think that you should not have done what you did, or the way you did it."

"I understand what you are saying, but the episode only adds to the difficulties we face. And now, just as we are ready to organize a company, Chanute is criticizing us again, and almost certainly we will have to sue Curtiss over patent infringement. His AEA group sold an aeroplane to the New York Aero Club just a few weeks ago, on June 26. We know that his machine benefited from help we provided, and since it was a commercial sale, that certainly violates our patent. Another concern for us is that Curtiss has formed his own aeroplane company, in partnership with Augustus Herring, and Herring is another individual I distrust. I can only ask you to wait even longer until Orville and I have had the time to deal with these issues."

Ellen felt crushed on hearing that statement. She had difficulty breathing and felt herself weaken.

"I need to sit down," said Ellen. "It seems there is always something working against us. I keep coming back to the time when we first declared our love for each other. I thought then, and still think, that we could overcome any obstacle or opposition to us. Now all I hear is that we must wait even longer. I think it is time that we acted independently and not allow events to control us. If you still want to marry me, let us do it this year."

"I do want to marry you," said Wilbur. "I have loved you for four years, and nothing that has happened has changed that. I had already determined that I would defy, if that is the right word, my own family. I know we can never get everything in perfect order, but I will need more time to settle these patent and business matters. That is the only way I will ever have a chance of lessening my family's opposition. I have continued to discuss my feelings about you with Orville and Katharine, of course."

"Do you think there has been any change in their positions?"

"No. Their views are quite rigid. They remain hostile to the whole idea, as does my father, for that matter. At least Lorin does not indicate any opposition. I don't know if it simply is that marriage doesn't reflect their plans or expectations for me or if there could be something specific regarding you, but I don't see how it could be the latter. It is more likely that they regard any other involvement by me as a hindrance to our work and violates their view of our family. What I do know is that it is depressing; I never wanted to subject you to this."

"I knew about your family four years ago," said Ellen. "It didn't stop me from loving you then, and it doesn't stop me now. You are a man of accomplishment, and we are both mature. That is enough."

"I will talk to you again soon," he replied, "after we have made a decision on the patent infringement matter and have finished organizing our company, which should be in a few weeks. Then I will try to make myself free, regardless of my family."

They dined together that evening, trying to recapture the pleasure of each other's company they had experienced before. They agreed not to dwell on their current problems but instead to discuss other events of the past year. Wilbur filled her with details of their honors in Washington and of his experiences in Europe, and Ellen told him news of her family and of developments at the *Reporter*. She also asked him about the homecoming celebration in Dayton, and Wilbur admitted that he had enjoyed all the festivities, regretting only that she could not be there.

Wilbur departed for Dayton the next morning, August 2, the same day their new flyer was accepted by the Army. Ellen bid him goodbye at the station, with a fervent pledge to see him soon and to help resolve their situation. He in turn expressed his regret to Ellen at having to postpone speaking with her father. She had been disappointed that Wilbur could not remain longer, but she knew that business took priority once again.

***

As before, Ellen followed Wilbur's activities closely in the press. With his return to America, and having determined that they had sufficient evidence of patent infringement on the part of Glenn Curtiss and others, he and Orville initiated a series of infringement lawsuits. Wilbur again asked Ellen for her support and patience as he dealt with the pressing legal and business matters that had befallen him at once. He emphasized to her that he would have to bear the brunt of the legal work, since he knew both the law and the process from his extensive experience in helping his father with litigation over church matters.

A complication was that Orville was preparing to leave for Germany with Katharine soon to deal with the German company and to conduct flight exhibitions. Both had extracted a promise from Wilbur that he would do nothing further with regard to Ellen during their absence.

Wilbur returned to Washington on August 14, traveling from there to New York to initiate patent suits against Curtiss in federal court. With Orville's absence, he instigated the lawsuits alone. Even as the suits against him proceeded in the United States, Curtiss won prizes for speed records at the Reims international exhibition in France on August 28. Wilbur told Ellen that he had entered three Wright flyers in the Reims contest and was surprised when Curtiss won.

Ellen, again feeling dejected by the new delays and the lack of resolution on their future, continued to devote herself to her reporting duties. She wrote about, but did not cover from the scene, the violent steel strike outside Pittsburgh on August 22, in which three law enforcement officers were killed. She had wanted to be there, but Theodore Rutledge still held concerns over allowing her to visit sites of news events in which she could be placed in personal danger.

Wilbur continued to inform Ellen of his activities. Among other duties, he traveled to Detroit on September 7, meeting with investor Russell A. Alger, a former Secretary of War, who was to participate in the Wright Company that was being organized. Wilbur divided his time increasingly between Washington and New York, attending to both Army and business matters. He traveled to New York again on September 18, then to Washington to begin the training of Signal Corps pilots. As Orville was extending flight records in Germany, Wilbur staged a notable flight on October 4, taking off from Governor's Island off lower Manhattan and flying up the Hudson River to Grant's Tomb and back, as part of a major civic celebration combining the three hundredth anniversary of Henry Hudson's voyage and the one hundredth anniversary of Robert Fulton's *Clermont*. Wilbur was awarded a prize of $12,500 for the flight. He gave an interview to *Scientific American* about the flight on October 23, then returned to Washington immediately afterward to continue the training of Army pilots. He next traveled to New York again on October 29 to deal with investors, returning immediately to Washington.

Another major event that affected Ellen, of which Wilbur had written her, was when Orville and Katharine arrived in New York from their European trip on November 4. Orville had been successful in everything he had attempted, including taking Crown Prince Friedrich Wilhelm for a flight. Wilbur had met them at the pier, greeting both warmly, and Orville enthusiastically reported that he had been pleased with his flight records there. Wilbur told them details of his own record flight as well as of his progress with training Army pilots. He decided not to mention Ellen at the time, and neither Orville nor Katharine made any reference to her. They remained in New York for two more days, concentrating on completing the organization of the Wright Company, which would control series production of their flyer design as well as the operation of flying schools and other aviation activities. With Katharine, the brothers returned to Dayton, arriving on November 7. Ellen, considering all that Wilbur had told her, was pleased at their success, of course, but still felt apprehensive about how their plans now might impact their future.

The Wright Company, backed by several prominent investors, was incorporated on November 22. The brothers were in New York to preside over the event. Wilbur was appointed president and remained in New York temporarily, while Orville, as vice

A Romance of Flight

president, returned to Dayton to manage production at the new factory then under construction. They received forty percent of the stock as well as a cash payment of $100,000 for their patent rights, making them relatively wealthy.

Ellen arranged to travel to New York early in December, soon after the incorporation, having requested and received an assignment reporting on plans of New York financiers to make major investments in building projects in Pittsburgh. Although she had never been to the city before, and in other circumstances would have been excited at the visit, she paid little attention to New York's attractions, instead heading directly to the Wall Street area and meeting appointments for interviews on her story. On her second day in the city, she met Wilbur. They met happily, but she found him still troubled by the old French allegations and by the pressures of business and legal proceedings. He escorted her to his office, and after proudly showing her its furnishings, he began to speak.

"I am increasingly disturbed by the actions of Chanute," he said. "In August, he publicly opposed our patent infringement suit against Curtiss and further alleged that we had taken credit for his ideas. I find his criticisms particularly hurtful because I had considered him a loyal friend, but now he appears to have taken the side of Curtiss. He charged that we not only took credit for what he claims were things he developed but also that we blundered in suing Curtiss for using similar ideas. I maintain that Chanute is wrong, because we always gave him full credit for his help to us and always acknowledged that we could not have succeeded without his encouragement. He is also wrong in claiming credit for our wing-warping control mechanism. Above all, I find it discouraging that Curtiss is so well regarded by the public after his success at Reims, while we are being criticized solely for the fact that we are pursuing legal action against him."

Ellen had known that both Wilbur and Orville had been deeply concerned over what they regarded as Chanute's lack of discretion in disclosing details of their design to others in France and elsewhere. She also recognized that the entire conflict with Chanute was a particularly heavy burden for Wilbur, coming at a time when he was involved with the company organization and patent suits concurrently, and with Army pilot training at its peak, and she assured him again of her understanding. He acknowledged her warmly, but then paused. He assumed a demeanor as serious as Ellen had ever seen as he began to speak again.

"Added to all these problems is that I am feeling absolutely exhausted. I have never worked so hard in my life, and I can't see an end to it. I don't know how much longer I can keep this up. I feel I am suffering the fate of Prometheus: I have given the world fire, but instead of being rewarded, I am being tormented for doing so. Now, on top of all this, it appears that the French are catching up to us in development. There certainly is far more interest in aviation over there than here, and Bleriot's flight across the channel led directly to the success of the Reims air show in September. Maybe I made a mistake by not staying to attempt the channel crossing."

He paused again, appearing to collect his thoughts.

"I would never want you to think that I don't still love you, but it just appears that our prospects for a future have been overtaken by events outside our control. Another point is that, as you know, I remain deeply affected by Orville's crash at Fort Myer. I need to remind you again of the dangers of flying. Not only was Selfridge killed, but Orville almost was, and I could be as well. I have come around to viewing flying as strictly business, but Orville loves flying for its own sake. We are different in that respect, I suppose.

"Ellen, I returned from France with you first in my mind. But with the way things have worked out, I am finding myself thinking increasingly that, with your being so young, perhaps you should consider building a life elsewhere. It is just unfair for you to keep waiting on me, and things have just gotten beyond my control in the space of a few weeks."

Ellen felt that she had almost been struck a physical blow at

Wilbur's statement, but she was determined to respond calmly. Gathering her composure, she replied, "I have no interest in a life elsewhere, Will. I want only a life with you."

"I've been reflecting on how we have accomplished everything we set out to do when you came into my life four years ago," said Wilbur. "We perfected our flying machine, we received a patent, we won the Army order, and we have initiated production in Europe. Now we have formed our own company and even have accumulated a large sum of money. But I remain deeply troubled, even tormented. We are now criticized in the press and by the public for our stand on the patent infringement question, and I have been subject to unsavory gossip. I have a hard road ahead."

"I know," replied Ellen, "but I support you, and I will be at your side. You must never forget that. Just tell me how I can help."

"The only thing I can tell you with certainty is that I cannot consider marriage anytime soon. I feel I have to give all my attention to these concurrent crises. I will be returning to Dayton soon, and I will write you from there."

Ellen had earlier come to the conclusion that the brothers had made a mistake in their relentless pursuit of the patent infringement suits. Now, having heard Wilbur's views, she decided to speak out in a way she would have never expected of herself earlier.

"I'm going to say something I didn't plan to say, Will. I believe that you should back away from pursuing these patent suits. It's not that you don't have a case, but I think they are just not worth the effort they will take or the grief they will cause. You still have the lead in flying machines, and I believe you will keep it. Even if others have made use of your ideas, you can withstand the competition. Just go ahead with your plans and don't worry about anything else."

"I appreciate what you say," he replied, "but things have progressed too far. Orville is adamant about the suits as well. I don't see any way we can withdraw now. We both see this as a matter of right and wrong."

"As do I, for that matter, but I want you to know that I do not give up on our future. I still cannot contemplate a life without you."

"I appreciate that more than I can say," said Wilbur. "That is just another reason why I love you. Perhaps equally important, it is why I admire and depend on you. I don't know of anything else I could say or do that would make things better for you. I only ask you to keep supporting me."

He escorted her down to the street where he told her he would need to work late at his office. They parted with mutual promises to speak again soon. As she walked to her hotel, Ellen reminded herself that she should not have been surprised that Wilbur remained determined to pursue the lawsuits, but she still felt she had been correct in expressing her opposition. She found that she felt as pessimistic as Wilbur, however, realizing that there were strong external forces acting against them.

Ellen completed her reporting assignment the next day and returned to Pittsburgh. She did not say goodbye to Wilbur as she left. On the trip home, her thoughts turned increasingly toward the conclusion that Wilbur simply possessed a depressive or pessimistic personality, always making more of obstacles and delays than another reasonable person might. But her major concern was that he, while a man of maturity and accomplishment, simply might not possess the ability to stand up to his own family.

She had requested her parents not to meet her at the station, and she made her way home alone by trolley. After dinner, Ellen told her parents how her meeting with Wilbur had gone and informed them that she did not know when or if he would be calling. She found she could report all these things unemotionally, and she did not attempt to describe the pain she felt. She said she looked forward to another Christmas with family.

Wilbur arrived in Dayton on December 17, the six-year anniversary of their success at Kitty Hawk.

CHAPTER FOURTEEN

LITIGATION, RESOLUTION

WASHINGTON, NEW YORK, DAYTON, PITTSBURGH, 1910-1911

Ellen was acutely aware that the new year was also the start of a new decade, but she could not generate a high degree of optimism for its promise after her last meeting with Wilbur. Her paramount concern continued to be for him, but he had written her comparatively little in the past several weeks and even on those occasions had said nothing about their future. She followed whatever she could from infrequent letters and news reports, and there were positive developments.

The brothers concentrated entirely on business as the new year began. After completing the training of Army pilots in Washington, Wilbur divided his time between New York and Dayton with the administration of the Wright Company. Orville continued to spend most of his time in Dayton, managing flyer construction and training civilian pilots at Huffman Prairie. Both devoted increasing effort to the patent infringement litigation which, while directed at several experimenters in addition to Curtiss, was most strongly contested by him. Even though Orville helped in many respects, Wilbur continued to carry the heaviest workload in the lawsuits. His limited time away from work was spent primarily in the company of his family. He had informed them of his meeting with Ellen in New York, but he did not disclose all the details and declined to say anything more about her or about their plans. Despite the continuing tensions caused by his original announcement, the family seemed as close as ever otherwise, and Wilbur felt gratified by that.

The patent dispute began boiling when the Wright Company gained a restraining order, effective in January 1910, against the Herring-Curtiss Company, removing Curtiss as a competitor for the time. Curtiss, however, immediately organized a new company under his sole control. Another complication for the brothers was that other experimenters and former associates had come forward demanding from them some recognition or compensation for their alleged contributions. Despite the intensifying legal activity as well his necessary attention to business, Wilbur still found time to travel south on February 11, 1910, in search of an additional training school site, as the company sought to expand flying training to a warmer climate. He selected Montgomery, Alabama, then returned to New York on February 19 to continue his work on legal matters.

Wilbur and Orville remained deeply troubled over Octave Chanute's public criticism of them and their patent infringement suits. Chanute's accusations about their motives were followed by allegations that they had profited by his ideas. Wilbur and Chanute exchanged detailed letters in which they outlined their respective positions on the matter of due credit and recognition. In particular, Wilbur took issue with Chanute's accusation that they were primarily motivated by a desire for wealth. With further communication, Chanute appeared gradually to become more conciliatory, leading Wilbur to think for a time that the rift would heal. Soon afterward, however, Chanute's health declined, and he discontinued correspondence.

Hailed as national heroes only a few months earlier, Wilbur and Orville found that they had since become targets of widespread public criticism stemming from their pursuit of the patent suits. The public appeared to support the Chanute position, and publicity regarding them was largely negative. The brothers were increasingly viewed as holding a fixation on becoming wealthy by building an aviation monopoly, resulting in a sharp decline in their popularity, while Curtiss gained in public sympathy. Wilbur's letters to Ellen reflected his distress at the turn of events.

Business activity increased, even in the face of the patent infringement litigation. The new factory in Dayton was nearing completion, and the Wright Company School of Aviation, with flying schools at Huffman Prairie and in Montgomery, Alabama, also was formally established. Wilbur, accompanied by Charlie Taylor, traveled again to Montgomery on March 24 to open the flying school, and both locations became extremely active in the training of new pilots. The first cadre of pilots trained by the brothers themselves then transitioned into training others, as the number of aspiring pilots steadily increased. Wilbur gave major attention to the Montgomery location, both with administration and with the training of pilots.

* * *

Completing his work in Montgomery at the end of March, Wilbur traveled to Pittsburgh on his way to Dayton. He had informed Ellen of his schedule, and she was waiting when he arrived at Pennsylvania Railroad Union Station. They embraced warmly, but she could sense immediately that he was melancholy. Despite the chilly weather, they strolled along the Allegheny as had become their custom. Ellen first asked about his progress in Montgomery, to which he responded positively. He then stated that he needed to discuss what he knew was uppermost on their minds. Ellen thought that he appeared to brace himself before he spoke.

"Ellen," he began, "I have devoted a great deal of time to thinking about our future these past several weeks, even though I have been extremely busy."

"You know that I have thought of little else as well," she said. "I hope we can at last move ahead. What does your family think now?"

"I have to tell you that nothing has changed. I haven't dwelt on the matter with them, but they have made it clear that they are still opposed to the idea of my marrying you. I sense that they still regard you as an interloper."

"I knew they felt that way, of course," said Ellen, "but I held out hope that they would soften their opposition after they had taken more time for reflection. I still can't believe they would attempt to deny you happiness."

"I don't think they mean to make me unhappy, but rather they believe they are saving me from a mistake. I say again that it is just a peculiarity of my family. Certainly, I differ with them on this, as you know, but I still feel a strong family loyalty and a sense of duty. The demands of the patent litigation are weighing heavily on us, and I am afraid that process will take longer than I ever expected. As you know, the major burden of the litigation is still on me, but both Orv and I share the pressures of managing and building the company at the same time. Those burdens alone would be enough to overwhelm most people. Now, the public seems to regard us as villains."

"I have been following those developments as well, and I know how much it must distress you. But remember that you still have me. I can understand the pressures you are feeling, but your life has consisted of overcoming obstacles, and you can overcome these."

Wilbur turned to gaze across the river, leading Ellen to recall the mannerism she had first observed in him at Huffman Prairie.

"I wonder if I can," he said. "I feel too discouraged. I am no longer in control of events. It seems that what I used to say just to deflect questions about my bachelor status may have been right all along, that I don't have time for a wife and a flying machine. I thought I had put that behind me after I met you, but now, after everything that has happened, it appears that my original view represents the reality more than ever. It is just too late for me."

He turned again and faced Ellen. "This is what I have been agonizing over, and why I haven't written you very often. I have dreaded this moment, but I cannot avoid it any longer: We just can't have a future together. Probably I am too old for matrimony anyway. You are young, not yet twenty-eight, and I am in middle age. I don't think I could ever make you happy with all the difficulties we are facing. Among other things, I shall have to travel constantly. It never looked easy for us, but after making you wait for four years, I will not ask you to wait longer. My family's views aren't going to change, of that I am certain, and I think in years to come you will see that it was the best choice to forget me and build your life in a different direction."

He paused and turned away again.

"Do you really mean that you don't think we can ever marry, then?" she asked, her voice trembling.

"Look at the record. We thought four years ago that we could marry in a year. When the next year came, it became the year after that, and so on. Even though Orville and I have attained the success we sought, it has not come with any peace of mind. The rewards of our work just have not been realized, and now we are in danger of losing everything through infringements of our patent. I feel too torn and burdened by what we must do now, and I don't know where you can fit in my life. As I said, I just do not feel in control anymore."

"I know where I am, Will. I am with you in spirit, and I still love you."

"And I love you, but that is not the question. The problems with my family will never go away, and then there are all these business and legal problems. I am just not strong enough to handle it all. That is why I must tell you to look elsewhere for your future."

"You know I have always supported you," said Ellen. "I have always tried to see things from your perspective, and I will continue to do so. But I will also say that I don't feel as young as you may think I am. I am almost at the point that people will consider me an old maid. I will accept what you tell me to accept, but I will not seek a new life. I shall continue to love you even if we are not together."

Wilbur paused, forming his thoughts, then said, "There has been another development. Recently, and as a family, we bought property in Oakwood, where we will build a large home, really our dream house. We had been discussing that for some months. Orville and I, Katharine, and my father will live there. They insisted that I be a part of the new home, and I think that is my destiny."

"I suppose this is goodbye, then?" Tears welled up in Ellen's eyes as she spoke, but she did not sob.

"In my view, it has to be. I am sorry."

Struggling with her emotions, Ellen spoke, "I hope you will understand how devastating this is for me. I have devoted almost my entire life to you over these past five years, even if mostly in secret, and now it has come to nothing. But in one sense I do not regret it. I really believe that what we have felt rarely happens to others, and I want to think we will always have our memories."

She paused, still tearful but struggling to maintain her composure, then spoke again. "I shall always love you, Will, but I never expected you to give up everything else in your life for me."

She took him in her arms and kissed him.

"Yes, we will have our memories," he replied, "and you have changed my life in ways that I never could have imagined. Please try not to be bitter toward my family. They are good people, and they never wanted anything but the best for me either."

"I will try," she said, "but at this moment, it is an effort. I know it will take time for me to sort out my feelings about the way things have happened. Even though I will never regret my love for you, I suppose that someday I will start to think about how my life might have evolved otherwise."

"Please remember that it's not just my family; it is also our legal problems that have almost overwhelmed me. I realize that all this has been very unfair to you, and I keep remembering what you told me about how your parents wanted you to marry. I hope you do not regard it as too late. I don't think it is."

Ellen did not respond.

A Romance of Flight

"I suppose it would be best if we didn't write anymore," he added. She agreed.

They walked back to his hotel. Neither had much to say. Ellen then accompanied him to Union Station. Wilbur did not kiss her. As they parted, Ellen found herself becoming reconciled to the outcome. That she felt so accepting surprised her to a degree. As Wilbur's train was called, she said simply, "Please go quickly."

He said nothing in response but did turn and give her a last look as he boarded.

When Ellen informed her parents that evening, she did so in an even voice. She did not attempt to describe her emotions, but felt nothing less than grief. She did not cry any more. Afterward, sitting alone in her room, she tried to tell herself that such an outcome was almost inevitable, or possibly she should have foreseen it from the start. But she could feel only an overwhelming sense of loss.

Her parents said little further about the matter. Several days later, she visited Julia and informed her of what had happened, this time giving way to tears. Julia told Ellen she was distressed for her but assured her that she would overcome the disappointment and still enjoy a bright future. Ellen thanked her, but responded that she couldn't see that at the time.

* * *

Ellen could only imagine how happy the Wright family would be, and of course they greeted Wilbur warmly on his return. All exchanged pleasantries as he began to relax at home, principally conversing about business developments. After dinner, Wilbur invited Orville, Katharine, and Bishop Wright to join him in the parlor, stating that he had something to say to them.

"Probably not to your surprise, I went by Pittsburgh on my return from Montgomery. Ellen and I met and had a long talk. I told her what I had already decided, that due to our mounting legal pressures and due to family considerations, I could not see her any more. A marriage is now out of the question. We are both quite unhappy about it, but she recognizes that there are many complications in my life. In any event, I am home and it is done. I will continue to divide my time between here and New York and to focus my attention entirely on business matters."

"I am glad to see that finally you have put family and business first," said Orville. "This certainly will enable us to concentrate on our problems without distraction."

"That is the way I have come to view it, and that is what I agree to do," Wilbur replied, although with a tone of resignation.

"Has Miss Hobson accepted your decision?" asked Katharine.

"She has. I must say that it is a mark of her character that she wants only what is best for me and for our endeavors. She has promised to continue to support us as much as she can as a reporter, but she will not initiate any contact with me in the future. She has always been acutely aware of your opposition to her coming into the family, but she promised me that she would try not to feel any bitterness toward you."

"I don't think any of us doubted her character or motives, Will," added his father. "We were just concerned about what would be best for you over the rest of your life. We all agreed that your work with Orville should remain your first priority and that you should live here with us as part of the family. These legal problems you are now facing simply have reinforced that."

Wilbur acknowledged the statement, then spoke again. "I hope you will understand, however, that Ellen is extremely grieved by all this. She has devoted most of the past five years to me when she could have taken another path. You should also realize that her life probably has been disrupted to a greater degree than has mine."

"I think we are aware of all that, Will," said Orville, "but I feel greatly relieved that you have done the right thing for your family. You can turn your full attention to pressing matters here, and there are things that have happened during the time you were away that need our immediate attention. I applaud your putting this episode behind you."

Wilbur said nothing in direct response. After a brief pause, he stood to go to his room, then said, "I will be ready to begin work in the morning, but I say to all of you that I will never tolerate any slighting or negative remarks about Ellen. Do you all agree?"

They agreed. From that point, her name was not mentioned in the Wright household.

***

Wilbur, adding to his busy schedule, returned to flight testing at Huffman Prairie, making what would be his last solo flight on May 21. Wilbur and Orville flew together for the only time on May 25, in their new Model B for the Army and for European production. Also on that day, at age eighty-two, Bishop Wright flew with Wilbur for the first and only time in his life and to his great enjoyment. Wilbur ended flying thereafter in order to focus entirely on business and legal matters as the pace of company activity accelerated. Walter Brookins, a young pilot Wilbur had trained, flew a record 192½ miles from Chicago to Springfield, Illinois, with Wilbur following by train to meet him at his arrival. Orville continued as a pilot and actively trained others. He first tested the Model B, equipped with wheels, in July 1910. The new factory was completed in November, and construction started on three Model B flyers for the Signal Corps against a new order, for delivery early in the coming year. Business, including income from their exhibition team, increased steadily, and the company was profitable. The brothers grew increasingly wealthy and still enjoyed considerable celebrity in their home city, even as they endured the national controversy brought about by their patent litigation and controversies.

Octave Chanute, in steadily declining health for months, died in Chicago, aged seventy-eight. Wilbur attended the funeral on November 25, 1910, and paid public tribute to Chanute as an inspiration to Orville and to him and to their work. Chanute's public criticism of the Wright brothers and his opposition to their patent infringement suits against Curtiss, while angering them at the time, were forgotten and never mentioned again.

Ellen continued to experience success with the *Reporter*. She wrote little on aviation but became increasingly active in coverage of other business and scientific developments. She gained interviews with industrial leaders of Pittsburgh and reported on significant business stories. During the course of her duties, she noted a news report that former president Theodore Roosevelt had taken a ride in one of the Army Model B flyers on October 11, 1910, becoming the first president to fly.

Not having developed any interest in living on her own, Ellen remained with her parents. She thought, with some irony, that she and Wilbur had that in common, both being entirely devoted to their families. Her grandmother Ryan died in November of 1910, reducing the household to three. Ellen had expected her death but mourned more at the loss of a source of stability in her life than over her grandmother as a person. She became a devoted aunt to her brothers' growing children and also enjoyed Julia Albright's two small children. Julia's son, now three, regarded Ellen as another aunt. Ellen still thought of Wilbur constantly, but she maintained her determination not to contact him and did not speak of him to her parents. She continued to enjoy many of her reporting assignments and had become one of the most valued members of the staff. Of concern for her, however, were the rumors circulating that Theodore Rutledge was beginning to consider retirement. She wondered who might replace him.

As the Christmas season approached, Roy Graham, rather to Ellen's surprise, invited her out to lunch. He had never done so before, although they had lunched together from time to time in the *Reporter* cafeteria. She agreed, immediately thinking that he might be planning to discuss the possible retirement of Rutledge. It was a sunny afternoon, unusual for December, and they walked to a nearby busy restaurant.

After they had ordered, Roy looked directly at her, and spoke. "Ellen, we have worked together for more than six years now, and I think you know that my personal and professional respect for you has always been high."

A Romance of Flight

"I appreciate that, Roy, and I have always regarded myself as fortunate that you have been a friend. I could not have succeeded here without your support."

"I appreciate that as well, and I'm glad that we are agreed. I have the sense that you plan to remain with the *Reporter*, regardless of any changes at the top. At least, I hope that is the case. I certainly don't have any indication that you plan to marry or move away or leave the profession."

She nodded her agreement that that was the case. She sensed that Roy appeared to become nervous as he prepared to speak again.

"Well, I'll come to the point. Knowing you as I have for these past six years, I have been thinking about what you have come to mean to me on a personal level. I would hope that I could call on you some time. You know that I have never married, and I have not seriously contemplated such a step for years. I suppose what I am asking is if you think you could regard me as a suitor. I don't know how to express it otherwise, only that I would be honored if you would consider me."

Ellen was stunned, not only at the substance of his message but also at his sudden and direct expression of it. She waited for a moment to compose herself.

"I must confess that this has caught me off guard, Roy. Yes, I have the highest regard for you as a person, but I had no idea that you might think of me in this way. I have never considered you as anything other than a valued friend and colleague."

She wondered if he had heard any rumors about her and Wilbur. She had never mentioned anything of that nature to anyone in the office, but she also understood that such news had a way of traveling.

"All I ask is that you just consider what I have said. I am thirty-eight years old, and I suppose if I am ever to move in that direction, the time is now. I hope you will not reject me."

"I would never reject you, Roy, and I am deeply honored by what you have said. It is just that I don't think at this point that I could ever consider you, or anyone else for that matter, as a suitor.

It has nothing to do with you as a person, but there have just been some things happening in my life that have led me to drop any consideration of marriage in my future."

She knew that Roy would almost certainly react if he had any knowledge of that to which she had just referred. He did not give her any such indication, however.

"Perhaps I made a mistake by speaking as I did," he continued, "but I felt the time had come for me to say something. I gather that you give me no encouragement, then?"

"I suppose in the way that you are thinking, no, I do not. I will say again that I shall continue to regard you as a friend."

"Then I will not inquire about anything that may have happened in your life. I suppose that is not something I should be asking anyway."

Ellen did not respond specifically. They finished their meal quietly, then walked to the office. Ellen felt almost sorry for Roy, thinking that her response might have been humiliating to him. She realized that she knew almost nothing about him other than professionally; she did not know where or how he lived in the city, anything about his family, or what his interests were outside the newspaper business. As they entered the *Reporter* building, Roy mentioned to her that he knew nothing about any retirement plans of Mr. Rutledge. He thought that Rutledge was nearing the age of sixty-five but hoped that he would stay as editor another two or three years. Ellen thanked him for that information, adding that she hoped Mr. Rutledge would remain longer as well.

That evening, Ellen decided not to mention the incident to her parents, but she did decide to tell Julia. Julia's reaction was that Ellen should have encouraged Roy. Ellen knew that Julia felt strongly that she should move on with her life and that her opportunities for marriage would diminish with each passing year. Ellen countered with her view that the episode had at least indicated that she might indeed have a life after Wilbur if she chose, but she would not be able to consider what that might be for a long time.

Roy greeted Ellen pleasantly in the office the next day, but he did not mention their lunchtime conversation again, nor did she. She maintained a friendly demeanor toward him as always.

* * *

Wilbur devoted himself entirely to work in partnership with Orville, including writing further articles about their aviation developments. By 1911, there were some three dozen Wright patent infringement suits filed in both the United States and Europe. But the brothers did not neglect business priorities even as they pressed the suits. They traveled together to New York on January 4 for the company board of directors meeting. Afterward, Wilbur traveled alone to Washington on governmental matters, returning to Dayton on January 16. Both returned to New York for another board meeting February 8. One decision emerging from that meeting was to close the Wright Exhibition Team, which while profitable to the company, had become regarded as too risky; several exhibition flyers had been killed.

Construction of the family's Oakwood mansion also began early in 1911, and both brothers contributed to the plans. Wilbur traveled to Paris again in March, remaining there until August to oversee business matters and to pursue the European patent infringement suits. After returning, he traveled widely in the United States as well, often in connection with patent lawsuits. He and Orville remained as close as ever. They were in agreement on virtually every matter relating to business, aeronautical development, and patent litigation.

* * *

In the course of her duties, Ellen noted news of the Supreme Court order breaking up the Standard Oil Company on May 15, 1911, in turn causing her to remember that Ida Tarbell's reportage on that company had been an early inspiration to her. The report also made her recall that Wilbur was still engaged in patent litigation in the courts. She had not changed her view that the brothers had made a mistake in their pursuit of such litigation, and she still thought with some bitterness that the patent question had contributed to the collapse of her hopes and plans.

Work remained the primary focus of Ellen's life. Despite her deep involvement in her reporting efforts, she could not avoid becoming dispirited at times, and her success and recognition as a reporter still left her unfulfilled. One result of that recognition and of Ellen's expanding professional contacts was that she received an offer during the summer of 1911 to join a large newspaper in New York, the *Herald*. She considered the offer, which of course would have involved a major move and reordering of her life, but eventually declined.

Chapter Fifteen

An Unfulfilled Life

Pittsburgh, Dayton, November 1911-June 1912

Since parting from Wilbur, Ellen's daily life consisted of an almost unvarying routine. In addition to remaining as dedicated to her work as ever, she maintained her close relationship with her family. From time to time she considered that she should make some plans for her life. While she told herself that she could not and should not continue living as she did indefinitely, she still could not motivate herself toward any definite change. The year 1911 seemed to pass slowly for Ellen, a situation that served to remind her that it was rather similar to life during her first year as a fledgling reporter.

Ellen still followed news reports on aviation developments, although passively, and became particularly interested in the exploits of Harriet Quimby, the first female aviator, who began setting records during 1911. Ellen had also followed other aviation achievements and flight records. She read of the record flight in a Wright flyer of an aviator named Calbraith Rodgers, who completed the first coast-to-coast flight in November, after forty-nine days.

She was especially interested to learn that his mechanic was Charlie Taylor, who had left the Wright Company to assist Rodgers in his attempt. She had not corresponded with Charlie in over three years, but she felt proud for him that he evidently had found a rewarding position.

Toward the end of the year, and somewhat troubling for Ellen, Walter Carrington came back into her life. She had learned from Julia some months ago that Walter's young wife had died of influenza the previous winter. For that reason, she did not feel entirely surprised when he contacted her, but she still felt ambivalent at the development. Walter called on her one Sunday afternoon, and she received him graciously, expressing sympathy for his great loss. He led a pleasant but inconclusive conversation and emphasized that he felt he was over his mourning period. He made another visit the following week, and as he departed, he asked if he could resume seeing her periodically. Ellen agreed to see him at her home but stated clearly that that was all she would promise. He began calling regularly, but their visits still consisted only of polite discussion of people and events; they did not go out to the theater or to other public entertainments. He was always extremely courteous to her parents, and they were gracious to him.

Ellen reflected on the fact that one side of her still held a desire for marriage and children, but she could not develop any interest in a future with Walter Carrington. But as Christmas approached, and as feared by Ellen, Walter in fact raised the question of marriage. He did not make a formal proposal, but he told Ellen he would do so if he sensed she would be receptive. Ellen was not surprised at his question, of course, and thanked him. She gave him no encouragement, explaining in deliberately vague terms that her life had changed greatly since she had first known him. As he left, he indicated that he would speak with her again after Christmas.

She had kept her parents advised of developments with Walter, knowing both that they were interested in his renewed attentions and that they held other views on the matter.

"Ellen, I wish you would not reject Walter again," said her mother one evening as they discussed his intentions. "After what he has been through, I think he would make an even better husband for you than he would have earlier. He is an excellent young man with a good station in life, and he would treat you well."

"I know all that, Mother," she replied, "but my feelings haven't changed, and I am not going to enter into a marriage of convenience."

"It is your life, of course, but you are approaching thirty, and your options are going to narrow. This could be one of your last chances, unless you have determined to live a life of spinsterhood."

"I have always been as strongly oriented toward marriage and children as anyone, but as you say, it is my life. I will still receive Walter, but I have made it clear to him that there is no point to it with regard to marriage."

"Do you still love Wilbur Wright, then?" she asked. Wilbur's name had not been mentioned in the house for some time, but Ellen was not surprised that her mother would mention him again.

"Yes, Mother," she replied, "even after all the things that made it impossible for us to marry. Someday my feelings may change, but not today."

Her mother did not pursue the matter further.

Walter Carrington also accepted Ellen's unchanged views and ceased calling on her.

* * *

By April 15, 1912, news of the *Titanic* disaster had spread throughout the country. Theodore Rutledge dispatched Ellen to New York to interview survivors who had been transported into the harbor by rescue ships. The story held a particular relevance to Pittsburgh, since many of its citizens were among the lost. Ellen conducted numerous interviews of survivors, then returned to write a long story including the first-person accounts for the *Reporter*. Once again she gained praise for vivid and timely reporting. While she felt satisfaction in that recognition, it did little to offset her overall feeling of dejection.

News reports on the activities of the Wright Company and of progress with the patent infringement suits came across Ellen's desk periodically. Theodore Rutledge offered her the assignment of covering the litigation, but she declined, explaining that she felt it was time she should move away from aviation as a specialty. Early in May, she saw in one such report the information that Wilbur Wright, while in Boston dealing with legal matters, had become ill and had been forced to return to Dayton for medical treatment and convalescence. The fame of the Wright brothers had grown to the point that even that event was news. By that time, Ellen had not seen Wilbur for more than two years, and she tried not to dwell on the matter. She knew her parents worried for her future, but she still declined to discuss her feelings with them in any depth.

* * *

Ellen was spending the quiet Friday evening of May 24 at home, as was her habit, when the telephone rang. Her mother walked to the entry hall and answered. Though her mother's voice was muffled, Ellen sensed immediately, and with rising anxiety, that the call was for her. Her mother called to her.

"Ellen, it is for you, a long-distance line. It sounds rather urgent."

With a premonition of distressing news, Ellen walked to the phone, took the receiver from her mother, and answered. Through the crackling over the line, she instantly recognized the voice of Orville Wright.

"Miss Hobson . . . Ellen, this is Orville Wright. I must inform you that Wilbur is seriously ill, and he has asked to see you. Are you able to travel to Dayton?"

Ellen was immediately overcome with grief and began fighting back tears. Her voice breaking, she said rapidly, "I shall come as soon as I can, of course. I had seen a brief news report of an illness, but I tried not to think about it. How serious is it?"

"It is quite serious," replied Orville. "It is typhoid fever, and I am convinced it was brought on by the extreme stress he has been under in the patent litigation."

"I only wish that I could have been there to help him." Ellen made the statement so quickly and instinctively that she had not considered that it might have been taken as an affront by Orville.

But he did not respond directly. Recovering, she added quickly, "I'm sure you have obtained the best care for him. How did the illness start?"

"He had been working nonstop on litigation from the first of the year to the time he fell ill. We think he was already exhausted when he traveled to Boston for that court appearance. He reported feeling ill some three weeks ago and came home immediately for treatment. That probably was the news report you saw. I was still in Washington on Army business, and I was told he was recuperating and that he seemed to feel better, so I didn't return home at the time.

"At first, we thought that the illness was brought on by eating contaminated shellfish, but then he was diagnosed with typhoid on May 8, about two weeks ago. He did not want to become bedridden and still wanted to move about, so he made a trip to Oakwood to look at the construction of our new home. But he was too weak to do anything and had a turn for the worse two days later. He underwent typhoid fever treatment immediately."

"I'm sure his doctors are the best, but what do they say now?" asked Ellen, hoping for some word of encouragement.

"You are correct that he has had the best medical care, and the doctors reported that he appeared to improve for several days afterward, but then he had another relapse just four days ago, on Monday. That was the day I returned from Washington. He has been bedridden since then and has been getting worse. The doctors are deeply concerned about his prospects, and I have hardly slept the last two nights. Then today, Will asked me to call you."

"I will leave on the next train. I know it is best that Will is with his family, and I can only pray that my presence will do something to help him. I will call you tomorrow morning with my schedule. And Orville, thank you for making the call yourself. I know that in many respects it wasn't easy for you."

Orville hesitated a moment before replying. "My only concern is for Will. I shall wait by my telephone."

"Until tomorrow, then."

Orville bid her goodbye.

She placed the receiver back on the hook and gave way to tears. All the emotions she had accumulated over almost seven years overwhelmed her in an instant. Her mother, who had left the parlor, returned when she heard Ellen weeping. Her father also came into the room. Ellen managed to compose herself enough to recount the information to her parents. She told them what she had told Orville, that she prayed it was not too late for her to help. She told her parents again how deeply she lamented the way events had worked out. Her mother gathered her in her arms and tried to console her.

After several minutes of being comforted by her parents, Ellen had composed herself enough to call Theodore Rutledge at his home. As he answered, she took a deep breath and spoke. "Mr. Rutledge, I have never made such a request before, but I must ask you for an immediate leave for personal business. I hope you will be understanding."

He gave his approval without hesitating, as she had hoped. "Do you know how much time you will need?" he asked.

"No, sir. I will need to travel, but I simply don't know how long I will be away. I will certainly inform you as soon as I know more. I just don't have anything more specific to tell you at this time."

Rutledge asked for no further details. She thought later that he might have heard of Wilbur's illness and perhaps might have deduced that that was the reason for her request, but she felt relieved that he did not press her for details.

She immediately called the Pennsylvania Railroad office and learned that the next available train to Dayton departed late the next morning.

Ellen followed her mother's suggestion that she drink warm milk before retiring, but she still slept only fitfully that night. Upon rising, she felt exhausted but forced herself to proceed with travel preparations, hoping that she would be able to sleep on the train. Once packed for her trip, she called Orville to report her schedule. He answered on the first ring.

"This is Ellen," she said. "My train leaves here at eleven, and I should arrive in Dayton about five in the afternoon."

"I will be waiting for you at the station and I will arrange a place for you to stay."

"I appreciate that. Is there any change in Wilbur's condition?"

"There is none, but the doctors are still trying every treatment known. Other family members have arrived, and they all agree that Wilbur's illness had been exacerbated by the stress of the patent litigation and other business problems. I told him that I had called you, of course, and he comprehended."

"I will see you at five, then."

Orville bid her goodbye, repeating her arrival hour.

Ellen hung up the receiver, and her tears returned. She had no doubt that Orville was correct about the stress of the patent litigation on Wilbur, but she still tried not to dwell on what might have been.

Ellen's parents took her to the Pennsylvania Railroad Union Station. Neither questioned her determination to make the trip, and from their support, she knew that both understood why it was imperative for her. They waited with her until her train was called. She promised to telephone them as soon as she knew more, then boarded. The train maintained its schedule, and the journey was without incident, but Ellen found herself impatient at its pace. Although she kept her eyes closed for much of the trip, and was largely oblivious to her surroundings, she still was unable to sleep. Her grief for Wilbur threatened to overwhelm her. She struggled to remain composed, as she did not want to attract the attention of fellow passengers. From time to time, she reflected on her first trip alone to Dayton, almost seven years before, and how it had changed her life, but she felt relatively calm as she remembered several pleasant episodes during past trips. In many respects she felt fortunate that she had been able to pursue the story she did, despite the unhappy ending.

At almost six hours, the duration of the trip was agony to Ellen, given the anxiety she felt. But by the time the train approached Dayton, she had successfully overcome her initial instinct to feel bitterness toward Orville, fully realizing that he was suffering as she was. When the train finally arrived at Union Station, she hurriedly stepped down onto the platform. She immediately saw Orville waiting, neatly dressed as always. Not having seen him for four years, she thought he had visibly aged but reminded herself that she had as well. He offered his hand, greeting her sympathetically and even warmly, for the first time in her experience.

"Miss Hobson ... Ellen, I am glad you have come. I know Wilbur needs you."

"It is good to see you, Orville," she said, extending her hand in return. She found that she had no difficulty acting graciously toward him, and she believed that he deserved that much, given that he had made the call for her to come.

Orville took Ellen's luggage and escorted her to his new automobile for the drive to the Wright home. Ellen observed that he walked with a slight limp and assumed that it stemmed from his injuries in the crash almost four years ago. Neither initiated a conversation immediately as they situated themselves in the automobile and began the drive. Ellen sensed that the situation was awkward, but she knew that Orville could see her intense grief, and she in turn sensed his deep concern.

It was only a short distance to the Wright home, but she could wait no longer before asking Orville for news of Wilbur. "Please tell me Will is better."

"I cannot," he replied, his voice rising and trembling with emotion. "The fever is too far advanced. The doctors hold out no hope."

Ellen no longer struggled to maintain her composure and began weeping, softly but uncontrollably. She stated again through her tears that she only wished she had been with Wilbur earlier and that she believed somehow that her presence could have been of some aid and comfort to him. Orville, to her surprise, agreed.

"I really regret the way things have worked out," he said. "Blame it on the peculiarities of my family if you want, but I am now sorry that we were not more accepting of you. I have come to realize that you would have made a great difference in Will's life, and now we are faced with losing him."

A Romance of Flight

Orville again expressed intense bitterness against Curtiss and the court system for the burden his actions had imposed on them. He maintained that Wilbur, being a chronically nervous person, had become extremely fatigued by the litigation, and in his view, that had made him more susceptible to illness.

They arrived at the Wright home momentarily, and with difficulty, Ellen composed herself again. Orville escorted her inside, and she exchanged hurried greetings with family members gathered in the parlor, first with the aged Bishop Wright.

"Thank you for coming," he said simply.

"Thank you, sir," she responded. "I only hope I can be of some comfort to Will."

She turned to greet Katharine and, surprising herself, hugged her. Although she had not seen Katharine in more than six years, it did not seem nearly that long, since their lives had been so intertwined through Wilbur. Katharine also welcomed her and returned her embrace, but neither said anything further. Ellen had visited the Wright home only once, almost seven years ago, but found herself feeling that it had been only recently. The surroundings and furnishings seemed very familiar to her.

Orville then introduced her to Dr. Daniel B. Conklin, the principal physician. They exchanged greetings, and Dr. Conklin escorted her upstairs to Wilbur's room. He made no specific personal comments to Ellen, but she assumed he knew who she was and why she was there.

She entered the dimly lit and simply furnished room where Wilbur lay in his bed. Ellen had expected to see him in a weakened condition, but as she approached, she could not avoid being shocked at his gaunt appearance; his eyes appeared dull and almost lifeless. He was barely conscious, but he turned toward her, and she could sense the recognition in his eyes. She could also see that he clearly was dying. Dr. Conklin looked briefly at Wilbur, then stepped outside. Wilbur weakly extended a hand to her. Ellen enclosed his hand in both of hers and said, "Will, I am here, and I won't leave you."

She leaned over and kissed him on the cheek, realizing almost as an afterthought that she was still composed and dry-eyed. She then held up his head and shoulders with one arm and gave him a drink of water, which he sipped slowly. With extreme effort, he spoke. "I should have married you. I should have married you five years ago, when I so wanted to. Perhaps life would have turned out differently for us."

"Don't think about the past. The only thing you need to know now is that I have never stopped loving you. You were always first in my thoughts even when we were apart. Now, please rest. You know that I will be here when you wake."

Wilbur soon drifted into sleep, his hand still in Ellen's. She sat quietly, watching his labored breathing. After a time, Dr. Conklin returned and briefly checked Wilbur's vital signs.

"Please get some rest, Miss Hobson," he said. "There is nothing you can do for him this evening. I will inform you immediately of any changes."

"Thank you," she replied, "but I will remain here through the night. I promised Will I would stay at his side."

Dr. Conklin acknowledged her statement and went back downstairs with no protest. As Will slept, Ellen began to look around the rather plain room. Her eyes focused immediately on the dresser where she saw her picture displayed—the same picture she had given Wilbur six years ago. That sight only caused her grief to intensify.

After perhaps an hour, Katharine came to the door.

"Please come downstairs and join us for dinner. I know you must be hungry."

"I am hungry, but please have someone bring a meal to me. I do not want to leave Will's side."

Katharine acknowledged her request, and after several minutes, Carrie Grumbach came upstairs with a plate and glass on a tray.

* * *

Ellen remained at Wilbur's side almost constantly, even sleeping in the armchair, and ministering to him as she could. Other family members looked in regularly, and Ellen continued to receive food at normal mealtimes, although she had little appetite. On Sunday evening, Ellen's second day at the Wright home, Orville informed her that Charlie Taylor and his wife had arrived, and Ellen came downstairs and greeted Charlie warmly. Charlie introduced his wife Henrietta, explaining to her that Ellen was a friend. It came as almost a shock for Ellen to realize that although she had not seen Charlie for years, she also regarded him as a real friend.

"It's so good to see you again, Charlie," she said, with her eyes moistening. She turned to Henrietta Taylor. "I am also happy to meet you, Mrs. Taylor. I have such pleasant memories of Charlie's work with Will and Orv, and of how much he helped me as well."

Charlie did not respond specifically to her statement, but Ellen knew that he understood what she meant. He explained that he had just returned to the Wright Company and that he wanted to be with the brothers in their time of crisis. As they talked further, Ellen mentioned her awareness of the coast-to-coast flight of Cal Rodgers and congratulated him on his part in the achievement. Neither made an explicit reference to the reason why she was there. She presumed that Charlie had learned everything from Wilbur, but she realized that there was no purpose to discussing anything of that nature that evening. She escorted them upstairs to see Wilbur. He recognized Charlie but was unable to say anything.

Ellen did not remember to call her parents until Monday, after she had been there almost two full days, and then spoke with them only for a moment. She still had not gone to the boarding house where Orville had arranged a room for her. Later that afternoon, when Wilbur was asleep, Ellen went downstairs to visit with the family, primarily Orville.

"Orville," she began, struggling to maintain her composure, "I'm so sorry I can't do anything for Will. It looks inevitable that we will lose him after all."

"I think we must accept that," he replied, his voice reflecting his grief. "I just hope your presence has been of some comfort to him."

Ellen silently appreciated Orville's response. Bishop Wright in particular treated her with respect and consideration and again expressed his gratitude for her presence. She thanked him again and did not allow herself any thoughts about his past opposition to her. She knew that he was grieving deeply, even while maintaining the stoic manner that she had come to regard as characteristic of the family.

Ellen began to sense that even Katharine was somewhat sympathetic to her, although still without warmth. Their conversation did not progress beyond exchanging pleasantries, and Ellen wondered if on some level Katharine still regarded her as an interloper.

Reuchlin and Lorin Wright soon arrived with their families. Upon their reintroduction, Lorin made mention of their earlier meeting, and he and Reuchlin and their wives were gracious in their remarks to her. By that time, however, all had conceded that Ellen's presence would not work the miracle they had hoped for. Wilbur turned more critical that evening, and Dr. Conklin announced to the family that he might not survive the night. But Wilbur lingered, drifting in and out of consciousness. He continued to recognize Ellen during his periods of consciousness and spoke to her with the final reserves of his strength. After a sleepless night at Wilbur's bedside, Ellen finally went to the boarding house on Tuesday afternoon, but only long enough to sleep for a few hours and then refresh herself. Upon rising, she returned to the Wright home and Wilbur's side.

She decided to remain there through Wednesday night, knowing the end could come at any moment. Dr. Conklin remained also. After midnight, he came downstairs and warned the family.

"It appears that Wilbur's last breath is approaching," he said simply.

All family members present gathered at Wilbur's bedside. Ellen decided that her place was to defer to the immediate family,

A Romance of Flight

and she stood quietly behind them. Dr. Conklin, after a recheck of Wilbur's pulse, announced that the end would come any minute. Ellen edged closer to the deathbed.

Wilbur Wright died early Thursday morning, May 30, aged forty-five. Ellen could not decide if she was unconsciously trying to present herself as a figure of strength and calm, or if she had exhausted her capacity to show grief, but she remained composed, as did most family members, after Dr. Conklin made the pronouncement of death. All she could feel was a kind of numbness. She wanted to comfort the family, Bishop Wright first of all, and expressed condolences to him with a steady voice. He acknowledged her words graciously, still maintaining his composure as she had expected. She then turned her attention to Orville, knowing him to be the most deeply affected of anyone in the family. He also acknowledged her attempt at comforting words. Dr. Conklin called undertakers. Ellen remained with the family in the parlor, but as dawn approached, and belatedly realizing how exhausted she was, she accepted the offer of Katharine's bed. For the first time in almost a week, Ellen had an unbroken sleep, lasting through the remainder of the day.

* * *

Wilbur Wright's untimely death generated heavy publicity and news coverage throughout the world. All earlier criticism of the brothers over patent suits and other controversies were forgotten by the public. Wilbur was regarded not only as a national hero but a world hero. Messages of condolence and acclaim poured in from abroad as well as from throughout the country. President Taft added a gracious tribute to his fellow Ohioan. A public funeral with eulogies was to be held on June 1, with the service to be held at the First Presbyterian Church in the center of Dayton, even though Wilbur had no affiliation with that church.

Ellen did not remember to call her parents again until the morning of the funeral. The Wright family telephone had been in use almost constantly, but they permitted her time and privacy for the call. Her parents had closely followed the news of Wilbur's death, so their attention was entirely focused on her. She spoke only briefly with them, but she did remember to say that she was unsure what day she would return. She had remembered to pack a black dress for mourning when she left Pittsburgh, knowing that it probably would be needed, and she notified the Wright family that she would return to the boarding house to dress.

The family insisted that Ellen travel with them to the church, and as they approached, she was astonished at the size of the crowd, which she later learned numbered almost twenty-five thousand and which had poured out onto surrounding streets. The family had invited her to sit in the pew immediately behind them, and she quietly followed them in. As she slid into her pew, she found that she was seated only a few places away from Charlie and Henrietta Taylor. They nodded to each other in silent and solemn greeting. She had not shed tears for the past two days, and she still felt what she could regard only as numbness. She tried to concentrate on the service but could not sustain her attention to anything said, even the eulogies. Her paramount concern was for the Wright family.

After the service, Wilbur's body was carried at the head of a long procession to Woodland Cemetery, where he was to be buried next to his mother. The procession took almost two hours to reach the burial site. The service was short and simple, as Ellen knew Wilbur would have wished. His grave was to be marked by a simple headstone. She again stood behind the immediate family.

At Orville's invitation, Ellen accompanied the family back to the Wright home. She paid her respects to all, then made an announcement.

"I want you to know I shall always appreciate your many kindnesses to me during this ordeal. Now, I just want to be alone for a few hours. I will return this evening, if that is agreeable."

Orville and Bishop Wright acknowledged her wishes. She departed and walked to the boarding house, where she changed from her mourning clothes into the dress she had traveled in. She looked in a mirror and was mildly shocked at her appearance, thinking that she looked years older. She sat in her chair and gave way to tears, something she had not done for several days. Composing herself yet again, she left and made her way to the city center where she boarded the Interurban electric trolley and traveled once again to Huffman Prairie.

Ellen Hobson walked the short distance to the field, now with more buildings and two flyers at the ready, for only a brief last look, knowing that she would never return. The Wright Flying School was established at the field, and there were signs of recent high activity, but of course there was no flying that day.

Epilogue

October 5, 1962

Ellen Wagner arrived in Dayton on schedule after her flight from Florida. She checked into her room which she had reserved at a downtown hotel. The exhibition hall housing the new National Aviation Hall of fame was nearby. She decided to take a short walk around the central city to observe how much it had changed over fifteen years, and it had changed.

The next day, she attended the opening ceremony, observing quietly. The presence of Milton Wright and Ivonette Wright Miller, children of Lorin and effectively protectors of the Wright legacy, brought back vivid memories to Ellen. Both were now in their sixties. She approached and spoke to them after the conclusion of the induction ceremony. Neither had remembered her visit in 1905, of course, but they were aware of her reporting of their uncles' achievements. Ellen reflected the long controversy over the presentation of the original 1903 flyer to the Smithsonian Institution in 1948. Ellen also knew that the old Wright Field of 1926, now Wright-Patterson Air Force Base, had been named for Wilbur specifically.

After the ceremonies, Ellen traveled to West Dayton to visit the sites of the Wright residence and the bicycle shop. The original structures had been sold to Henry Ford in 1936, not without some controversy in Dayton, and restored for inclusion in his Deerfield

Village preservation project in Dearborn, Michigan. Charlie Taylor, then living in California, had been brought back to participate in the restoration of the bicycle shop.

After touring numerous historical sites and monuments, Ellen reflected with satisfaction at how the brothers had been recognized and remembered. She planned to return to her Florida home the next day, feeling fulfilled at her trip. Her husband was buried at a cemetery near her home, and she was prepared for the day when she would be buried next to him.

Afterword

Wilbur was never to live in the Oakwood mansion, which in any event was not completed until 1913. After its completion, and named Hawthorn Hill, Orville, Katharine, and their father lived there as a family. Bishop Wright died in 1917 at the age of eighty-eight. Carrie Grumbach continued to serve the family loyally in the mansion for years.

Orville succeeded Wilbur as president of the Wright Company but proved no more comfortable with management responsibilities than had Wilbur. In 1914, after conflicts with other investors, he began buying out their interests, then sold the company the next year, becoming a millionaire in the process. He remained active in aviation as an experimenter and consultant.

Katharine lived on in the mansion with Orville until 1926, when, at age fifty-two, she married. She had been courted by Henry Haskell, an old friend, for more than a year, without disclosing the relationship to Orville. The couple moved to Kansas City, Missouri. Orville was so incensed by the marriage that he never spoke to Katharine again, only relenting when he visited her deathbed three years later. By then she was too ill to recognize or respond to him.

* * *

All the Wright patent infringement suits were eventually won by Orville and by the Wright Company, but collecting royalties would prove more difficult.

*　*　*

Charlie Taylor remained active in aviation the remainder of his life. He died on January 30, 1956, at the age of eighty-seven.

*　*　*

The National Aviation Hall of Fame was established in Dayton on October 6, 1962, with the Wright brothers as the first honorees. Charlie Taylor was inducted into the hall in 1965.

About the Author

Donald Pattillo served in the US Air Force after graduating from the University of Alabama. He later earned a PhD in International Business at Georgia State University and pursued an academic career for some twenty years. He then turned to his first love, aviation history, and has published three books and a major scholarly article in the field. Always a romantic about aviation, he conceived the idea of a romantic novel involving the Wright brothers some twenty years ago and has worked on it since. *A Romance of Flight* is the result.

He lives in Marietta, Georgia.

Other Books
by Donald Pattillo

Pushing the Envelope:
The American Aircraft Industry

A History in the Making:
80 Turbulent Years in the American General Aviation Industry

The General Aviation Industry in America:
A History (Second Edition)